A *Woman* SCORNED

BOOK THREE OF THE SYDNEY LEGAL SERIES

CHRIS TAYLOR

LCT Productions Pty Ltd
18364 Kamilaroi Highway, Narrabri NSW 2390

ISBN. 978-1-925119-50-3 (Paperback)

A Woman Scorned is a work of fiction. Names, characters, places, brands, media and incidents either are the product of the author's imagination or are used fictitiously. Any resemblance to actual persons, living or dead, events, or locales, is entirely coincidental.

Published in the United States of America.

BOOKS BY CHRIS TAYLOR

THE MUNRO FAMILY SERIES
(In order)

The Profiler
The Investigator
The Predator
The Betrayal
The Deception
The Negotiator
The Christmas Vigil
The Ransom
The Defendant
The Shooting
The Maker
(Available in Audio)

THE SYDNEY HARBOUR HOSPITAL SERIES
(in order)

The Perfect Husband
The Body Thief
The Baby Snatchers
The Final Bullet
The Debt Collector
The Lab Test
The Stolen Identity
The Cliff-top Killer
The Likeable Fraudster

THE SYDNEY LEGAL SERIES
(in order)

An Accidental Murderer
At the Hand of Her Father
A Woman Scorned
Lies and Deception
Ordinary Evil
The Ties That Bind
The Perfect Crime
Malicious Love
Toxic Inheritance

THE BARRINGTON FAMILY SERIES
(in order)

Broken Lives
Broken Promises
Broken Bonds
Broken Spirits
Broken Vows
Broken Minds
Broken Dreams
Broken Hearts
Broken Homes

THE CRAIGDON FAMILY SERIES
(in order)

Callum
Joel
Isabella
Nicholas
Sophia
Flynn
Noah
Logan
Elizabeth

Get a FREE book when you sign up for Chris Taylor's
newsletter at: www.christaylorauthor.com.au

Love Audiobooks? Check out Chris Taylor Books on audio
on Audible.com, Amazon.com and the iBooks store.

Join Chris Taylor's Facebook reader group/fan page and be
among the first to receive news of book releases, read and
review books prior to release and other amazing offers. Join
Now at: www.facebook.com/groups/1758023621144744/

Find out more about all of Chris Taylor's books, by visiting her
website at: www.christaylorauthor.com.au/about/books

DEDICATION

This book is dedicated to each and every one of my loyal and dedicated readers and especially Jenny Diggens and those of you who write and tell me how much my stories have touched your lives. It is for all of you that I write. I hope you enjoy A Woman Scorned.

And as always, to my very own knight in shining armor: my husband, Linden. I love you.

ACKNOWLEDGMENTS

As usual, no book comes into being without a lot of help and support by my friends and family. A world of thanks must go to my wonderful editor, Pat Thomas. Thank you for everything that you do to make my stories even more amazing than I could ever dare to dream. To former Detective Superintendent Michael Kilfoyle, thank you for lending my story credibility. Any mistakes are wholly my own.

To Damon Freeman, Alisha Moore and all of the staff at damonza.com, thank you for yet another fantastic cover. To my sister, Nicole Guihot and to my friend, Ally Thomson, thank you for your excellent editorial comments, proof reading skills and suggestions. I hope you like the final result.

To Amy Atwell and her dedicated staff at Author E.M.S. who are so much more than book formatters. Amy, once again, thank you for your magic.

To the fantastic writer organizations such as Romance Writers of Australia, Romance Writers of

America and Romance Writers of New Zealand for all the help, support and encouragement they offer new and aspiring writers, including me.

To my readers, thank you for your support and love for my stories. Your encouragement and enjoyment make this journey all worthwhile.

And lastly, to my friends and family, especially my husband and children. Thank you for putting up with late dinners and even later conversations as I've emerged day after day from the sometimes scary but always enthralling world I've created on my computer.

PROLOGUE

The night was well upon her. In fact, it was closer to morning than night. If she looked up, past the buildings that towered above her, she could see the faintest glimmer of stars. The moon was a mere sliver of light, barely discernible in the darkness. It was even blacker in the close confines of the alleyway where she hid. The foul odor of rotten food, dank drain water and a myriad of other offensive smells burned her nostrils, but she couldn't leave. At least, not yet.

With the back of her gloved hand, she pushed at the damp strands of hair that were plastered across her forehead. A faint breeze tinged with the scent of salt and summer drifted through the narrow opening. Instead of relief, the air brought with it another wave of stench. Her stomach churned in protest and she swallowed convulsively.

Where the hell was he? He should have been there by now. From her experience, his routine never changed. This was his favorite bar, his regular haunt. In ten minutes, it would be closing time. He never stayed past last call.

As if her thoughts had conjured movement, the back door that led from the bar into the alleyway opened with a noisy protest. Light spilled out onto the dirty pavement and glinted off the barrel of the gun in her hand. Her heart skipped a beat and she flattened herself against the wall in an effort to conceal herself in the shadows. Her fingers tightened around the trigger.

A drunken patron stumbled through the doorway and stepped out of the building and onto the uneven surface. He tottered, and for a moment, she thought he would fall. She stared hard at his shadowed face, but knew even before she registered the heavy beard and long hair that he wasn't the one she sought.

Keeping to the shadows, she remained still and quiet and waited for the man to depart. The door protested again and a second man left the bar. With his gaze fixed on some point in the distance, he stumbled down the alleyway in the direction of the street.

It wasn't him. Another false start.

She let out her breath on a shaky sigh, her belly tight with nerves. The gun felt heavy and awkward, as if it resisted her evil intent. Her heart thumped slow and heavy. Now that she was there, she wanted to get it over with; do the deed and then simply disappear into the blackness, never to be seen again.

But first, she needed the victim...

CHAPTER 1

Detective Constable James Shepherd reached across his desk and pulled a fresh stick of gum from the packet that sat near a stack of files he'd tossed there hours earlier. Wishing it was a cigarette but determined not to break the forty-six days he'd managed this time to stay away from nicotine, he shoved the gum into his mouth and hoped it would distract him until the wave of cravings eased. It was just as hard as it had been the last two times he'd tried to quit. He just had to keep reminding himself of the health benefits and the money he'd save.

It was times like this that were the hardest. He was doing the graveyard shift. The clock on the wall told him it was a little past two. Four hours to go. The night had been uneventful. He'd even managed to file most of the paperwork that sat in haphazard piles on his desk. Sometimes a night spent in the office was a relief, but time could drag and then he'd find himself thinking about smoking again...With a grunt of disgust, he forced his attention back to the paperwork.

"What are you so unhappy about?"

James looked across at his colleague who was seated a short distance away, behind a similarly overcrowded desk. "Nothing in particular," he replied.

Detective Constable Hung Wang had been with the City of Sydney detectives for years and had been partnered with James for the better part of six months. It was long enough for James to trust him but also to realize the man had no interest in being friends or even being friendly. Taciturn to the point of rudeness—for Wang it was all about the job.

The man regularly worked eighty-hour weeks and was among the first to volunteer for a double shift whenever they were short staffed, which occurred with regular monotony, like now. Wang spent hours on the computer researching cases, looking for clues. Despite the man's standoffishness, James felt a reluctant admiration for the sheer amount of hard work his fellow detective put in—and all that overtime—for no more than the standard pay. Then there was Wang's enviable success rate. In the short time he'd been partnered with James, Wang had solved more than half a dozen cold cases. There was no arguing the man was a dedicated and clever investigator, if a little odd.

The phone at James' elbow pealed, breaking the silence. Reaching across, he answered it.

"City of Sydney Police Station. This is Detective Shepherd."

"Detective, this is dispatch. We've received an emergency call. There's been a shooting in an alleyway off Bathurst Street. No word on how many people are involved. First responders are on their way."

After taking down the details supplied by the dispatcher, James hung up the phone and turned to Wang. "At last, a little action. There's been a shooting downtown."

Wang immediately looked interested. "Guess we'd better get over there, then," he said and pushed away from his desk.

"Guess so," James replied and followed his colleague out of the squad room.

James breathed in through his mouth in an effort to avoid the stench of rotting garbage, rank storm water and God knows what other filth that lined the broken pavement and gutters on either side of the narrow alleyway running between two crumbling buildings on Bathurst Street in downtown Sydney. The bright emergency lights flashed blue and red and white from police and paramedic vehicles. The lights pulsed in the night sky and bounced off the walls of the buildings.

He pulled out his flashlight and directed the beam through the darkness in front of him. A rat scurried into the shadows.

"What do we have?" he asked, approaching one of the uniformed officers who had helped secure the scene and was now standing watch over a body that lay on the ground.

"White male, mid-thirties. Shot through the head with a single nine millimeter bullet. This wasn't done by an amateur."

"Did we recover a shell casing?"

"Yes. Right beside the body. It's been bagged already. I gave it to your colleague."

The officer indicated with his head in Wang's direction. James saw a plastic evidence bag in his partner's hand. He returned his attention to the officer. "Anyone see what happened?"

The officer shook his head. "No. All we have is the girl who called it in. Apparently, she'd just stepped out of the bar next door and heard a gunshot. She saw someone dressed in black and riding a motorbike come out of the alleyway shortly afterward. She noticed something lying on the ground and went to take a closer look."

James acknowledged the officer's information with a nod. "What's her name?"

"Jo-Beth Gregson. She's just over there."

James looked over in the direction the uniform indicated and saw a petite, dark-haired girl who barely looked legal. Sheer, tattered black stockings encased pale, skinny legs. A short black leather skirt, barely covering the essentials, was teamed with an equally brief sleeveless midriff top. Heavy makeup made her look older than she was. If he had to guess, he'd put her about the age of his younger sister.

The woman stood hunched against the concrete wall of one of the buildings. Her hands were jammed in her pockets. She stared at her feet. *Why wasn't she tucked up safe and sound in bed instead of out on the streets in the middle of the night, turning tricks and being front stage center, witnessing a murder? Where were her family, the people who cared?* James bit back a sigh and looked back at the officer. "I guess I'd better go talk to her. Do we have an ID on the vic?"

"We found his wallet on him. Still had sixty bucks in it, so we can probably rule out robbery as a motive. Driver's license says he's Douglas Michael Hanley. Lives in Granville. Thirty-six years old."

Once again, James acknowledged the officer's comments with a nod of thanks. As he stepped away, something pale caught his eye. Bending low, he picked up a business card that lay close to the body. He turned it over and with the aid of his flashlight, read the embossed writing.

SALLY-ANN LI
ATTORNEY AT LAW
SYDNEY LEGAL

There was an address and on the back, other contact details, presumably work numbers. He wondered if the card had any significance to the murder and pulled out an evidence bag. Dropping the card inside the plastic, he stuffed it back inside his jacket pocket. It might not be anything, but he'd learned through years of experience that it was better to err on the side of caution. In the filthy alleyway, it was impossible to decipher what was trash and what could be important, but the white card was still crisp and reasonably clean. It didn't look like it had been there long.

Glancing across to where the witness stood, he pulled out his notebook and pen and moved over to stand beside her. She looked even younger up close.

"I'm Detective James Shepherd. I understand you heard a gunshot."

The girl's dark eyes were huge in her small, pale face. Black mascara had run down her cheeks, like she'd been crying. After a decade in the police service, James had become immune to violent crime scenes, but he was sensitive enough to realize the average civilian didn't react quite so calmly to the presence of a dead body, not to mention the shock of the realization that if she'd exited a few moments earlier, she might have been caught up in, or witnessed, the death.

The girl gave a hesitant nod, her fear evident.

James did his best to put her at ease. He gave her a friendly smile. "It's Jo-Beth, right?"

"Yes," came the soft reply.

"What can you tell me, Jo-Beth?"

"I... I already spoke to the officer over there. I told him everything I know."

James nodded. "I'm sure you did, but I'd like to hear it again. You came from the direction of the bar, right?"

She shot him a furtive glance and he couldn't help but wonder if she was worried he might bust her for being under age. Under normal circumstances, he'd probably give her a lecture, but right now his concerns lay only with the man who'd died on the filthy street.

"Look, Jo-Beth," he said. "At the moment, I don't care if you're sixteen or sixty-six; if you were in the bar turning tricks or whatever it was that you were doing downtown in the middle of the night. All I'm trying to do is solve a murder. Got it?"

She flinched. His tone was harsher than he'd intended, but time was ticking away. The longer it took to gather the information, the more time the perpetrator had to get away, hide evidence, disappear. Swallowing a sigh, he did his best to curb his impatience and tried again.

"Where were you when you heard the gunshot?"

"I... I'd just stepped out of the bar. I left through the front entrance. The bartender had announced last call. People were getting ready to leave. I was hoping someone might—"

She broke off. James didn't need her to spell it out. "You were hoping to pick up a john, right? I get it. So when that didn't happen, you stepped outside, onto the street. Were you alone?"

She grimaced. "Yes. The guy I'd been chatting up decided he had to go home to his wife."

"How many shots did you hear?"

"One."

"What else did you hear?"

"A motorbike. One of those really loud ones, or maybe it just sounded that way because the streets were so quiet and the buildings are really close. Sometimes that can magnify the sound. The bike came out of the alleyway toward me, all black and shiny and rumbling."

James made some notes and then continued. "What else did you see?"

"The figure on the motorbike was dressed all in black. I think the helmet was black, too."

"Could you tell if the rider was a male or female?"

"No. It was too dark and I only saw them for a few seconds. I still didn't realize someone had been shot."

"Could you describe anything about the biker? Were they tall, short?"

"Not tall, I don't think. Their legs didn't seem too long."

"What about their build? Broad, narrow? Thin? Fat?"

The girl scrunched up her face in thought, like his sister did when she was thinking hard. It made her look even younger. "Average build, I guess. Not skinny, but not fat, either."

Once again, James took down her responses in his notepad before turning his attention back to her. "Anything else?"

"No."

"What about the motorbike? What do you remember about that?"

"Just that it was big and black and shiny. I don't know much about motorbikes."

"What about paintwork? Markings? Any kind of badge?"

"No, I'm sorry. It happened so fast. I heard the gunshot and was still processing that when this motorbike roared out of the alleyway. It took me a few minutes to realize there was a man lying on the ground and that he'd been shot." She shuddered and hugged herself. The fear was back on her face.

"It's all right, Jo-Beth. You've done well. Can you tell me which direction the bike took once it cleared the alleyway?"

"Yes. It turned left, but Bathurst Street is a one-way street, so there wasn't much choice unless the rider wanted to go against the traffic and I guess that would have drawn unnecessary attention."

James nodded in agreement. In the back of his mind, he acknowledged Jo-Beth's summation and wondered again how she'd ended up on the streets. It was obvious she wasn't stupid and she spoke like someone who'd received a reasonable education at some point in her life. *Where had her life gone off track?* It saddened him to know she was just one of many young people living on the streets after their lives had taken an unexpected turn. He wished there was something he could do to help her, but right now, he had bigger problems to solve.

Reaching into his jacket, he pulled out his wallet and handed her his card. "Thanks for talking to me, Jo-Beth. If you think of anything else, give me a call."

She took the card and slipped it inside her shirt. James' gaze swept over her skinny form. "You eaten tonight?" he asked.

She shook her head. Once again, he reached inside his wallet. This time, he pulled out a couple of ten-dollar bills and handed them to her.

"Go and get something in your belly."

The money went the same place as his business card. She sniffed and he caught a glint of tears.

"Thanks," she said.

He brushed off her gratitude. "Do me a favor," he replied, his voice gruff. "Call home. Let them know you're okay."

She grimaced. "I don't have a home. There's no one."

James sighed. After taking down her contact information, which consisted of nothing more than her full name and a cell phone number, he turned away. The late hour, coupled with the hopelessness of the young woman's situation had worn him down and he still had a murderer to catch. He and Wang returned to the station.

Dragging his keyboard toward him, James opened a new file in the name of Douglas Michael Hanley. Once they located his family, a formal identification would be made, but for now, the driver's license would have to suffice. The vic looked enough like the photo on his identification to satisfy James that they had the right man. Despite the fact he'd taken a bullet to the head, it had been a clean shot, entering in the middle of his forehead and exiting through the back.

To James' surprise, the victim was listed in their database. Douglas Hanley had a handful of minor assaults and three DUIs. The most recent one was only a few weeks earlier. According to the police database, he lived with his mother. James didn't relish being the one to bring her the bad news.

He glanced at the clock on the wall. It was

going on for five. Thinking about Jo-Beth's life brought to mind his sister. Lizzie had had a falling out with their step-mother and had been staying with him for the past few days. Feeling the sudden need to message his little sister, he sent her a text.

Thinking of u. xx

A moment later, his phone *dinged* with an incoming text. He glanced at the screen.

That's what I love about u, big brother. Ur always looking out 4 me. Xx

He shot back a reply. *Ur meant 2 b asleep.*

He didn't have to wait long for her response.

Ur meant 2 b at work.

I am.

Then why r u texting me?

A reluctant smile tugged at his lips. *Just checking ur ok*, he texted.

I'm fine.

Good, go back 2 sleep.

Yes, Dad.

He bit back another smile. He could almost hear her snarky tone. He sent off another reply.

Hey, ur the 1 who wanted 2 stay with me. I can always send u home.

The reply was swift and short.

No!

James sighed. She was barely seventeen. It wasn't like she could hang out at his place forever. He said as much in his next text.

U need 2 give some thought to going back home.

Please, James! Anita and I need some space. I'll behave. Promise.

He bit his lip. He wasn't that old that he didn't remember what it was like to be seventeen—no longer a kid, but not yet an adult. It was a difficult time in a person's life, filled with conflicting emotions and expectations. Coupled with the fact their father had remarried six years previously and Lizzie and her step-mother, Anita, didn't exactly see eye to eye...

He sighed again and sent off another text.

All right. U can stay another night or 2. Now, go back 2 sleep. U have school in the morning. I'll b home in a couple hours.

Can u bring bagels???

He read her text and shook his head and this time, he let his smile break free.

Ur incorrigible!

???

He laughed.

CHAPTER 2

Sally-Ann Li swiped a brush through her long, straight hair and left it loose. Though she often tied it back into a sensible bun, or at least a braid, after sleeping past her alarm she didn't have time for anything else. A slash of red lipstick, a spray of her favorite perfume and she was almost ready. Hurrying back into her bedroom, she riffled through the bottom of her closet for shoes.

The silver ones with the four-inch heels were cute and oh so stylish, but they were much too uncomfortable to wear to work. She had to be in court for most of the day, which meant a fair amount of time on her feet. The black suede wedges would be a far more sensible choice. Decision made, she slipped on the shoes, collected her phone from the nightstand and headed for the kitchen. She was just reaching for the oatmeal when her phone rang.

Glancing at the screen, she answered it. "Hi, Aimee. What's up?" Her greeting was met with silence and then the unmistakable sound of a sob. The realization that her older sister was crying sent a shard of panic straight to her heart.

"Aimee? What's the matter? Is everything all right? Oh, God! It's Mom, isn't it?" Sally-Ann held her breath, dreading the answer. Their mother had been suffering a serious bout of influenza. Sally-Ann feared it had moved to her lungs.

"No, no! It isn't Mom. She's fine. Well, she's still got that cough, but otherwise she's okay. At least, she was when I spoke to her yesterday."

Sally-Ann let out her breath and then realized she still hadn't been told why her sister was upset. "Then what?"

"Oh, Sal! It's Doug!"

Sally-Ann frowned. "Doug Hanley? *Your* Doug Hanley?"

"Yes! How many other Dougs do I know? Oh, Sal! I just received a call from his mother. He's... He's dead!"

Sally-Ann gasped. It was the last thing she expected her sister to say. "What do you mean, he's dead? He's only in his thirties. Was he in an accident?"

"No! He's been...*murdered!*" Aimee let forth another round of sobs.

Sally-Ann shook her head slowly back and forth in confusion and disbelief. "Murdered? Who'd want to murder Doug?"

"I don't know! He was found shot in an alley in the city. The police asked his mother to formally identify him. Now she's accusing me of having something to do with his death!"

"You? That's ridiculous! You and Doug have been divorced for years! Why would she think you had a part to play in this?"

"I don't know, but she told me she's already pointed the police in my direction! She said I never forgave Doug for putting me in a wheelchair. She said I've just been waiting for the right opportunity to get back at him!"

"She's crazy!" Sally-Ann replied, still shocked to hear her ex-brother-in-law was dead.

"Absolutely, but what am I going to do? What if the police come asking questions? What will I tell them?"

"You'll tell them the truth—of course—that you had nothing to do with Doug's death. Besides, you haven't seen him for years."

Silence greeted her on the other end of the phone. Sally-Ann frowned. "Aimee? It's true, isn't it? You haven't seen Doug since the divorce settlement."

"Y-yes. N-no," Aimee stuttered.

Sally-Ann's frown deepened. "Which is it, Aimee? Yes or no?"

Her sister sighed heavily in her ear. "It's true, I hadn't seen him for years, not since the judge handed down his decision, but a few weeks ago, Doug called me. It was straight out of the blue. I nearly fell over when I realized it was him."

"What did he want?" Sally-Ann demanded. Dead or not, her ex-brother-in-law had been a loser through and through. He'd never deserved her beautiful, sweet-natured sister—then or now. Sally-Ann had been pleased to see the back of him.

"He wanted to see me. He... He told me he still loved me, that he was sorry. He... He wanted to know if there was a chance we might get back together."

"*What?*" Sally-Ann practically yelled the word into the phone.

"I know what you're thinking, Sal, but until the accident, we were happy...really happy."

"He ran off with your rehab nurse! Did you forget that?"

"No, of course not and he hurt me very much when he did that, but we'd just been told I was a paraplegic. I was never going to walk again. It was a lot for him to take in. Too much."

Sally-Ann shook her head, aghast. "I can't believe you're making excuses for him! That lowlife walked out on you and your marriage when you needed him most! And to make matters worse, *he* was the reason you were *in* a wheelchair!"

"It was an accident, Sal. Even the police agreed. He was never charged, remember?"

Sally-Ann made an impatient sound of disgust in the back of her throat. "And you know exactly how I felt about that, how I *still* feel about that!"

Aimee sighed quietly. "It happened so long ago, Sal. You need to let it go. I have." She paused and then added softly, "It was nice to speak with Doug that day. He sounded so pleased at the thought of seeing me again. Now...he's dead."

"Hang on a minute, didn't he marry that little tart he ran away with?"

"The nurse? Yes. Apparently things didn't work out. They split a few months ago."

"Oh, Aimee! Surely you didn't give him any hope that you and he...?"

"No, of course not, but...I did meet with him." She paused and then, in a voice that was ragged with emotion, she continued: "You don't understand what it's *like*, Sal. Most people I meet won't even look me in the eye and those who do often look at me with pity. Doug knew me, knew the woman I was, from before. He didn't see a damaged woman in a wheelchair. He saw *me*."

Aimee's voice broke and Sally-Ann's heart clenched with pain. She couldn't imagine what life was like for her sister. She wanted to think that Aimee was living a life just as happy and fulfilled as she had prior to the accident, but she knew she was kidding herself.

For one, Aimee had lost her mobility and with it, a fair portion of her sense of self. She'd been a talented gymnast. She'd been good enough to qualify for the Olympics. Instead, she'd gone to college and studied psychology and sports science and had met Doug Hanley there and fallen in love. Dreams of being an Olympian had faded, but she'd still maintained her fitness with regular visits to the gym and competing in friendly local gymnastics competitions. She'd also volunteered at a sporting complex close to where she lived, teaching and encouraging young kids to achieve their dream.

Now Aimee was a paraplegic and she'd never walk the beam or swing off the high bars again. That part of her life was over and it wasn't the only major upheaval she'd faced. It was easy for Sally-

Ann to feel aghast over the fact her sister had behaved civilly toward her ex-brother-in-law. Sally-Ann's life wasn't the one that had been turned upside down.

And now Doug was dead...murdered.

"Do the police know for sure it was murder?" she asked.

"He was shot in the head at close range. I don't know all the facts, but apparently they've ruled out suicide." Her voice hitched. "It's just so *sad!* I can't believe it! Who would want Doug dead? It doesn't make sense! I only saw him the other day. We met for coffee. I barely recognized him. He'd lost a heap of weight."

"Two divorces might put you off your food," Sally-Ann said dryly.

"It was more than that," Aimee insisted. "He'd changed in other ways. He was nicer. More gentle. He was so sorry for what had happened. For the first time, he actually apologized."

"Well, that's big of him. The son of a bitch ought to be sorry. He's the reason it happened."

Aimee sighed again. "Oh, Sal. No one's forgotten how I came to be in this wheelchair—least of all me—but I've long since forgiven him for the accident. Even so, I told him it wasn't ever going to work out between us, no matter how sorry he was. That part of my life's over."

Sally-Ann blew her breath out on a quiet sigh of relief.

"How did he take it?" she asked.

"Not very well. He actually got a bit teary. Told me again how sorry he was, how I was the only woman he'd ever loved, and on and on."

"I still don't understand why his mother would think you'd had anything to do with his death."

When Aimee replied, her voice was heavy with sadness and resignation. "Maureen Hanley never liked me. We all knew that. She thinks I've been biding my time since the divorce, just waiting for the opportunity to seek revenge."

"She didn't know you very well if she thought that," Sally-Ann commented dryly.

"That's the problem," Aimee replied. "She didn't know me at all. From the first moment Doug brought me home to meet her, she treated me coldly. She didn't want her son married to an Asian girl."

Anger rushed through Sally-Ann at her sister's words, fueled by the knowledge that what Aimee said was likely true. While Australia prided itself on being a multicultural country, there were still many people who harbored racist attitudes. Sally-Ann had often been subjected to such narrow-minded attitudes in the school yard. Her high school years had been sheer hell.

With an act of will, she forced the nightmares away. She refused to be dragged back down that path, helpless and weak, voiceless, accused of crimes she didn't commit. That was the reason she'd become a lawyer and worked in the Children's Court. She wanted to champion the causes of some of the most vulnerable in society; be their voice during their hour of need.

"Sal? Are you listening?"

Sally-Ann blinked and forced herself to

concentrate. "I'm sorry, Aimee. What did you say?"

"I said that Doug's mother told me I was the last person he called on his phone. That's another reason why she thinks I had something to do with his death."

Sally-Ann frowned. "I thought you said you met with him a few days ago? Surely he's made other calls since then?"

"You'd think so, but that's not what his mom said."

"Do you think she's telling the truth?" Sally-Ann asked.

"I don't know. I certainly didn't notice a missed call from him and the last time we spoke was the day we met for coffee when I told him— Hang on, there's someone at the door."

Sally-Ann poured oatmeal into her bowl and added milk while she waited on the line. She was just about to spoon some into her mouth when Aimee spoke again. This time, her voice sounded panicked.

"Oh, God, Sal, it's the *police*. They want to come in and talk to me. What do I *do*?"

"Aimee, take a breath and let it out. Stay calm. You've done nothing wrong. Let them in and talk to them. They're just doing their job."

"What if they think I had something to do with Doug's death?" she wailed.

Sally-Ann heard the increasing panic in her sister's voice. She understood Aimee's reaction. Their father had fled China with his wife and daughters sixteen years earlier, fearing for their lives, hunted by the Chinese authorities for crimes he didn't commit. He'd instilled in both girls a healthy fear and distrust of the police.

Over the years, in her capacity as a criminal lawyer, Sally-Ann had learned to deal with the police and often came into contact with them in the course of her job, but her sister was a psychologist. Aimee probably never had cause to speak with law enforcement officers. And after that news from the mother of her ex, no wonder she was so freaked.

"Do you want me to come over?" Sally-Ann asked.

"Would you?" Aimee pleaded.

Sally-Ann thought of the work piled up on her desk and the hearing she was meant to be fronting up to in court later that morning. Perhaps she'd be able to deal with her sister's crisis and still make it to the courthouse on time. She'd try her hardest. The worst that could happen was that she'd have to call in a favor at work and ask someone else to attend the hearing. Her friend and colleague, Abby Fitzgerald, might be free...

The thoughts rushed through Sally-Ann's head. She sighed. "All right. I'm on my way. Don't say anything until I get there."

"How long will you take? What if they pressure me to speak?" Aimee cried.

"I'll get there as fast as I can," Sally-Ann replied, her mind now firmly committed to helping her sister. "Just tell them you're waiting for your lawyer."

James Shepherd stared down at the petite, attractive Asian woman in the wheelchair who looked at him with an expression that was part fear, part defiance. Douglas Hanley's mother had mentioned that her son's ex-wife was Asian, but she hadn't revealed the woman was bound to a wheelchair. James wondered if it were a permanent affliction, or if she'd injured herself temporarily. He noticed the woman held a cell phone in her hand.

"Mrs Aimee Hanley? I'm Detective James Shepherd. We'd like to talk to you about Douglas Hanley."

"That was my lawyer," the woman said in response, indicating the phone. "She advised me not to say anything until she arrives."

James' eyebrows flew up in surprise. They were merely making preliminary inquires. He would have been taken aback by her forceful attitude if he hadn't spied the flash of fear in her dark eyes. Now she was lawyering up. *What the hell was going on?*

"Mrs Hanley, we're just here to ask a few questions," he said in a conciliatory tone.

"My name is Aimee Li," she shot back. "My husband and I divorced five years ago. I no longer go by the name Hanley."

James nodded. "That would be Douglas Michael Hanley, correct?"

"Correct."

Wang stepped forward. James moved aside to allow his partner a little room. The woman still hadn't invited them in.

"Miss Li, I'm Detective Hung Wang. I work with Detective Shepherd. Douglas Hanley was found murdered last night. In fact, it was the early hours of this morning."

The woman didn't look surprised.

"You've heard already," James stated.

She looked at him and nodded. "Yes. His mother rang a little while ago with the sad news."

Wang shot her a quizzical look. "Is it? Sad news?"

"Of course," the woman replied defensively. "Just because Doug and I fell out of love and I chose to go back to my maiden name doesn't mean I'm glad he's dead. In fact, I still find it very difficult to believe."

James eyed her solemnly. She appeared to be genuine. Still, the mother of the deceased was adamant her son's ex-wife was involved. James' thoughts circled back to the wheelchair. If the injury were genuine, this woman obviously wasn't the shooter. Still, she could have arranged the hit...

"How long have you been in a wheelchair?" he asked.

"Five years. I'm a paraplegic," she stated flatly.

Once again, her response surprised him. "Five years... The same time you've been divorced. Is there a connection?"

Her mouth twisted into a grimace. "I was injured in a boating accident. My ex-husband was behind the wheel. Our marriage didn't survive my injuries."

James frowned. He couldn't recall any such notations about a boating accident in Hanley's file. He kept his gaze on her. "Was he charged over the incident?"

She lowered her gaze and shook her head. "No. It was ruled an accident."

Once again, James studied her closely. Though it appeared she had every reason to be bitter, he couldn't detect that emotion in her tone. *Perhaps she was clever at hiding it?* After all, her ex-husband, the man who'd caused her serious permanent injury, had just been found murdered. It wouldn't do to hand the police a possible motive.

James had been a detective long enough to know that all types could be criminals. The most innocent-looking person could turn out to have a heart as black as the night. He'd learned never to take anything or anyone at face value. Besides, she'd already made contact with her lawyer and then there was that flash of fear... What it all meant, he had yet to learn, but he was far from through with Aimee Li.

"Did your ex-mother-in-law tell you how her son was killed?" he asked.

The woman nodded. "Yes. Maureen said he was shot."

James kept his gaze trained on her. "Yes, he was shot. In the middle of the forehead. Do you know how to shoot, Miss Li?"

"No."

"Because this person knew what they were doing. The gun was fired from a reasonable distance and yet the bullet landed dead center, killing your ex instantly. We're sure it wasn't by chance."

Once again, he eyeballed her, but she remained unflustered. Either she was very good at keeping calm under pressure, or she was telling the truth.

"What's your relationship like with Doug's mother?" Wang asked conversationally.

The woman turned her attention to James' colleague. "I have no problem with Maureen Hanley, though I can't say she feels the same way about me."

"You're right," James replied. "In fact, she was the one who sent us to your door. She's convinced you're involved in Doug's murder."

Anger flickered in the dark depths of Aimee's eyes. "Then I guess I ought to be thankful she's not in charge of this investigation," she replied, her tone laced with sarcasm.

"You and your ex-mother-in-law didn't get on?" James guessed.

The woman let out a bark of laughter. Her mouth tightened. "Oh, we got on just fine. As long as I stayed well out of her way. She was ashamed and upset her son had the audacity to marry an Asian woman. Maureen Hanley, fine upstanding Christian lady who volunteers twice a week at a church-run soup kitchen can't stand the thought of her precious son being tangled up with a woman born in China."

And there it was. The bitterness he'd expected earlier. It was strange how it hadn't manifested itself during discussions about her ex-husband. No, it was the ex-mother-in-law who'd triggered it. *Interesting.* Just as interesting as Maureen Hanley's certainty her ex-daughter-in-law was responsible for her son's death.

As if belatedly realizing she'd let her tongue run away with her, the woman in the wheelchair collected herself and then, reversing the wheels of her chair, turned and headed down a wide hall. Taking her up on her unspoken invitation, James and Wang followed behind her.

The hall ended in a bright and airy open concept kitchen and living room. James noticed the kitchen countertops had been customized to accommodate the height of the wheelchair.

The overall color scheme was white and buttercup yellow. Furniture was sparse, but what there was had been selected with care. The room was decorated with style and flair and could have been taken from the pictures of one of those glossy home design magazines his sister sometimes flipped through. Whatever Aimee Li did for a living, it paid well.

The woman in question sat in her chair on the far side of the room. Her back was to the window. Morning sunlight spilled over her shoulder, throwing her face in shadows. She appeared to have regained her calm façade and any indication that she'd been upset by their line of questioning was gone. A knock sounded at the door. Her expression reflected her relief.

"That will be my sister," she said.

James frowned. "I thought you were waiting for your lawyer?"

"My sister *is* my lawyer. Please, will you show her in?"

James concealed his surprise and headed back down the hall. Reaching for the knob, he opened the door and was immediately taken aback. The young female who stood in the entryway was the most beautiful woman he'd ever seen and she was spitting fire. She barely came up to his shoulder, but she stared at him with all the attitude of a mother lion who was hell-bent on protecting her cub.

"I'm Sally-Ann Li."

James' head spun. He'd thought Aimee was attractive; this woman was stunning. Dark, almond-shaped eyes flashed with anger. Coal-black hair that shone like a satiny curtain hung loose around her shoulders and fell halfway down her back. A luscious mouth painted in bright red lipstick drew his gaze over and over again. And then his mind snagged on her name.

Sally-Ann Li.

The name on the business card he'd picked up at the scene. His heart thumped. *Coincidence?* Hardly. But what did it mean? Belatedly, he shook her proffered hand. It was small and slim, but her handshake was strong and firm.

"Detective James Shepherd," he said in reply.

She narrowed her eyes at him. "I'm representing Aimee Li and you want to hope like hell you haven't elicited any information from her without me present."

She wore a tailored, charcoal-gray suit and pale gray blouse. The outfit looked like it cost more than a month's wages. Belatedly, he noticed her four-inch black wedges. Though they elevated her somewhat, she was still tiny, but with her shoulders thrust back and the light of challenge gleaming in her eyes, it was obvious what she lacked in stature she made up for in attitude.

He stepped back and allowed her to enter. A wave of expensive perfume wafted toward his nose. Her wedges clacked at a brisk pace along the wooden floorboards. He followed at a more leisurely pace, enjoying the view from the rear. It was every bit as pleasing as the front. He was suddenly very interested to learn more about Sally-Ann Li.

Chapter 3

Sally-Ann leaned down to peck her sister on the cheek and used the time to slow down her heartbeat. The sight of the sexy detective on the other side of the door had sent her pulse into a flurry of activity. It was like a frisson of electricity had passed between them. It felt so real, she'd almost gasped at the impact. She was sure he'd felt it, too. Still, this wasn't the time or place to get distracted by a handsome face and a pair of startling green eyes.

"How are you doing?" she whispered to Aimee.

"I'm fine," her sister replied.

"Have you told them anything?"

Aimee blushed guiltily. Sally-Ann frowned. "I thought I told you not to speak to them until I got here?" she whispered furiously.

"You did and I didn't tell them very much. They just started asking questions and I... I answered them."

Sally-Ann shot another narrow-eyed look in the direction of the good-looking detective and then focused back on her sister. "I guess it doesn't matter. It's not like you have anything to hide, right?"

Aimee nodded. "Right."

Sally-Ann cleared her throat and returned her attention to the detectives who stood a short distance away. She'd barely noticed the Chinese detective on her way in. The man was older than his colleague. Sally-Ann guessed him to be in his mid- to late forties. His short black hair was graying at the temples and crows' feet lined the skin around his eyes. He stared at her with eyes that were as black as midnight. The younger detective stepped forward and made the introductions.

"Ms Li, this is my partner, Detective Hung Wang. We're here to talk to your sister about the murder of her ex-husband."

Sally-Ann nodded. "Yes, Aimee called me a short while ago and told me about Doug's death."

James moved closer to her sister. "We have some more questions, Miss Li."

Aimee shot a look at Sally-Ann, who nodded. "Ask away," Aimee said.

"How long were you married to Douglas Hanley?" James asked.

"Seven years," Aimee replied. "We got married right after my twenty-second birthday."

"And you've been divorced for five, right?" Shepherd asked.

"Yes. I'm thirty-four, Detective, in case you need help with the math."

The detective allowed himself a small smile. Sally-Ann caught a glimpse of even, white teeth that were in stark contrast to the tanned skin around his mouth.

"When did you last see your ex-husband?" Wang asked.

Once again, Aimee looked toward her sister and once again, Sally-Ann nodded in encouragement. As much as they'd been raised to be suspicious of the police, for the most part, Sally-Ann knew the law enforcement officers were just trying to do their job. From her experience in court she knew things often went smoother if you cooperated, and with nothing to hide, there was no reason not to answer their questions.

"Doug called me a few days ago and wanted to see me. We met for coffee at the Westfield Mall," Aimee replied.

"Which mall?" James asked.

"The one in Parramatta."

"You've been divorced for five years. How often did you speak with your ex?" James asked.

"We didn't speak," Aimee replied quietly. "At least, not until a few weeks ago. Doug's call came from out of the blue. Until the other day, I hadn't seen him since the divorce was finalized."

Shepherd frowned. "So you hadn't seen or heard from him in all that time and suddenly, he calls you and asks you to meet. Is that right?"

"Yes."

"What for?"

Aimee's brow furrowed in confusion. "Excuse me?"

"Why did he ask you to meet with him?" Wang clarified.

Color spread across Aimee's cheeks. She stared down at her hands where they were folded in her lap. "He wanted to talk to me. He wanted to apologize for...the accident. He told me he still loved me and that he should never have walked out. He wanted us to get back together."

"And what was your response?" Shepherd asked.

"I was flattered and a few years earlier I might have taken him up on his offer. I was heartbroken when he walked out on our marriage. It took me a long time to heal, not only from the accident, but the emotional pain took a long time to get over. But... I'm finally in a place where most of the time I'm happy with who I am and where I am in life. I have a good job, a nice apartment, a small group of close friends. And I did it all without Doug. I've moved on; I don't need him in my life. I told him as much."

"And how did he take it?" Wang asked.

Aimee sighed. "Not very well. He tried to convince me to give him another go. He promised he'd try harder this time."

"And what did you say?" Wang asked.

"I told him no."

"Where were you last night?" Shepherd asked.

Sally-Ann tensed. She was certain her sister was innocent of any wrongdoing, but she'd forgotten to ask her if she had an alibi.

"I was here, at home," Aimee replied.

"Alone?" Shepherd asked.

"Yes."

"Can anyone verify that?"

Aimee shrugged. "I spoke to my mother a little after eight. I was watching Seinfeld reruns. Mom loves that show. We talked about it. I went to bed around ten and didn't wake until Doug's mom telephoned me early this morning."

"Did you speak to anyone in your building last night? Anyone who can confirm you were here?" Shepherd continued.

Aimee fell silent a moment and then shook her head. "No. Unless one of the neighbors saw me alight from the cab I always take from work. You'd have to ask them."

Shepherd and Wang shared a look. Sally-Ann had seen that look before. It immediately set her on edge. She moved so that she stood between Aimee and the detectives and crossed her arms over her chest. She eyed the men defiantly.

"My sister lives alone. She was at home last night watching television and then went to bed, like she does most nights. It's not her fault there might not be anyone who can verify her movements. It's not like she was given any warning that she'd need an alibi." She clenched her teeth together and glared at the good-looking detective. "Where were *you* last night, Detective? Is there anyone who can verify *your* whereabouts?"

Seemingly unperturbed by the challenge in her tone, the detective in question shot her a lazy look. Sally-Ann could have sworn she saw a glint of amusement in his mesmerizing eyes.

"As a matter of fact, Ms Li, there *is* someone who can verify my whereabouts."

Her belly tightened with disappointment. He was married…

"I was doing the graveyard shift from six to six, alongside Detective Wang," he added, surprising her. "That's how we caught your ex-brother-in-law's case. I guess we got lucky."

His tone was liberally laced with sarcasm. Heat spread up Sally-Ann's neck and crept across her cheeks. *What was she doing?* It was madness to challenge the detective. He was in charge of a murder investigation, an investigation that put her sister in their sights. Of course they were wasting their time in that respect, but right now the detectives were pursuing every line of inquiry and unfortunately, that included Aimee. The sooner she gave them the answers they sought, the sooner they'd realize she couldn't have committed the murder and then they'd be on their way.

"Where was Doug when he died?" Sally-Ann asked, modifying her tone.

Detective Shepherd's gaze remained steady on hers. "He was shot in the forehead in an alleyway in the city."

Sally-Ann gasped then shook her head slowly back and forth. "Detective, does my sister look like someone capable of doing that? She doesn't even know how to shoot, let alone get herself into an alleyway in the middle of the night to murder her ex-husband."

The detective looked unperturbed. "It doesn't mean she didn't get someone else to do it."

Sally-Ann's lip curled derisively. "You watch too much TV, Detective. My sister wouldn't hurt a fly.

She abhors violence."

The detective's expression remained unchanged. "Your ex-brother-in-law ruined your sister's life. What's worse, it appears the law didn't see fit to punish him for it. That's a fairly strong motive, Counselor."

Sally-Ann held on to her temper. There was nothing to be gained by letting the detective know how much his words rankled. "My sister has been in a wheelchair for five years. That's a long time to wait for revenge."

"Perhaps an opportunity didn't present itself earlier?" the detective continued in a mild tone. "Your sister told us she recently met up with her ex-husband. Perhaps the meeting dredged up old memories and renewed long-dormant anger and pain... Who's to say?"

"What about Janice Carter?"

The quietly voiced question broke through the silence. As one, Sally-Ann and James turned to face Aimee.

"Who's Janice Carter?" James asked.

Aimee grimaced. "I see Maureen Hanley didn't fill you in on *everything*."

James looked at Wang and then returned his attention to Sally-Ann's sister. "I don't believe she mentioned that name."

"She's Doug's ex-wife," Sally-Ann stated and felt a shard of satisfaction at the surprise that flooded the faces of both detectives.

"Hang on a minute," Shepherd said. He turned to Aimee. "I'm confused. I thought *you* were the ex-wife?"

"I'm Doug's first wife. He left me for Janice."

Detective Shepherd nodded in comprehension. He made his way over to the two-seater and lowered himself onto it. The action brought him down to Aimee's level. Sally-Ann caught a whiff of his spicy cologne. It tickled her nostrils. Annoyed that she'd noticed how good it smelled, she hovered protectively nearby.

"Tell me about Janice," Shepherd said quietly.

Aimee drew in a deep breath and eased it out on a sigh. "Janice Carter was a nurse at the Sydney Harbour Hospital. That's where I was hospitalized after the accident. I spent months there—between the days in the Intensive Care Unit and the weeks in rehab, the hospital became my second home. Doug visited me often, right up until the day he told me he'd fallen in love with one of the nurses who was involved in my treatment. He was leaving me for Janice. Life as I'd known it was over and at that point, apparently so was my marriage."

"It must have come as a shock," Shepherd said sympathetically.

Sally-Ann was grateful for his sensitivity toward her sister. Aimee had been desperately hurt by her husband's betrayal and even more so because it came at a time when she'd needed him the most.

"Yes, it did," Aimee admitted quietly. "Apart from the accident, it was the worst thing that had ever happened to me. Coming right on the heels of being told I'd be confined to a wheelchair for the rest of my life, it was a little tough to take."

Her sister said the words lightly and even

managed a shaky smile, but Sally-Ann wasn't fooled. The whole sad episode had sent Aimee spiraling into a depression so deep, her family had despaired that she'd ever find a way out of it. But, to her credit, Aimee had found the strength to pull herself together and over the years, she'd learned to live with her disability. She'd even returned to work and now ran a successful counseling business in a medical center attached to the Sydney Harbour Hospital.

"When did Doug marry Janice?" Shepherd asked, his tone still low and respectful.

Aimee sighed. "I'm not sure of the exact date. They were together from the time Doug left me. He filed for a divorce from me a few months later and a year down the track, the final papers were issued. When I spoke to him the other day, he said he and Janice were over. From what he said, I gathered the break-up was recent."

Shepherd frowned. "What made you think that?"

Aimee shrugged. "Just that he said Janice had taken the break-up hard and was hopeful they'd reconcile. He wanted no part of that. In fact, like I already told you he wanted to get back together with me."

"Did you and Doug have any children?" Shepherd asked.

Aimee shook her head sadly. "No. Doug caught the mumps when he was fifteen. The illness left him infertile. Unfortunately, neither of us knew about the infertility until we started doing some medical investigations. We'd tried for a family for a couple of years before we decided to go to a doctor."

"That must have been tough," Shepherd said.

Aimee looked across at him. "Yes, it was."

"Do you think that contributed to the breakdown of your marriage?" Shepherd asked.

"Maybe. It certainly put a strain on things, though I would never have left Doug over it. I hadn't married him for his ability to provide me with children. I didn't think it was something we couldn't get past. Then I got hurt…"

Sally-Ann cleared her throat. She couldn't see how this line of questioning was relevant. All it was doing was dragging up painful memories for her sister and Aimee had already been through enough.

"Detective Shepherd, are we nearly done here?" she asked.

He shot her a look that was loaded with challenge. "What do *you* think about the boating accident that left your sister a paraplegic?"

Sally-Ann bit her lip against an instinctive protest. She hated that people referred to it as an accident. Okay, the police hadn't seen fit to lay charges against her ex-brother-in-law, but even all these years later, she fumed against the injustice that he'd walked away without being punished. As far as she was concerned, his reckless behavior had caused the injury to her sister. He should have been made to pay. Still, it wouldn't do to alert the police to the anger and resentment she still felt toward Doug. Not when he'd just been murdered. She chose her words with care.

"Naturally, my family and I were incredibly upset when it happened. Despite the police findings, I think he acted irresponsibly and should have been held accountable. Our parents feel the same way. It doesn't mean we wanted him dead."

Wang straightened from his slouched position up against the wall and stepped forward. "Who are your parents?"

"Chao and Fen Li. They live in Leichardt," she replied.

"We'll need to interview them," Wang stated and took down their address.

Sally-Ann swallowed a sigh. *Great.* The last thing her parents needed was a visit from the police. Her dad would freak. She needed to call him and warn him.

"We'll also need to speak with Janice Carter," Shepherd said. "How certain are you that she still works at the Sydney Harbour Hospital?"

He directed his question to Aimee. She shrugged. "I'm not at all sure. When Doug and I spoke the other day, he didn't mention where she worked. He only talked about the fact they were over."

Shepherd acknowledged her comment with a nod and then reached inside his jacket. He pulled out two business cards and handed one to Aimee and gave the other to Sally-Ann. Their fingers brushed and tingles ran down Sally-Ann's arm from the contact. She averted her gaze and murmured her thanks.

"Please call me if you think of anything that might help with the investigation. According to Maureen Hanley, your sister was the last person to speak with the victim. Or at least, she was the last person he called." The detective turned back to Aimee. "Did you speak with Doug last night?"

"No. It didn't even show up as a missed call. You can check my phone if you like."

Shepherd nodded and Aimee wheeled away toward the counter. Her phone was lying on the low bench. She picked it up and gave it to the detective. Shepherd checked the screen and then handed the phone back to her.

"It's locked."

Aimee entered her passcode and then handed the phone back to him. In silence, he flicked through the screens and then handed the phone to his colleague. Wang repeated the action and a moment later, shook his head.

"There doesn't seem to be any call logged to the victim last night. In fact, the only calls I can find that relate to him are the ones made and received three days ago."

"That's when Doug and I agreed to meet. I already told you about that."

Shepherd nodded, appearing to be satisfied. "Yes, you did, Miss Li and we appreciate your cooperation. We'll have to check Doug's phone. It was collected as evidence at the scene. Anyway, like I told your sister, if you think of anything else, please call me."

With a final glance in Sally-Ann's direction, Shepherd headed toward the front door. Wang followed him. The door clicked on their departure and Sally-Ann's shoulders slumped on a sigh. She looked at Aimee. "We need to call Dad."

CHAPTER 4

Sally-Ann pulled the phone out of her jacket pocket and dialed her father's number. Both of her parents worked shift work at the local supermarket. She wasn't sure if either would be at home but, with the police heading in their direction, she couldn't take any chances. She needed to warn them.

Her father had been so proud when she'd graduated from law school and she understood why. Back in China, he used to be a lawyer. When the family had fled their home country in fear of their lives, her mom and dad had taken up low profile jobs and the whole family lived a quiet existence in the suburbs of Sydney—so as not to draw attention to themselves.

Sally-Ann had been thirteen when she arrived in Australia and she remembered well the costly tailored suits and expensive shiny black leather shoes and matching briefcase her father used to wear. She wondered if he missed having such an important, intellectually stimulating job.

Though her father had explained to his daughters years earlier why he was so fearful of the Chinese police, Sally-Ann thought he was a little too paranoid when, in whispered tones, heavy with fear, he spoke of being hunted by the Chinese authorities. Still, she and Aimee knew better than to make light of his concerns. And that was the reason she needed to warn him of the impending visit from the two detectives. Besides, her mother had been suffering a serious chest infection that could easily spread to her lungs. Sally-Ann didn't want the shock of an unexpected visit from law enforcement to jeopardize her mother's recovery.

"Hello?" The sound of her father's cautious greeting filled her with relief.

"Dad, it's Sal. I'm afraid I have some bad news." She relayed the fact that Doug had been found murdered in the early hours of the morning.

"Well, I didn't want to see the man dead, but I can't say I'm unhappy that he's finally gotten what he deserved," her father replied.

"Dad! Don't say that! Did you hear what I said? Doug was murdered! Someone shot him in the head."

"After what he did to your sister, surely you can't expect me to feel sorry for him?" came the caustic reply.

Sally-Ann blew out her breath on a sigh. She understood where her father was coming from and she didn't blame him for his antagonism. The hurt and pain Doug had caused her sister was still a festering wound for her parents. They couldn't understand how the police didn't hold him responsible for the accident. It had only served to strengthen their belief the police couldn't be trusted.

"The thing is, Dad, two detectives have been to see Aimee this morning. In fact, they left not long ago. They questioned her about Doug."

"Surely they can't think our Aimee had anything to do with it!"

"No, Dad. I don't think so. I guess they're following all lines of inquiry. She was his ex-wife and Doug's mother very kindly pointed the police in Aimee's direction."

Her father made an angry sound of disbelief. "That wicked, conniving woman!" he spat. "She never did like our Aimee. How dare she accuse my little girl of doing something like that! I should go over there right now and give her a piece of my mind. Does she still live in Granville? Just wait until—"

"Dad! Stop! You can't go over there. You'd only make things worse. We both know Aimee had nothing to do with Doug's murder. Let's just leave the police to do their job."

"Bah! The police! What do they know? They—"

"Are on their way over to your place now. At least, I think they'll arrive sometime today. They want to talk to you and Mom about Doug and about the accident."

"Why would they want to talk to us? That accident happened five years ago."

"Yes, well, they're covering all bases. Apparently Maureen told them how we blamed her son for what happened. I guess they're checking it out. After all, someone was angry enough at Doug to murder him."

"Oh, yes! I was angry enough to murder him. I lost count of the number of nights I lay awake, thinking of ways to kill him. But why would I wait five years? It doesn't make sense."

Sally-Ann drew in a sharp breath. "For heaven's sake, Dad. Don't go telling the police things like that! You'll go right to the top of their suspect list!" She paused and sighed quietly, knowing as a lawyer he would already understand that. "Just acknowledge how upset you were about the accident, but impress on them that it was a long time ago. You've learned to accept what happened and we've all moved on, including Aimee."

"But—"

"No, Dad. Trust me on this. The less you say to them, the better. At the moment, it appears they're just following up on inquires and it's my guess Maureen is largely behind this. Once they realize she has her own ax to grind against the Li family, they'll leave us all alone. I just wanted to call and warn you they might be on their way, so you can be prepared."

"Yes, well, thanks, Sal. I appreciate the heads-up. I'll warn your mother. She'll need some time to steel herself against a visit from the police. We might have fled China more than a decade and a half ago, but the nightmare of those last weeks in our home country is still very much in the forefront of our minds. It's not something either of us will forget. Still, I won't give the police any cause for suspicion. I promise to keep my temper under control."

Sally-Ann breathed out a sigh of relief. "Thanks, Dad. Would it help if I was there when they come to speak with you?"

"No, honey. I'll be fine. Besides, you're at least an hour away and you don't even know when they're coming. Don't you have to be at work?"

"Yes, you're right. I do." She sighed again. "I should have been there already. I had to call in a favor from one of my colleagues to take over my cases until I can get there. Even so, I need to show myself before too much more time passes."

Once again, her father reassured her. "Go, Sal. I'll be fine. If I start getting into trouble, I can always play the 'I don't understand English' card and request an interpreter. That would delay things long enough for you to get here."

Sally-Ann thought of the Chinese detective who had accompanied Shepherd. "Unfortunately, one of the detectives involved in the investigation is Chinese. It would be our luck he speaks Mandarin."

Her father chuckled. "That would be unfortunate. Look, honey, I'll be fine. Don't worry."

She gnawed at her upper lip, reluctant to bring their conversation to an end until she'd voiced the question that had occurred to her the moment she heard Doug had been shot.

"Dad... Y-you didn't do anything stupid, did you? The detective said Doug was shot in the head. I know how much you love your firearms and you've held a grudge against Doug for a long time..."

"No, of course not! I already told you. I'm not going to pretend I'm sad he's dead, but I had nothing to do with it. You don't have anything to worry about on that score, honey."

The band of tension around Sally-Ann's chest eased. After urging him once again to phone if he needed her, she ended the call.

"What did he say?" Aimee asked.

"He wasn't unhappy to hear about Doug's untimely death, but he insists he had nothing to do with it."

Aimee stared at her with dark shadows filling her eyes. "Do you believe him?"

"Yes, I do," Sally-Ann replied and realized she meant it. "To this day, Dad blames Doug for putting you in a wheelchair, but I don't believe he had anything to do with Doug's murder."

Aimee nodded, relief flooding her face. "Good. I'm so glad. I couldn't stand it if Dad went to jail for something he thought he was doing for me. Especially murder." She shuddered and Sally-Ann was reminded of all her sister had been through. It had been a tough five years. The last thing any of them needed was to be caught up in a murder investigation.

"How are you holding up?" she asked softly, coming over to rest the back of her hand against her sister's soft cheek.

Tears glinted in Aimee's eyes. "I'm fine. I'm just so sad for Doug. I loved him for so long. I thought we'd be married forever. When he ran off with that nurse, I was devastated, but on some level, I understood. I was a paraplegic. He hadn't signed up for that. He—"

"Don't you dare make excuses for him!" Sally-Ann was appalled her sister could even think like that. "He was a no-good, lying, sneaking son of a—"

"Maybe he was," Aimee interrupted, "but he was also hurting and in shock and struggling with his guilt. Every time he saw me, he was reminded all over again about what had happened and how he was responsible for it. The police might not have held him criminally liable, but that didn't mean Doug felt the same way. He told me. It tore him up inside. Running away was his only escape."

"Oh, well, too bad for him!" Sally-Ann replied sarcastically. "Poor little Doug. Too gutless to stick around and live with the consequences of his actions." She shook her head in disbelief. "Don't expect me to feel sorry for him."

Aimee looked at her sadly. "I don't expect you to understand. I guess the only way I could get through those awful weeks, months, *years* was to accept that he did what he had to do. I learned to forgive him."

Sally-Ann stared at her sister and was overcome with guilt. *How could she be related to such a sweet and kind and giving person?* Aimee made her feel ashamed. Sally-Ann wasn't in a place where she could forgive her ex-brother-in-law and now that he was dead, she wasn't sure that she ever would.

"That afternoon, a few days ago, when Doug and I met for coffee... We had such a nice afternoon. We chatted about things that had happened years earlier, back before things went so wrong. He was upset about the break-up of his second marriage, but not in a devastated kind of way. As I said, he kept telling me how much he still loved me and wanted us to get back together. He seemed to be in a good place and was hopeful about the future, even after I let him down as gently as I could." She paused and then added, "I still can't believe he's dead... Murdered... No one deserves to die like that."

Her voice hitched on a sob and Sally-Ann's heart went out to her. She bent down beside the wheelchair and gave her sister an awkward hug. Aimee drew in a deep breath and eased it out slowly.

"I'm okay, Sal. Promise. It's just been a bit of a shock. I was only speaking with him a few days ago..." She shivered. "I didn't like that detective."

"Which one?"

"Wang. There's something about him that made me uneasy. He kept staring at me."

Sally-Ann was annoyed that she hadn't noticed. She was supposed to be there protecting her sister and most of her attention had been stolen by Shepherd. She offered Aimee a reassuring smile. "Don't worry. I'm sure they're taught to be like that in detective school. He was probably trying to intimidate you into a confession."

Aimee laughed without humor. "Well, he can stare at me all he likes. He won't get a confession from me. I didn't do it."

Sally-Ann stood and hugged her sister again. "I know. You're the sweetest, kindest girl in the world. You put me to shame." She checked the time and winced. She was so late. She only prayed Abby Fitzgerald had located her clients and reassured them they were in good hands and that her more difficult cases were lower down the court list.

"I have to go, Aimee. I'm late for work."

Her sister gave her a grateful smile. "Thanks for coming, Sal. I really appreciate it."

Sally-Ann smiled back at her. Despite the five-year age difference, they'd always been close. "No problem. Anytime. Call me if you need anything. I'll see you soon."

James and his colleague strode toward the double glass entry doors of the Sydney Harbour Hospital. A few patients congregated in the designated smoking area off to one side, all in hospital gowns, some with IVs in their arms. Another sat in a wheelchair. With cigarettes in their hands and clouds of smoke rising above their heads, it was all James could do not to inhale deeply as he and Wang walked past.

Resolutely ignoring the craving to light up, he reminded himself it was forty-seven days since he'd quit, and headed toward the information counter that stood off to one side of the grand foyer. Wang followed a few steps behind him.

James greeted the elderly volunteer with a friendly smile.

"Hi, I was wondering if you could point me in the direction of the general manager's office."

The woman smiled back at him and touched her fingers to her cloud of snowy hair. "My, aren't you a handsome one! Are you a new doctor on staff? Wait until I tell Dottie! She's going to be disappointed she missed meeting you. Still, if this is just your first day, there's a chance she'll see you again. I—"

"I'm sorry," James interrupted, acutely aware of Wang who stood just a short distance away. "I'm not a doctor. I'm—"

"Oh, my mistake! You're a nurse! I shouldn't have assumed you were a doctor. It's just that you look more like a doctor in that nice suit and that tie... Is that Italian silk? It looks like Italian silk. My Reginald *loved* Italian silk ties. He—"

"I'm sorry. I'm not a nurse, either. In fact, I'm not a member of staff." He pulled out his wallet and showed her his credentials. "I'm Detective James Shepherd. I'm here to speak with a staff member."

The old woman's hand came up to her mouth and she looked taken aback. "Oh... Oh...I see. I-I'm sorry. Here I was rabbiting on. I... Oh, dear! I'm so embarrassed. You're a police officer. You're not a doctor. You—"

"Please," James interrupted for the third time. He gentled it with another smile. "I really need to speak to the general manager. It's Deborah Healy, isn't it?"

The woman beamed. "Yes. She's held that

position for some years now and a more stylish woman you'll never meet."

James gave a curt nod of acknowledgment and tried to curb his impatience. "Do you mind giving me directions?"

"Of course, Detective. Go back toward the entryway and just before you reach the glass doors, you'll see a staircase off to your right. Go up one floor and you'll find Ms Healy's office, two doors down on your left. There should be someone there who can help you."

James nodded his thanks. The elderly volunteer gave him another smile. "Well, Detective, I hope you have a lovely day. It was very nice chatting with you!"

"You, too," he replied and then turned away. Wang fell into step beside him and together, they headed back in the direction they'd come. They walked in silence. Wang was the first to break it.

"What did you think about the Li woman?"

"Aimee? She certainly has motive. I mean, her ex put her in a wheelchair and even though she came across all sweet and forgiving, could anyone really feel that kindly toward the man who'd ruined her life? Still, there's no way she was the one on the motorbike and she told us she couldn't shoot. We can check if she's ever held a firearms license, but unless we can find a link between her and a killer for hire, she's a fair way down our list."

"What's your take on the sister? She's very protective of someone who apparently has nothing to hide. I mean, she felt the need to be there even though this was only a very preliminary visit. I found that odd. Who calls their lawyer if they aren't afraid of saying the wrong thing?"

"You're right," James agreed. "The sister was an altogether more interesting proposition. For a start, she isn't in a wheelchair and she was definitely still pissed at the ex-brother-in-law for the part he played in her sister's injury. It would be worth looking into her background—a firearms check, along with a check into whether she owns a motorbike."

"And then there are the parents," Wang added. "They also appear to have a reason for wanting to harm our victim."

"You're right. The whole Li family should be on the suspect list in some form or other. They definitely had motive. Let's see if we can find means and opportunity. In the meantime, we'll ask a few questions of our vic's *second* ex-wife."

Reaching the staircase, the men climbed the flight of stairs as directed. The executive suites were in an older part of the hospital and still showed signs of the grandness and style that had gone into the design of the building more than a century and a half ago. Original stained glass windows were surrounded by heavy wooden frames that were painted a forest green color. The morning light that filtered through them fell softly onto the polished wooden stairs beneath James' feet.

They turned left at the top of the stairs and walked until they came across a closed door embossed with the words *General Manager*.

James knocked on the wooden panel. It opened almost immediately. The middle-aged woman who greeted them was smartly dressed in a white linen pantsuit. A silk blouse in pale pink complemented the outfit.

"Good morning, I'm Detective James Shepherd and this is my partner, Detective Hung Wang. Are you Ms Healy?"

The woman chuckled. "Good heavens, no! I'm Veronica Blackwell, her receptionist. Do you have an appointment?"

"No. This visit is a little spontaneous. We're following up on some inquires in relation to a murder in the city last night."

Veronica's eyes widened momentarily. "I'll let Ms Healy know you're here and see if she has time to speak with you. Please, come in and take a seat."

James and Wang entered the room. The waiting area was small but tidy, with a dark leather sofa against one wall. A pile of magazines were artfully strewn across the glass top of a wooden coffee table.

"Ms Healy will be with you in a moment," Veronica advised. "Can I get you something to drink? Coffee or tea?"

James glanced at Wang and answered for both of them. "No, thanks. We're fine."

The woman nodded and returned to her seat behind the counter. A moment later, a door to their left opened and a tall, slender woman wearing a tailored, navy-blue suit and a blouse the color of clotted cream strode into the waiting room. Without pause, she came straight up to where they sat and put out her hand.

"Detective Shepherd, I'm Deborah Healy."

James stood and shook the proffered hand. The general manager turned her attention to Wang.

"And you must be Detective Wang." Wang nodded and returned her handshake.

With the preliminaries out of the way, the general manager inclined her head in the direction of her office. "Shall we?"

She turned on her four-inch, black leather heels and headed back the way she'd come. Her short red hair bounced slightly with the movement. James' gaze was drawn to her shapely butt. She must have been in her early fifties, but she was trim and toned and had a pair of stocking-encased legs that would put women half her age to shame.

They followed her into a corner office that overlooked the front entryway of the hospital, a floor below. The room was large and airy. Sunshine poured through the tall windows that lined the wall behind her desk, flooding the room with natural light. Potted plants that were not only real, but appeared to be flourishing, stood along the window ledge. Deborah Healy had a green thumb.

"Please, take a seat."

Two chairs stood opposite a large wooden desk. James and Wang did as she asked. Deborah took a seat behind her desk. Folding her hands in front of her, she looked at them expectantly. "Now,

Detectives, I must admit I'm at a bit of a loss as to the reason for your visit. Veronica mentioned you wanted to speak with me about a murder in the city last night. How I can help you?"

James cleared his throat. "Douglas Hanley was found murdered in an alleyway off Bathurst Street in the early hours of this morning. We're following several lines of inquiry, including speaking to those who were close to him. We understand his wife, Janice Carter, works here."

Comprehension filled the general manager's eyes. She acknowledged James' comments with a brief nod. "She might very well work here. I'm sure you can appreciate with more than a thousand staff employed by the hospital, I'm not familiar with each and every one of them, but if you give me a moment, I can have Veronica verify that this woman works here and give you permission to speak with her if she's on duty today."

"Thank you," James replied.

Deborah reached for her phone and spoke quietly into it. James' gaze scanned the general manager's desk and came to rest on a large black-and-white photograph of a good-looking older gentleman who smiled widely for the camera. The picture was familiar and all of a sudden, James recalled where he'd seen it.

Deborah hung up the phone and James eyed her steadily. "I'm sorry for your recent loss. I understand your husband was a fine surgeon."

The woman's lips tightened, as if she was working hard to hold back her emotions. She gave a jerky nod. "Thank you. Yes, he was. There are many heart surgeons in this country who owe their skill and expertise to my husband. Cancer took him away from us way too soon."

James recalled seeing a story on the prominent surgeon's passing a couple of months earlier. It had been all over the news. Richard Healy had been given the honor of a state funeral. It had been attended by thousands. A special pew had been set aside for some of his former patients who owed their lives to the man's skill as a surgeon. James could remember feeling sad that such a brilliant man's life had been ended by cancer.

The phone at Deborah's elbow pealed, interrupting James' thoughts. The general manager answered it and listened to the caller in silence. A few moments later, after a murmur of thanks into the receiver, she ended the call.

"It appears you're in luck. Janice Carter is in fact employed here as a nurse and she's currently rostered on the morning shift. You should find her on Ward A5. It's a rehabilitation ward."

James pushed his chair away from the desk and stood. "Thank you, Ms Healy. We appreciate your cooperation." He put out his hand and once again shook hers.

Wang nodded his thanks and together, the two of them left the office and headed back down the stairs.

CHAPTER 5

After explaining to Janice Carter's supervisor the need to speak with her, James and Wang waited outside the rehab ward for the nurse to appear. It was interesting that she still worked in the same ward where she'd met Aimee Li and her husband. Either the nurse really liked working there, or it didn't matter to her that the relationship that had started in that very ward had since died a sad death. From what Aimee Li had told them, the break-up hadn't been Janice's idea.

A tall, blond, busty woman James guessed to be in her late twenties, rounded the corner and headed toward them. She was dressed in a blue nurse's uniform, but she didn't look like any nurse James had ever seen. Perfectly applied makeup, including thick black mascara and shiny, hot-pink lips, was teamed with a mass of blond hair artistically arranged in a loose pile of curls atop her head. James guessed it was some kind of bun, but the golden tendrils that curled enticingly over her head and across her ears seemed so much more than that.

She approached them somewhat cautiously and James could only guess that she'd already been filled in by her supervisor. He introduced himself and Wang and got down to business.

"Ms Carter, we're sorry to inform you that your husband Douglas Hanley was murdered last night."

James watched closely for her reaction. She gasped in shock and her mouth formed a perfect O.

"Oh, no! Not Doug! Please, you must be mistaken!"

Wang shook his head. "I'm afraid not, Ms Carter. He's been formally identified by his mother."

Once again, the woman gasped in shock. This time, she brought an elegantly manicured hand up to her mouth. The hot-pink polish matched the gloss on her lips. "H-how?" she stammered.

"He was shot in the head," James stated flatly. "By someone who knew what they were doing," he added.

"Where were you last night, Ms Carter?" Wang asked.

Her eyes grew wide. "You can't honestly believe *I* had anything to do with it!" she cried.

"We're covering all bases, Ms Carter," James replied as he pulled out his notebook and pen. "We understand you and Mr Hanley were estranged, is that correct?"

She opened her mouth as if to protest and then

closed it again and offered a reluctant nod. "Yes. But we were working things out. We were going to get back together! It was only a matter of time! I bet that bag of a mother of his told you we were finished. She never liked me. If you ask me, she was jealous of what Doug and I had together. She couldn't stand to see him happy. We... We loved each other!"

Tears glinted in her eyes. James resolutely ignored them even as he applied a softening in his approach.

"I'm sorry, Ms Carter. I'm sure this is very distressing for you, but I'm afraid we have a few more questions."

"Where were you last night?" Wang repeated.

The woman dug around in the front of her uniform and produced a tissue which she dabbed at her eyes before replying. "I worked until eleven and then I went home."

"Where do you live?" James asked.

"I live in Granville."

"That's where Doug lived with his mother," James stated.

"Yes. We bought a house together only a few blocks from her. Doug was very close to his mother and her husband died a year ago. Cancer. After his death, she lived alone. Doug didn't want to move too far away from her. He visited with her most days. When we...decided to take some time apart, he moved back in with her."

"Whose idea was it to end your relationship?" James asked.

Janice grimaced. "It was Doug's. He...he was struggling with my desire to start a family."

James started in surprise. Aimee Li had said her ex-husband was sterile. *Had Doug withheld that information from his second wife?*

"You see, Doug was infertile," Janice continued, answering James' unspoken question. "He caught the mumps when he was young," she explained. "I wanted to use an anonymous sperm donor. Doug was against it. Lately, we seemed to argue about it incessantly. That's why he moved out."

"He told his first wife that you and he were over. In fact, according to Aimee Li, your husband wanted to rekindle his relationship with her."

Her cheeks turned a vivid red. Anger flared in her eyes. "That's a filthy lie! There's no way Doug would go back to her!"

James shrugged. "If you say so."

"I don't only say so. I *know* so! Sure, Doug felt sorry for the woman. After all, he'd been driving the boat when she had the accident that put her in a wheelchair, but that was as far as it went. He loved *me!* I'm the one he's spent the past five years with! *Me!*" Her bark of laughter sounded harsh in the silence of the corridor. "What man in his right mind would choose her over *me?*"

James compressed his lips against a response he might regret and instead steered the conversation back to the matter at hand.

"You say you went home to Granville after your shift last night. Can anyone verify that?"

Janice shook her head. "No. I... I live alone."

"Did you take public transport?" Wang asked.

Once again, the woman shook her head. "No."

"What time did you arrive home?" James asked.

"About half-past eleven. Traffic is quiet at that time of night."

"What time did you start work this morning?" Wang asked.

"Seven. I left home at six-fifteen. I always allow a little extra time in the morning. Peak-hour traffic and all that."

"Do you own a motorbike, Ms Carter?" James asked, changing tack.

The woman looked a little confused. "Yes."

James glanced at Wang. He could tell from the sudden interest on his colleague's face that the man had also picked up on the significance of Carter's reply.

"Is that how you get to and from work?" James asked.

"Yes. Most of the time."

"Did you ride your motorbike to work yesterday?" Wang asked.

"Yes."

"What about this morning?" Wang added.

"Yes. The only time I don't ride is when it's too wet. The roads get slippery and visibility is bad. Motorists tend not to notice motorbikes as much in the rain. They're concentrating on the challenges the bad weather presents. It's not much fun on a motorbike in the rain. On those days, I catch the train."

"Do you mind showing us your motorbike now?" James asked.

The woman shrugged. "No, I guess not. It's parked in the staff parking lot. I'm due for a break soon. I'll take you there."

"Thank you," James replied. "When did you last see Doug?"

Once again, tears welled up in Janice's eyes. "I haven't seen him for more than a month. He stopped taking my calls! He refused to see me! I tried to speak to his mother, to get her to talk sense into him. She never much liked me, but I was sure if anyone could bring him round, Maureen could. I told her we were trying for a baby. I thought that might be enough to get her to convince him to take me back, or at least to talk to me."

"Did it work?" James asked.

Janice shook her head sadly. "No. Maureen couldn't care less about grandchildren. She knew he was sterile. I guess she figured we were talking about using a donor. She said it was between Doug and me. She refused to get involved. If you ask me, she was pleased that we'd split up. She had him all to herself again."

James pondered the comment and filed it away. "Ms Carter, Doug was shot once in the head. There were no signs of robbery. Do you know who might have wanted him dead?"

The woman shook her head, her eyes wide with distress. "No! I don't have a clue who might have wanted Doug dead! He had a good job and got on with his work colleagues. In fact, he got on with everyone. The only people who ever felt ill will toward him were members of the Li family."

James stilled. From the corner of his eye, he noticed Wang had also become alert. "Why do you say that?" James asked, striving to keep his voice casual.

Janice's lips turned up in a sneer. "He put their daughter in a wheelchair! Do you think they were happy about that? For the first few months after Doug and I got together, his phone never stopped ringing. It was always Chao Li calling to scream abuse at Doug for what he'd done to his daughter, his precious little girl. Poor little Aimee! Confined to a wheelchair. And according to her father, it was all Doug's fault!"

The woman shook her head. Anger still flashed in her eyes. "I mean, how could it be Doug's fault? The stupid bitch fell badly while she was water skiing. She broke three vertebrae in her lower back and suffered permanent damage to her spinal cord. How was that Doug's fault? Just because he was the one behind the wheel. The police investigated and ruled it an accident. They didn't lay any charges. It was too bad the Li family never accepted their findings."

"When was the last time Doug received a call from Chao Li?" Wang asked.

"I'm not sure. A while, I think. Unless Doug just stopped telling me about them. Every time he'd get a call from Aimee's father, he'd get depressed and feel guilty over what had happened. Make no mistake, he blamed himself. There was nothing me or his mother could say to convince him otherwise. It got him down sometimes."

"The accident happened five years ago. Do

you think the Li family would still be harboring anger and resentment over Aimee's injuries and Doug's part in causing them?" James asked.

"Who knows? But old man Li was relentless in his accusations for a long time. Maybe he was just biding his time. Waiting for Doug to let down his guard. Who knows? Maybe it was the sister. She was a bulldog where Aimee was concerned. I ran into her in the corridor of the hospital not long after Doug told her we were—"

Janice broke off and flushed crimson.

"Running off together," James finished.

Her embarrassment deepened and she stared at the floor. "Yes, well. It was just one of those things. We didn't plan it," she muttered. "We didn't mean to hurt anyone. It just happened. You can't help who you fall in love with, right?"

She glanced up at James, but he didn't respond. The last time he'd been in love he was in the third grade. He wasn't exactly the best person to consult on the subject. He glanced at Wang.

"What were you saying about Aimee Li's sister?" Wang prodded.

"Yes. Well, Sally-Ann—that's Aimee's sister—she was livid when she realized I was the other woman. She tore strips off me. I was scared she might even get physical. She only came up to my shoulder, but she was ferocious."

"Did she threaten you?" Wang asked.

The woman laughed without humor. "Threaten me? She looked like she wanted to tear me limb from limb! She was almost frothing at the mouth. I tell you, I thought she was going to attack me."

"Did you file assault charges?" James asked.

Janice shook her head and once again, looked away. "No. I... I guess I thought I deserved it. After all, I *had* run away with her sister's husband. I understood how she might be feeling a little angry."

James scrawled in his notebook and took down Janice's details, including the make, model and license number of her motorbike. He looked back at her.

"Do you own a firearm, Ms Carter?"

The woman kept her gaze fixed to the floor. "No," she muttered.

James made a mental note to check the Firearms Registry. Of course, there were always ways and means to procure a gun illegally if one knew how to go about it. He swallowed a sigh and pulled a business card out of his wallet and handed it to her.

"Thanks for your time, Ms Carter. Call me if you think of anything else," he said.

She sniffed and swiped at her nose with the back of her hand and then took the card and slipped it inside the front of her uniform. He was reminded of Jo-Beth Gregson, the young street girl who'd done exactly the same thing. He wondered how she was doing and whether she'd used the money he'd given her to buy food. He wanted to believe she had.

"Do you still want to take a look at my bike?" Janice murmured, breaking into his thoughts.

James looked at Wang who nodded. "Sure."

As they followed the woman out of the hospital

and made their way to the parking lot, Wang sidled up beside him.

"What do you think?" Wang asked, his voice pitched low enough that the woman who walked ahead of them wouldn't hear.

"I'm not sure," James replied. "She doesn't have an alibi and she was already in the city. We only have her word she left here and went home. She could have just as easily detoured via Bathurst Street. It's only half a dozen blocks away. She rides a motorbike and, considering it's her main form of transport, I'm guessing it's not a piece of junk. She denies owning a firearm, but we both know that doesn't mean she didn't get hold of one. She claims to have loved the victim, but they'd recently broken up and though she says differently, Aimee Li's convinced Doug was of the opinion they weren't getting back together. Could the break up have tipped Janice over the edge? Who knows?"

"I agree," Wang replied. "She's definitely a possibility."

Like James had already guessed Janice Carter's bike was an impressive Kawasaki Ninja 300cc. He was nearly blinded by the sun as it reflected off the gleaming black paintwork. It was a bike anyone would be proud to own and cost a pretty penny. Janice must have saved long and hard unless someone helped her out with the purchase. Interestingly, the big black machine fit the description of the bike given by Jo-Beth Gregson.

Moving forward, he bent and examined the bike up close, looking for signs of damage or any other evidence that it had been involved in a crime. There was nothing.

"Do you mind if I take a few pictures?" he asked Janice.

She shrugged. "Help yourself."

James took a few frames on his phone before thanking the woman once again for her time.

"Where to?" Wang asked as they made their way back to the unmarked squad car.

James glanced at his watch. "Let's go and grab a coffee and then head over to the Li house."

Wang nodded. "Sounds like a good plan."

Janice watched the departing backs of the detectives and tried hard to slow her racing heart. *Doug was dead!* She couldn't believe it! Had Todd come through for her, after all? The last time they'd spoken about it, he'd told her he thought her plan for him to do away with her estranged husband was stupid and he didn't want any part of it. He was still on parole for an armed hold-up. He'd done a ten-year stretch. He wasn't in a hurry to go back. Not even for her.

She'd cursed him out and called him all kinds of names, but in the end, there was nothing she could do. He refused to help her. But Doug *had* been shot dead in the night. It must have been Todd. It couldn't be anyone else. She needed to call him. Digging around in the pocket of her uniform, she tugged out her phone. The call went through to voicemail.

"Dammit, Todd! You need to call me right away. The cops have been here. They told me about Doug. You need to get rid of the gun. Do you hear me? Get rid of it. And keep your fucking mouth shut!"

She stabbed her finger at the screen and ended the call. Her heart still pounded in her chest. She drew in a shaky breath and smoothed out the wrinkles in her uniform in an effort to regain a level of calm. She glanced at her watch and noted the time. Her break was over. She was needed on the ward.

CHAPTER 6

Sally-Ann absently chewed the end of her pen while she waited for her next client. She was seated in one of the interview rooms set aside for members of the legal fraternity outside the Children's Court at Parramatta. It had been a busy morning. She'd made good time from Aimee's apartment and had met up with Abby partway through an interview with one of her young clients and was relieved to discover that the clerk had yet to call any of her cases. Now she was waiting for Ronnie Denyar to make an appearance. The boy was late and she was growing increasingly concerned he might not show.

She'd phoned his mother only the day before to confirm the time and date and Shirley Denyar assured her they'd be there. Ronnie had been on bail for a serious assault. Today he was due to be sentenced. Though Sally-Ann intended to do everything she could to keep him out of jail, given the seriousness of the charges, coupled with the fifteen-year-old's extensive criminal record for similar offenses, she hadn't given the family too much hope. She wondered if that was the reason they hadn't shown.

"Damn it!" she cursed under her breath. Surely they knew it would go even worse for Ronnie if he failed to appear? Not only would he be sentenced on the original charges, but he'd also be in breach of his bail, which was an offense in itself.

It reminded her of another teenager she'd represented six weeks earlier. Alexander Popov had been arrested on drug charges. According to the police, the sixteen-year-old had been supplying a number of his fellow students at his local high school. Alexander denied the charges and they'd gone to trial. The police had done their homework. They produced witness after witness who testified to the fact that Alexander had supplied them with drugs. Mostly ecstasy, but more recently, crystal meth. Despite her best efforts, Alexander had been found guilty.

His father had been furious. Viktor Popov was not a man to be messed with. At six foot four and weighing more than two hundred and fifty pounds, not only was he a mountain of a man, but Sally-Ann had heard whispers from the prosecutor's camp that the man had done time.

Though she'd been disappointed and saddened when her client was sentenced to three years jail, she was relieved Viktor Popov no longer had an excuse to be part of her life. From the first moment she'd met him, the man had unsettled her and his outburst of anger at his son's sentencing, in full view of those present in the courtroom, had been frightening to see. She shivered at the memory.

A knock at the door startled her. She looked up in time to see the door open and the clerk of the court filling the opening.

"Um, excuse me Ms Li, we just called one of your cases. Is Ronnie Denyar here?" the clerk asked.

Sally-Ann grimaced and shook her head. "It doesn't look that way."

"Too bad," the clerk replied. "Judge Harris is in a hurry. He has somewhere to be later this afternoon. He wants to get through the list before lunch."

Sally-Ann blew out her breath on a sigh. "So, what you mean is, he's not in the mood to give my client any more time to appear."

The clerk nodded. "That's the gist of it."

Sally-Ann glanced at her watch. It was heading on for twelve. In just over an hour, the court would break for lunch. Feeling the pressure, she tugged out her phone and flicked through her contacts until she found the entry for Ronnie's mom. Hoping like hell the woman picked up, she punched in the number and waited.

James pulled the squad car alongside the curb and killed the engine. He'd put the address given to him by Sally-Ann Li into the GPS and it had brought him and Wang to a modest red-brick bungalow in the inner west Sydney suburb of Leichardt. Though the paintwork around the window sashes and eaves was faded and peeling, the bones of the house looked solid, like they had stood the test of time—and they probably had. The houses that lined the street were mostly *circa* early 1900s. Many had been renovated to reflect modern styles and color schemes, but the house where the Li family lived looked largely untouched. James glanced at his colleague.

"This is it."

Wang nodded in acknowledgment and glanced at the house. "It's not quite what I expected, given the fact one daughter is apparently some hotshot lawyer and the other one lives in a very comfortable townhouse on the outskirts of the city."

James shrugged. "Perhaps they've put every spare penny into their children. Some people do."

"They work at the local supermarket. I can't imagine there are too many spare pennies," Wang said dryly.

James didn't reply. At this stage, he had no interest in the Li family finances. Instead, he opened the door and climbed out. Wang followed suit. The heat from the midday sun was almost unbearable after the cool confines of the air-conditioned car. It was hot on the back of James' neck and he wished he could take off his jacket. Surreptitiously swiping at the sweat that had gathered on his brow, he and Wang walked up the cracked concrete path to the front door.

James opened the screen door. It squeaked in protest. He rapped on the wooden panel and then stepped back. The door was opened almost immediately, as if the occupant had been waiting for him. A small gray-haired Asian man regarded them suspiciously, his eyes narrowed.

"Yes?" the man asked curtly.

James cleared his throat. "Are you Chao Li?"

The man frowned and shook his head. "No English."

James sighed and looked at Wang. "Do you speak Chinese?"

Wang grimaced as if in irritation. "There are more than two hundred individual dialects in China. We don't just speak Chinese."

James flushed, embarrassed at his ignorance. "I'm sorry," he muttered.

As if taking pity on him, Wang's expression softened. "It's fine. Don't worry about it. But just so you know, there are five main dialectical groups in the People's Republic of China. Mandarin, Yue—which includes Cantonese—Min, Wu and Hakka."

James nodded in acknowledgment. "Can you ask this man what dialect he speaks?"

Wang stepped forward and spoke to the man who stood in the doorway in a language James didn't understand. A moment later, Wang looked back at him.

"He speaks Mandarin."

Not wanting to re-offend, James chose his words with care. "Is that...? Is that a language you speak?"

"Of course," Wang replied impatiently. "It's the official language of the People's Republic of China."

Once again, James felt heat rise in his face. While he prided himself on treating everyone he came across the same regardless of their ethnicity, he was sorely reminded how little he knew about cultures other than his own.

"Do you want me to conduct this interview?" Wang asked bluntly, ignoring his embarrassment.

James nodded in relief. "Yes. Thanks. That would be great. If you can just keep me in the loop a little, let me know what's being said, I'd appreciate it."

Wang nodded and turned to the man who'd remained silent during their exchange. Wang asked the man something. James caught the words "Chao Li." The man nodded. Wang asked something else. Once again, the man nodded.

"He says he has two daughters—Aimee and Sally-Ann," Wang said to James.

"At least we know we have the right person," James replied. Wang nodded and turned back to Li. He asked another question in Mandarin and Li responded in kind. Once again, Wang told James what had been said.

"I told him we're here about the murder of Douglas Hanley. He said his daughter, Sally-Ann already called him."

James turned to look at the elderly man. Beads of sweat had gathered on his brow. His eyes darted from Wang to James and back again. Okay, it was hot, but there seemed to be more to it than a reaction to the heat. James wondered what had made the man so nervous.

"Ask him about his daughter's accident," James said.

Fury flashed in Chao Li's eyes and his face flushed red. James started in surprise and then narrowed his gaze at the man.

"You understood what I said, didn't you?"

The man lowered his head and stared at the ground. Slowly, he nodded. James cursed under his breath.

"What kind of game are you playing, Mr Li?" he asked in a voice that was dangerously low.

The man gulped and his face froze for a moment with fear. "I-I... I'm sorry. English isn't my first language. I know enough to get by, but..." He lifted his shoulders in a helpless shrug. "I'm not used to having the police show up at my door. I didn't want to misunderstand one of your questions. I prefer to speak in Mandarin."

Wang stared at him. "How long have you lived in Australia?"

"Sixteen years."

"Long enough to have picked up the local language," Wang stated, his eyes hard.

Li gulped again and wrung his hands. His skin took on a lighter shade of pale. James wondered again what the man was so nervous about. Surely the mere presence of police officers couldn't be enough to illicit such a reaction? Did the man know more than he was letting on? James was determined to find out.

"From here on in, we conduct this interview in

English. If there's something you don't understand, you ask me. Got it?"

"Y-yes. I-I understand."

"Good," James replied. "Now, you told my colleague here that your daughter already informed you of Doug Hanley's murder. She also might have told you that we spoke to her earlier today. In fact, we spoke to both of your daughters. Aimee told us about the boating accident that left her a paraplegic."

"Even after all these years, I refuse to believe it was an accident," Li muttered.

"Why don't you tell us what happened?" James offered.

The man blew out his breath on a heavy sigh. His shoulders slumped. "My daughter was a gifted gymnast. From the earliest days, she was determined to make it to the Olympics and she was good enough to make it. Even after we immigrated to Australia, she continued to pursue her dream."

"What happened?" Wang asked.

"She met Douglas Hanley. She fell in love and got married."

"You don't sound like you were happy about that," James stated.

"Mixed marriages present a number of difficulties. And then there was Doug's mother. She never liked Aimee. She never liked any of us."

"She didn't like Asians?" Wang asked.

Li looked up briefly at James' colleague and then looked away. He nodded. "That's right. She wanted her son to marry a nice Australian girl."

"Let's fast-forward to the accident," James said a little impatiently. They'd already established Maureen Hanley's racist attitude toward her Asian-born ex-daughter-in-law. According to Janice Carter, Doug's mother didn't like *her* either. Perhaps the woman just wasn't happy about her son being married. To *anyone*. Who knew? Until the woman's prejudice became relevant to the murder investigation, James couldn't be bothered wasting any more time on it.

"Aimee told us the accident happened five years ago," he said.

"Yes. Doug owned a speed boat. Aimee had taken up water skiing. With her athletic background, she was a natural and she loved it. The two of them spent many a weekend skiing up and down the Parramatta River."

"What happened the day she was injured?" Wang asked.

"We'd all gone out for a day on the water. Me, my wife Fen, Aimee and my youngest daughter, Sally-Ann. It was a beautiful day. I remember lying back on the grass of the riverbank and marveling that there wasn't a cloud in the sky..."

The man's voice drifted off. Once again, James tried to curb his impatience. "And," he prompted.

"Despite the beautiful weather, Doug was in a foul mood. He'd argued with Aimee over lunch and had given all of us the silent treatment. I wasn't sure what they were disagreeing about, but I guessed it had something to do with having a baby. Aimee had told me she was trying to convince Doug to try IVF with donor sperm." Chao glanced up at James. "Do you know about Doug's—?"

"Yes," James interrupted. "Aimee admitted it had caused tension in their marriage."

"Yes, well, I felt some of the tension that day by the river. Nevertheless, it appeared that Aimee was determined to enjoy the day. She asked Doug to take her for a ski. I volunteered to be the observer."

"So you were on the boat when Aimee was hurt?" James asked.

Chao nodded and his expression filled with sad resignation. "Yes. Doug was driving way too fast, behaving recklessly. At one point, he almost collided with another boat. I told him to slow down, to watch where he was going. Aimee was on a single ski behind us. She was a competent skier, but even competent skiers can fall off."

"What happened?" Wang asked.

Chao leaned heavily against the doorway. "Doug refused to slow down. He started acting crazy, swerving the boat left and right, stirring up the water."

"Let me guess," James said. "Aimee came off."

Chao nodded somberly. "Yes. She fell awkwardly and hit the water hard. She broke three vertebrae in her lower back and suffered significant other trauma to her spinal cord."

"And you think Doug was to blame," James said.

Anger flashed in Chao's eyes. "Of course he was to blame! He was driving irresponsibly and with a total lack of concern for my little girl. This would never have happened if he'd behaved sensibly and if he'd listened to my repeated requests."

"The police refrained from laying charges," Wang stated.

Chao's face twisted in an angry grimace. "The police! *Bah!* What would they know?"

As if suddenly becoming aware that there were two law enforcement officers standing in front of him, he flushed with embarrassment and once again averted his gaze.

"You still blame Doug for what happened, don't you?" James challenged the man with his gaze.

Chao lifted his head and stared at James, his eyes blazing. "Of course I blame him! I was there! It would never have happened if he'd only slowed down." Chao shook his head. "Accident! *Ha!* He was angry at my little girl; he was trying to scare her. I could tell. He had no concern for her safety. I'm not saying he meant to cause her injuries, but at that moment, he didn't much care if she got hurt. He was an idiot. She should never have married him. I told her not to. It wasn't a good idea. But she wouldn't listen! She's always been headstrong. She's been influenced too much by her friends. Where I come from, girls know how to behave, to listen to their fathers, to do as they're told."

"Mr Li, do you own a gun?" Wang asked, changing the subject.

Chao blinked and took a moment to adjust to the switch in topic. "Yes, I do."

James started in surprise. "What kind?"

"A nine millimeter Glock."

"I assume you're licensed," James added.

Chao looked affronted. "Of course."

"We'd like to take a look at your license," Wang said.

"Give me a minute. I'll go and get it for you."

Chao disappeared inside the house and returned a few minutes later. He handed his license to Wang who studied it a moment before handing it back.

"It looks legitimate," Wang said to James.

Once again, Chao puffed up with indignation. "Of course it's legitimate! What do you think I am? I like to go target shooting at my local pistol club."

"Does Aimee shoot?" Wang asked.

"No. Aimee was never interested in firearms."

"What about your other daughter?" James asked.

Chao turned to look at him. "Sally-Ann? Yes, Sal's an excellent shot." His smile was filled with pride.

James shot a look at his partner and then tucked the information away. "Do you own a motorbike, Mr Li?"

The man shook his head. "No, I don't own a motorbike."

"I noticed you have a garage down the back. Do you mind if we take a look inside?" James asked.

Chao shrugged. "I guess so. I have nothing to hide."

James and Wang made their way down the side of the house. Chao followed a few steps behind. The door to the garage was old and weathered. When James tugged on the iron handle, it squeaked in protest. Inside, the garage was as black as molasses. "Is there a light in here?" he asked.

"Yes." Chao fumbled along the wall and flicked a switch. A moment later, the space was filled with light.

An early model, white Nissan Pulsar sat just inside the garage. As James' eyes adjusted to the light, he spied a 650cc Suzuki Gladius motorbike parked in the far corner, near a stack of old chairs. The motorbike was strikingly similar to Janice Carter's Kawasaki and like the nurse's bike, it could easily fit the description given by their eye witness. He spun on his heel and glared at Li.

"I thought you told us you didn't own a motorbike," he stated flatly.

Li looked fearful. "I-I don't. That doesn't belong to me. It's... It's Sally-Ann's."

James frowned and shot a look at Wang. From his colleague's expression, it was clear Wang had also joined the dots. Sally-Ann Li owned a motorbike. Her business card had been found at the crime scene. She was also an excellent shot. Her father owned the same kind of gun that was involved in the murder of his ex-son-in-law, a man who was held in low esteem by at least some of the members of the Li family.

Had Sally-Ann pulled the trigger? And if so, had she done it of her own volition, or at the request of her sister? Where did their father fit in? It was obvious Chao Li was uncomfortable about the police presence on his property. What was he hiding? James was determined to find out.

CHAPTER 7

Sally-Ann pressed at the ache that had made itself known between her eyes and did her best to focus on what the judge was saying. Ronnie Denyar had failed to appear and a warrant had been issued for his arrest. Two of her other clients had been given harsher sentences than she'd anticipated and they'd looked to her with shock and anger in their eyes. Now it was Jaxon's turn.

Fourteen-year-old Jaxon Turnbull had been charged with one count of arson. The trial had ended a month earlier. There had been a mountain of evidence against him, including an eyewitness who'd testified that she'd seen him at the scene. One of the occupants of the house had woken and come downstairs for a nightcap right about the time Jaxon was setting fire to their den. It came as no surprise when the jury found him guilty.

Sally-Ann had advised him to plead guilty right from the outset. His early plea would be taken into account during the sentencing. He'd spend less time incarcerated. But at the time, Jaxon would have none of it. It was a common occurrence. Everyone wanted to delay the inevitable for as long as they could. Now, for Jaxon, his time was up.

"For such a young man, it troubles me that the defendant, Jaxon Turnbull, has such a long criminal history, including two previous convictions for arson," the judge intoned.

Sally-Ann clenched her hands together beneath the bar table and waited for the judge to hand the sentence down. From what she'd heard so far, it was going to be substantial. She flicked a glance at her client. Jaxon's expression remained stoic as he stared at the judge. Sally-Ann wondered what he was thinking.

Weeks ago, after he'd been found guilty, she asked him about lighting the fire. He told her he'd done it for attention. Apparently, he'd been bored. She'd asked him what family he had at home.

"No one," had come the surly reply.

"What about your parents? Brothers and sisters?" she insisted.

"I only have a sister. She lives with my aunty. Mom and her boyfriend—I don't know his name— come and go. Mostly she stays with him."

It broke Sally-Ann's heart to hear another sad story of a neglected child growing up way too fast, but Jaxon had done the wrong thing. The house had burned to the ground. People could have died.

She'd already explained to him he was looking

at a period of incarceration. How long? They'd have to wait and see. As the judge droned on about Jaxon's predilection for lighting fires, the dread in her belly increased. Finally, the sentenced was announced: eighteen months.

Sally-Ann couldn't prevent a wince. Keeping her head lowered, she scrawled the terms of her client's incarceration on the legal pad in front of her. As soon as the judge brought down his gavel and moved on to the next case, she stood and went to her client where he sat in the dock.

"Eighteen months, Jaxon. I'm sorry," she said quietly.

He shrugged and looked at her with the same stoic expression he'd displayed earlier. "Hey, you did your best, Miss. Don't worry about it."

She tried to think of something else to say, but came up empty. Her chest tightened on a surge of emotion. *He was fourteen!* What would become of him? Jaxon noticed her distress and offered her a slight smile.

"Hey, Miss Li, I'll be fine. I'll be out before I turn sixteen. Besides, it's probably safer than being at home and it's not like my mom's going to miss me."

The truth of his comment hit her hard. It was so unfair that some people got to be parents when they couldn't care less about their kids. Jaxon was a perfect example. She thought of her sister and her heart clenched. Aimee wanted so badly to be a mother and she would make such a great mom. And yet, life hadn't seen it that way. It was so wrong.

Swallowing a sigh, she bid Jaxon a solemn farewell and watched as the corrections officer led him away. Turning back to the bar table, she gathered her files and stuffed them into her briefcase, relieved that her day in court was done. Pushing her way through the door that led to the outside, she blinked at the bright sunshine that hit her in the face. Digging around in her handbag, she found her sunglasses and put them on.

Almost immediately, she spied the good-looking detective who'd visited her sister earlier. She wondered where his colleague was and then wondered if he'd spoken to her parents. The fact that he was there, obviously waiting for her, wasn't a good sign. Still, she refused to be intimidated. Neither she nor any member of her family had done anything wrong. It was time she convinced him of that.

James spotted Sally-Ann Li the moment she exited the glass doors that lined the entrance to the modern gray-and-brick rendered building that housed the Parramatta Children's Court. He'd called her office on his way back from her parents' place and had been informed by her secretary she was at court. Wang had returned to the station. James had volunteered to sit tight and wait. He was glad he had.

The effect her beauty had on him hadn't lessened in the time they'd been apart. Even from a distance, she was stunning. She wore the same charcoal-gray suit and gray blouse she'd worn earlier that morning. Her hair was still loose, but she'd tucked it behind her ears. Somehow, the simple action made her appear younger. A pair of designer sunglasses hid her eyes from his gaze.

Her sister was thirty-four. He guessed Sally-Ann was a little younger, probably closer to his age...

He knew the exact moment she spotted him. She stopped midstride and a frown creased the perfect smoothness of her brow. She whipped off her sunglasses and glared at him.

"Detective Shepherd. What are you doing here?"

He purposefully kept his voice light and even offered her a smile. "Hello, Ms Li. We meet again."

She grimaced in response. "I'll ask you again, what are you doing here?"

"I have a few more questions."

"I've already told you everything I know."

"Not quite. I didn't know you were an accomplished shooter."

Her expression remained defiant. "You didn't ask."

"I also didn't know you own a motorbike," he said. His voice was quiet, conversational, but he kept his gaze steady on hers, leaving no doubt about the seriousness of his question.

She stared at him pointedly. "Plenty of people own motorbikes. I don't see how that's relevant."

He saw the curiosity in her eyes, but refused to be drawn into giving an answer. "Do you own a gun, Ms Li?" he asked more forcefully.

"No. Whenever I go to the range, I use my father's—"

She broke off, as if becoming aware of what she was about to say and how it might appear. A wary expression filled her face.

"Don't worry, Ms Li. My colleague and I have already spoken with your father. He told us about the gun he owns."

"Then there's nothing more I have to say," she replied. Her tone was terse, the defiance was back in her gaze.

"I'm not finished quite yet, Ms Li," he replied and this time, his voice was lined with steel. "Where were you last night?"

She tightened her lips and took a moment to speak. "I was at home. I worked at the office until about half-past six. I came home, cooked dinner, watched a little TV and went to bed. I turned out the light before half-past nine. I slept through my alarm and woke around half-past seven. That's it."

"Can anyone verify that?"

"No. I live alone."

He absorbed the information. Ignoring the spark of excitement her words ignited in his gut, he continued. "Your business card was found at the crime scene. Can you tell me anything about that?"

Her eyes went wide in shock and for a moment, she was speechless. And then she regained her aplomb. "You're lying."

"No, I'm not. I was the one who collected the card off the pavement."

She shook her head slowly back and forth as if

trying to come to terms with the discovery. "I have no idea why my business card would be at the crime scene."

"Did you give it to Douglas Hanley recently?"

"No. I haven't seen or spoken to Doug since he divorced my sister."

"And yet the card was there."

She eyeballed him and he felt a reluctant admiration for her courage. "I don't know what you want me to say, Detective. I didn't give my card to Doug and I have no idea why it was found near his body."

"Do you speak Mandarin?"

She shook her head, as if impatient with the question, but answered. "Yes, it's my native tongue."

"When did you emigrate from China?"

"Not that it's any of your business, but I arrived here with my sister and parents when I was thirteen."

"And how old are you now?" he asked, glad he'd been given the opportunity to seek out that particular piece of information.

She crossed her arms over her chest and huffed out a sigh. "I'm twenty-nine, Detective. I've been in Australia for sixteen years. How is any of this relevant?"

Ignoring her, he forged on. "You did your high school years here. That must have been tough." He could only imagine what it had been like to arrive in a new country, struggling with a new language, a different culture, a foreign city and be thrust into the often cutthroat world of high school, with all its hazards and pitfalls.

As if reading his mind, her lips tightened. "Yes. Let's just say, it was...character building."

All of a sudden, an image of a much younger Sally-Ann Li filled his mind. Despite the fact there was no evidence of it now, it was conceivable she'd once been a gawky teenager. Still, awkward or not, those years were difficult for anyone, let alone a girl in Sally-Ann's situation. He felt a pang of sympathy.

Without a conscious decision, his thoughts turned to his sister, Lizzie, and the troubles she'd been having with their step-mom. He was sure it was a normal part of growing up and the fact Anita wasn't their mom added an extra layer of difficulty. The situation would be made even worse for Lizzie if she were having troubles at school. At least he didn't have to worry on that score. As far as he knew, she had a supportive network of friends and of course, she also had him to help steer her through the most challenging times. In fact, it was probably time he had a serious talk with her about moving back home. She couldn't stay with him forever and quite frankly, he was tired of fielding calls from his father begging him to make her see sense.

The sound of Sally-Ann clearing her throat and the look of irritation she threw his way snapped him back to attention.

"Are we finished now, Detective?" she asked caustically.

He wished he had more questions, could hold her attention longer somehow, but the truth was, though the recent discoveries had put her higher on the suspect list, they were a long way from having enough evidence to arrest her—or anyone, for that matter.

He grimaced and reminded himself that the real reason he was speaking with Sally-Ann was so that he could solve a murder. He best remember that before he got distracted once again by a woman so beautiful she stole his breath away.

She stroked the smooth, worn barrel of the handgun with a hand that trembled. The night her world changed forever came rushing back. Her chest tightened on a sob of anguish and she gasped in an agony of sadness and disbelief.

He was gone.

She couldn't believe she'd done it. She'd been so angry at him—furious, really. She hadn't fully thought her plan through. All she'd wanted was to inflict pain on him in the same way he'd inflicted pain on her. But now he was dead and it was all her fault. How was she going to live with herself, knowing what she'd done? Now she had no one.

Hung Wang stared at the 5 x 8 colored photographs of the four members of the Li family he'd obtained off the Internet. The daughters had been easy to find. Both of them had professional head shots on their LinkedIn profiles. He already knew Sally-Ann was a lawyer. LinkedIn had disclosed that Aimee was a psychologist. She ran a private counseling practice out of rooms that adjoined the Sydney Harbour Hospital.

Chao Li's picture had been found on Facebook. His employer had posted a picture of the man on their page, declaring him Employee of the Month. Chao didn't look too happy about having his picture taken. Hung couldn't help but wonder what kind of customer service the man provided when he looked so disagreeable. Still, whether or not Chao liked having his picture taken was hardly of consequence to a murder investigation.

Although Chao Li had told them his wife wasn't at home when he and Shepherd had called on her husband, Hung had still managed to track her down from a picture that had appeared recently in her local newspaper. It was a story about the upcoming Chinese New Year. Apparently Fen Li was clever with needle and thread and had been appointed head designer of the costumes for the parade that year.

At the thought of Chinese New Year, Hung was filled with melancholy. The New Year was a traditional time of family and celebration that made him long for his home country. Of all the holidays celebrated, the Chinese New Year was the most important for the Chinese.

Normally, the celebration would start on New Year's Eve and last for around fifteen days, until the middle of the first month. Before the celebration, people usually cleaned their houses from top to bottom and displayed traditional New Year's decorations. Hung could remember his mother doing that when he was a kid. Once again, he was filled with a surge of homesickness.

He glanced around him, relieved that the squad room was empty. He'd left his colleague waiting outside the Children's Court for Sally-Ann. The fact that she not only owned a motorbike similar to the one described by the eyewitness, but was also an experienced shooter had pushed her considerably higher up the suspect list. She'd also expressed her anger at her ex-brother-in-law and revealed that she blamed him for her sister's injury.

He understood Shepherd's insistence they speak again to the stunning lawyer, although he wouldn't put it past his partner to use it as an excuse to spend more time with the woman. There was no denying her beauty and the classy way she held herself. If Hung were a bit younger...

He fingered the simple gold band that adorned his ring finger. He wasn't really married. It was just for show. He liked to think it lent him an air of responsibility; that it engendered trust in those he met. That was also the reason he had a photograph of his non-existent wife and son on his desk. Well, he had an ex-wife and he did have a son, just not the boy in the photo. Still, the picture served its purpose. His colleagues saw it and assumed they were his family. It also helped stop some of the inevitable questions.

He picked up the photo of Sally-Ann he'd had enlarged. It was the same picture that had been used on the Sydney Legal website and he understood why. It was a good picture. Sally-Ann stared at the camera with the smallest of smiles playing around her lips. Her eyes sparkled with warmth and good humor. Her long black hair hung straight and shiny around her face; her skin was flawless. She looked like a woman you wanted to know better. She looked like a woman who enjoyed life.

Hung Wang turned his attention to the picture of Aimee. Much less confidence showed in her black-eyed gaze, but she was beautiful, just the same. There was no mistaking the two girls were sisters. And then there were the older members of the Li family. Hung guessed Chao and Fen to be in their mid- to late fifties. It was sometimes difficult to tell. Asian people tended to carry their age well, but given the fact they had a thirty-four-year-old daughter, he assumed the parents were older than they looked.

Were they involved in the murder of Douglas Hanley? They certainly had motive and then there was the eyewitness who'd seen the motorbike. Did members of this family have opportunity? Was it possible they knew Doug would be there, outside that bar, at that time of night? Aimee Li had admitted she'd met with her ex-husband only days earlier. Could he have told her then about his intention to visit the bar on Bathurst Street? And then another thought occurred to him and it made his heart thump hard.

Casting a second good look around the office to check that he was still alone, he took out a key from the top drawer of his desk and unlocked the one below it. Digging under the pile of papers and legislation he stored there, he pulled out a thick file from underneath. With his heart picking up the pace, he flipped open the folder and stared at the pictures inside.

The black-and-white 5 x 8s were worn and creased with age. A man and his wife were in one photo. In the other were two young girls. The photos had been taken sixteen years ago, when the girls were thirteen and eighteen. Hung looked at them closely and then looked again at the Li women.

There were certainly similarities. The young women in the black-and-white photos had long, straight black hair. They were both petite and showed promise of the beauty that was to come. Though the photos had been taken at a distance, he was almost sure the older one had a mole low on the side of her jaw, just like Aimee Li. Their names were Biyu and ChangChang Zhang and sixteen years ago in China, they'd simply disappeared. It was suspected they'd fled China with their parents, Yu and Lihua Zhang after Yu had been arrested for treason. Somehow the family had escaped before Yu could be brought to justice.

Weeks after the disappearance of the Zhang family, Chinese intelligence agencies had discovered they'd migrated to Australia. Within days, Hung received orders that came from the president of China himself charging Hung with the task of finding the escapees and bringing them home to face justice and the punishment they so richly deserved. It was made clear to him that he wasn't to return empty handed. In fact, he wasn't to return at all until he found them.

Sixteen years in and he was still looking. It had gotten to the point that he saw the Zhang family in every Chinese face he met, especially those ones who fit the basic information he'd been given all those years ago.

Could that be the reason his interest had been piqued by the Li family? Was it just that he was tired of living in a foreign country and longed to be home that he felt a stirring of excitement in his gut when he looked at the pictures and compared them with the ones he kept locked away in his drawer, or could the Li family be the one he had been searching for?

He looked at the photos again. The ages checked out and there were certainly similarities between the pictures. The parents, in particular, appeared to bear a close resemblance to the black-and-white prints.

But what if they were involved in the murder? What if they were convicted and sent to jail? He'd be destined to spend the rest of his days in this hellhole. His superior had made it quite clear: Failure wasn't an option. If Hung returned home without his captives, he'd be a pariah—exiled for the rest of his days. It would be no better than the life he lived now, demoted from his exalted position in the People's Liberation Army; isolated from whatever family he still had; alone.

He'd purposefully maintained his distance,

refusing to befriend his neighbors or anyone else he came into contact with. In the beginning, he'd done it out of the genuine belief that he wouldn't be there long. There had been good evidence the fugitives had passed through the international airport in Sydney. Their intelligence had been fresh and reliable. Compared to Beijing, the population of Sydney seemed laughable. He'd been confident he'd locate the family he hunted within a fortnight. Unfortunately, that hadn't been the case.

He'd underestimated the number of Chinese nationals residing in Sydney and he'd also underestimated the Zhang family's ability to disappear. Despite his best efforts, he hadn't found them by employing the means available to him. It was then he'd realized he'd have to delve deeper, get access to private records, government databases and the like in order to find them.

He'd pondered the problem for more than a week before he hit on a solution. Law enforcement officers had access to records unavailable to the average person. If he was a police officer, he'd be able to use that access to narrow down his search and hopefully locate the people he sought.

He spent time thinking about how best to go about it. He could apply to enter the New South Wales Police Service, but the course went for nearly two years. That was much too long to wait. He wanted to find the traitors, return home with them and resume his comfortable life. Then he looked into it further and discovered that international students were ineligible to apply. All of a sudden, becoming a police officer was no longer an option.

Still, Hung was nothing if not determined and he continued to toss around possibilities. Then, one evening, he'd met an off-duty police officer in a bar. Someone new to the area. They'd talked and arranged to spend some time together. The man was Chinese...

And then it had finally come to him, the solution he'd been looking for. He'd research and then replace the Chinese officer and then assume the man's identity. Westerners quite frequently mistook one Asian for another. To them, Asian people all looked the same. It was an ignorant attitude, but there was no denying its existence and now he'd use it to his advantage. In fact, he was counting on it.

The plan continued to develop over the days that followed until he was confident he'd found his target. He'd begun to hang around police stations as well—large ones situated in busy areas so his presence outside the building wouldn't look too conspicuous. The policeman new to the area was about the same age as he was. They were also of similar height and build. He followed the man home the next time they met and continued to do so until he had the man's routines down pat.

Over the ensuing weeks, Hung managed to befriend the man on his daily commute to and from work. He learned that his target lived alone and had no family in Australia. He'd come to

Australia a decade earlier, seeking a better life. He was now a New South Wales detective and had recently been transferred to the City of Sydney station.

He was perfect and Hung barely slept the night before he planned to make the real Hung Wang disappear. The idiot had confided that he'd put in for some leave and was looking forward to a few weeks' vacation. He hadn't had a holiday in more than a year and he was planning to head south to Hobart. The weather was cooler in summer and he'd been told the salmon fishing was great.

Hung had absorbed the information in silence and had barely been able to conceal his glee. He'd bided his time until the evening before the man was due to leave for his trip. It had been a simple matter to lie in wait outside the man's apartment that night and put a bullet through his brain while he slept.

It had taken Hung most of the night to clean up the mess and remove any evidence of the crime. He'd then assumed the man's identity, even to the point of residing in the man's home. He'd spent the days coming and going in and out of the apartment. He brought in shopping, took out the garbage, acknowledged his neighbors with a wave the way he'd seen the real Hung do. His plan had worked perfectly and nobody had questioned him when he arrived for work three weeks later. He'd been there ever since.

But now almost sixteen years later, it looked like he might have found the family he'd been ordered to find. There was something very familiar about the man. Was it possible Hung's days in exile were over? *Could* he have found them?

A surge of excitement went through him and with it, a renewed sense of purpose. He dragged his keyboard toward him. The Li family bore a definite resemblance to his fugitives. They most certainly required closer scrutiny and if it turned out they were responsible for the death of Douglas Hanley... Well, he'd deal with that complication, if and when it became necessary. Until then, he'd allow himself the slightest fantasy about how it might be when he returned to his homeland, triumphant.

CHAPTER 8

Sally-Ann acknowledged her secretary with a brief wave of her hand and hurried into her office. She closed the door behind her and made a beeline for her desk. Dropping her briefcase onto the polished wooden surface, she took a seat and pulled herself forward. Dragging the keyboard toward her, she went online and opened the page to a search engine.

Quickly, she typed in Doug's name and the word murder. It had been more than twelve hours since Doug had been shot. The incident should have been picked up by the news.

Sure enough, several media outlets had snippets of the story. She scanned the text until she found what she was looking for.

An eyewitness apparently reported seeing someone the police believed to be the perpetrator leaving the scene on a motorbike. Now the detective's question in that regard made sense, along with his attitude.

Only one article made mention of the gun.

Either the reporter had a good connection inside the City of Sydney Police or he was better at retaining and recording the facts. According to the story, Doug had been shot with a nine millimeter handgun, exactly like the one owned by her father.

Almost immediately, another thought occurred to her and with it, her belly filled with dread. She'd used that gun less than a week ago. She'd gone to the rifle range with her father. It had been so long since she'd taken the time to go with him, that she'd felt guilty when he reminded her of that fact moments after they pulled up in the rifle range parking lot. But she'd brushed off his comment with a smile and made a silent vow to spend more time with him in the future. After all, neither of her parents were getting any younger. They wouldn't be around forever.

Now a nine millimeter handgun had been used to murder her ex-brother-in-law. Her father had assured her he hadn't done anything stupid and she darn well knew it wasn't her. Aimee didn't have it in her to kill anyone, even Doug. She was like their mom that way.

No, the detective was only bluffing when he'd asked her those questions, insinuating she knew more than she'd let on. It must have been someone else who shot Doug. Someone else who had a beef against him. Someone else who owned or had access to a motorbike and a nine millimeter handgun. Someone else who just happened to carry her business card.

The phone at her elbow pealed and she

absently reached over and picked it up. "Sydney Legal. This is Sally-Ann."

"Sal, it's Dad."

He sounded breathless, like he'd run a block or two before making the call.

"Dad, where are you?"

"I'm at work. I had an afternoon shift. I'm on my break. I wanted to call you. I had a visit from the police."

"Yes, they told me."

"Oh, I see. They've spoken to you again?"

"Yes. They were very interested in the fact that not only can I shoot with some degree of accuracy, I also own a motorbike. I wondered why it had sparked their attention so I searched for the story about Doug online. Apparently the fatal bullet came from a nine millimeter gun and the shooter escaped on a motorbike."

Her announcement was met with dead silence. She knew the moment her father joined the dots.

"Oh, my God, Sally-Ann!" he gasped. "The police think it was *you!*"

"Apparently," she said dryly. "Or at the very least, I'm a person of interest."

"Oh, no! This is terrible!" her father wailed.

"Dad, don't worry about it. I didn't kill Doug. I must be one of at least a hundred people in this city who can both shoot and own a motorbike. If that's all they have on me, I'm fine."

"But they asked me about Doug. I told them how I blamed him for Aimee's accident. They might think you feel the same way."

"Yes, well, I kind of already told them that."

"Oh, Sal! What are we going to *do!* Now they have motive! This is terrible!"

Sally-Ann swallowed a sigh. She understood the fear and panic that laced her father's voice. He'd been looking over his shoulder for sixteen years. The visit from the detectives had rattled him.

"What did you tell the police?" she asked quietly.

"I thought I would be able to handle it—the interview, I mean. You'd warned me they were coming. Thankfully your mother had a morning shift at the supermarket. She wasn't there when they arrived. I tried to keep calm and act like there was nothing wrong, but when I opened the door and saw them standing there, I panicked... All I could think of was all the times I came under scrutiny by the Chinese authorities. First when your mother and I went against the one-child policy— we paid thousands of dollars to have them look the other way—and then when they came after me on the pretext I was selling state secrets to the US. Anyway, when the officers started to question me. I pretended to struggle with English, like you suggested, to buy time. Only, one of the detectives was Chinese. He spoke Mandarin."

"That would be Detective Wang," Sally-Ann supplied. "Was he short with black hair, graying at the temples?"

"Yes, that sounds like him. I didn't like him. There was something about him..."

Sally-Ann sighed. "I know what you mean. Aimee felt the same way."

"Yes, well, he started questioning me in Mandarin.

It was going fine until the other detective told Wang to ask me about Aimee's accident. You know how I feel about people referring to that as an accident. My anger must have shown in my face. The young detective realized I could understand English just fine."

Sally-Ann gasped in alarm. An image of the suave, sexy detective with the probing green eyes came to mind. "Oh, Dad! What did he say?"

"He was suspicious, of course, but I managed to allay his concerns by explaining how English is my second language and I didn't want to misunderstand any of their questions."

"Did he buy it?"

"I think so."

Sally-Ann sighed in relief. "What else did you tell them?"

"Nothing. Only the truth. I answered their questions with the truth."

"They asked you about owning a gun," Sally-Ann guessed.

"Yes. And a motorbike. I told them I didn't own a motorbike, but then they asked to have a look in the shed and...they found yours. I had to tell them you owned it."

Sally-Ann grimaced, but then forced the irritation away. It wasn't her father's fault and like he said, he was only telling the truth. She just hoped it wouldn't go against them.

"Where were you last night, Dad?" she asked calmly.

"I was home with your mother, of course."

"Doug was shot with a nine millimeter, Dad. The

same as yours. You might not own a motorbike, but we both know you have the spare set of keys to mine."

"It wasn't me, Sal! I swear! Every time I think about Doug and what he did to our Aimee, I get crazy all over again, but I didn't kill him! I'm telling you the truth!"

"Okay, Dad, I believe you," Sally-Ann said, hoping to calm him down. He wasn't a young man and the last time he went for a check-up, his blood pressure was high. She didn't want to be the cause of a heart attack.

"Where were you last night, Sal?"

The question was asked quietly and without inflection, but she gasped all the same. How could her father possibly think *she* had anything to do with Doug's death? Then her shoulders slumped on another sigh. For the same reasons she put that very question to her father.

"Don't worry, Dad. I was home in bed by half-past nine. Even the old Seinfeld re-runs Mom and Aimee were watching didn't interest me."

She thought about the half-bottle of red wine she'd polished off after picking at a TV dinner for one. It seemed like just another sad and lonely day in the life of brilliantly smart, but single, girl—Sally-Ann Li. She'd gone to bed feeling sorry for herself, depressed at the reminder of the teenager she'd once been: top of every class, but without a solitary friend. A few tears of self-pity escaped before she dashed them off her cheeks and forced herself to sleep.

"We need to be careful, Sal," her father warned,

his voice pitched low. "We can't afford to draw attention to ourselves. We need to—"

"I get it, Dad," she said, cutting him off. "It's been that way for sixteen years. 'Stay out of the way of police.' 'Keep a low profile.' 'Don't get in trouble,'" she mimicked. "I've heard it over and over since I was thirteen."

"And I meant every word of it!" her father snapped. "Listen to me, Sally-Ann! I know what I'm talking about! The police are bad news, whether they're Australian or Chinese. We can't afford to let our guard down, and especially not now. They're looking at us in connection with a murder investigation! They already know we were angry at the victim. Now they know we have access to a motorbike and a gun. It's not too far a stretch to see them making a case against us. You need to be careful. Please, Sal. *Please*, be careful."

She heard the anguish in his voice and was immediately overcome with guilt. His concern for her welfare came from a good place. He cared deeply for her and her sister and didn't want either of them to come to harm. Additionally, he didn't want them accused of something they didn't do.

She knew all about what had happened to him in China. She understood his fear of police better than anyone, and for that reason, she acceded to his request. Once again, an image of the good-looking detective flashed through her mind and she smiled sadly with regret. It pained her to think there could never be anything between her and the cute officer, but she loved her family more.

Her father would never accept a police officer as a son-in-law and she couldn't expect him to. Whatever fleeting fantasy she might have had about Detective James Shepherd needed to die a natural death. And quickly. There could never be anything between them. If her current situation was any indication, she was destined to many more lonely nights, yet.

———————

Hung Wang's fingers flew over the keyboard. It was late. His shift had finished hours ago and the skeleton night staff were gathered in the tea room. He should go home. But there was nothing and no one to greet him in his cramped and smelly flat and the only thing in the fridge was a dish of stale rice. Besides, he was focused on researching the Li family and what he'd already found was more than a little intriguing.

According to the Births, Deaths and Marriages Registry, sixteen years earlier, all four members of the Li family had legally changed their names. Their applications had been lodged the first week they'd spent in Sydney. That bit of information was more than interesting and had kept him glued to the screen long after he should have left for home.

Not everything was as it appeared... Just like with him. The Li family were as fake as his wedding ring. *Who were they and what were they hiding?* He was pretty sure, but he needed confirmation.

He tugged out the phone in his pocket and dialed a number he knew by heart. It was answered almost immediately. He replied in Mandarin.

James scrubbed a hand through his short hair and did his best to curb his frustration. It had been three days since the Hanley murder and they were no closer to capturing his killer. The urge to sneak outside for a cigarette was almost overwhelming and he clenched his jaw tight in an effort to suppress it. He was forty-nine days in on his quit program. He refused to let the pressures of work ruin all he'd achieved. With a groan of irritation, he strode over to the whiteboard that stood in one corner of the squad room and with his hands on his hips, stared at their list of suspects. The three members of the Li family—along with Janice Carter—completed the list.

He and Wang had finally caught up with Fen Li, wife of Chao, at the supermarket where she worked. She confirmed what Aimee had told them about watching Seinfeld on TV and though she'd appeared frightened by their presence, she was a tiny woman, barely five feet high. There was no way she could have climbed on board, let alone maneuvered the beast of a motorbike Jo-Beth had seen. And she didn't seem to have a motive. She appeared genuinely sorry that Doug had died and confided that she'd always hoped he and Aimee would get back together.

At that, James had started in surprise. Other than Aimee, she was the first member of the Li family who hadn't expressed residual anger at what Doug had done, or disappointment that he hadn't been punished. Fen had quietly told him how much Aimee loved her ex-husband and though her daughter declared to anyone who'd listen that she was over him, Fen knew better.

James had pondered the information, and though he still had Aimee on the suspect list, she was well below the others. In fact, he could almost remove her from it altogether. Wang agreed.

"I just don't see Aimee Li as our perp," Wang had told James when they spoke about it earlier. "I mean, the woman's in a wheelchair. She's obviously not our shooter and I checked the Firearms Registry database. She doesn't own a gun and she doesn't come across as the type to fraternize with criminals—something she'd have to do in order to procure the services of a hired killer. She only has her mother as her alibi and the fact that they were watching the same TV show, but that in itself supports her claim of innocence. If you're going to commit a murder, wouldn't you make sure you had someone who could vouch for your whereabouts at the time of the offense? Aimee Li, being the murderer, just doesn't make sense."

"I agree," James replied. "I also checked Doug Hanley's phone. It turns out the last phone call he made was to a cab company. His mother told us he'd called Aimee. I guess she was mistaken."

"Sounds like it," Wang replied dismissively.

James sighed. Clearing Aimee Li of suspicion didn't make solving his case any easier. He still had three viable suspects on his list and no concrete evidence that pointed to any of them. It was frustrating to say the least. And then he had an idea. He spun on his heel and faced Wang who sat at his desk a short distance away.

"Why don't we bring them all in for a polygraph?"

"Who?" Wang asked distractedly.

"Our suspects! Chao and Sally-Ann Li and Janice Carter!" James replied in exasperation.

"What's the point? Even if they fail, it's not admissible."

James bit his lip in frustration. Wang had gained a reputation among the detectives for being a top-notch investigator, but right at that moment, James failed to see any sign of his colleague's purported brilliance. Wang's decided lack of interest in their murder investigation was beginning to piss him off.

"Who cares if it's admissible?" he retorted. "It might shake them up a little. Who knows what they'll say? If nothing else, it could help us narrow the suspect list. So far, we have very little. There were no prints on the business card. Hanley doesn't appear to have any enemies, apart from the ones we know about and I wouldn't exactly call them enemies."

Wang shrugged disinterestedly. "Whatever you think. I guess it's as good an idea as any." He returned his attention to his computer screen.

James curbed his temper. Getting mad at his

colleague wouldn't help anything. He needed to focus on the facts, gather evidence, interview witnesses, do what he usually did when faced with a challenging case. This one was no different. If Wang wasn't interested in helping him solve it, he'd darn well solve it on his own.

CHAPTER 9

Sally-Ann hung up the receiver and stared at the phone. Her heart thumped. Detective Shepherd wanted her and her father to come down to the station and take a polygraph. She hadn't heard from him since their discussion outside the Children's Court and the knowledge that she and her father were still on his suspicious mind in relation to Doug's murder was unsettling.

Now he wanted them to take a lie detector test. He tried to convince her it was one way she and her father could remove themselves from suspicion. Of course, she'd declined. Even though the results from such tests weren't admissible as evidence in a New South Wales court of law, they provided the police with vital information and as a defense lawyer, she wasn't of a mind to provide the police with anything more than what was absolutely necessary.

She thought of her father and how he'd react if he knew they were still on the suspect list. He'd be beside himself with fear. He'd reiterate all the reasons why the police weren't to be trusted. He might even urge her to pack up her things and leave. It's what he'd suggested the last time they'd spoken. She'd downplayed his suggestion.

Still, she had to keep him updated. It was the right thing to do. With a sigh, she reached over and picked up the phone and dialed her father's number. He answered on the second ring.

"Sally-Ann, how are you?"

"I'm fine, Dad. Can you talk?"

"Yes, of course. I worked the morning shift. I've been home a couple of hours now."

"Where's Mom?"

"She's in the kitchen preparing dinner. She had a day off."

Once again, Sally-Ann sighed. Her father's tone changed immediately. His voice became tinged with alarm. "What is it, Sal? What's happened?"

"I'm sorry, Dad; it's really nothing. I just had a call from the police—Detective Shepherd. He wants us to take a polygraph."

Her father gasped. "A lie detector test!"

"Yes, Dad."

"What did you say?" His voice was now filled with panic.

"I told him no, of course."

"Why did you do that?" he exclaimed.

She started in surprise. "Because the police will go on a fishing expedition. It's obvious they have nothing. If we sit tight, they'll give up and move on to someone else."

"No! They'll think we're hiding something!"

"Dad, the results from a polygraph aren't admissible in court."

"I don't care about that! I just want to get them out of our lives! I want to take the test, Sally-Ann."

"Dad, as a lawyer, I advise you against it. You've been living a lie for sixteen years. These tests are very hard to beat. What if you fail? It would make things worse. I—"

"I know those things better than anyone, daughter, but you don't know the police like I do. They won't let this go. They think you and I had something to do with Doug's death. They won't be satisfied until they've proven it."

"We've been over this before, Dad. They have nothing on us! It's not like they can go planting evidence or making things up."

"Don't bet on it, Sal." His words held an ominous warning. Though the ambient temperature in her office was pleasant, she shivered.

"Well, I'm not going to sit the test, Dad. You can suit yourself. As your lawyer, I'm advising you against it, but you do as you like."

"That's your decision, Sally-Ann. You've never had the police chasing you, accusing you of doing something you've never done. It can drive you insane. Besides, I'm telling the truth about Doug. I had nothing to do with his murder and I want my chance to prove that."

She thought about all her father had been through and mollified him with her tone. "Would you like me to set it up?"

"Yes, thank you. I'd appreciate that."

Blowing her breath out on a sigh, she agreed to

call him back with the details and then ended the call. Scrolling through her contacts, she found the number for Detective James Shepherd and dialed it.

James stared down at the details of the appointment he'd just made for Sally-Ann Li's father to sit a polygraph test. Interestingly, she'd still declined to participate in one herself and she'd made it clear her father was acting against her advice. James only hoped the test would bring some results that would help them find the killer.

Janice Carter, the victim's wife, had also agreed to take the test. As a matter of course, James had investigated her story and had been surprised when it didn't check out. She'd told them she was working the night Doug Hanley had been murdered, but it turned out she wasn't.

Why would she lie about something so easily disproven? It didn't make sense. Janice owned a motorbike similar to the one seen coming out of the alleyway shortly after the shot was fired and though the Firearms Registry confirmed she didn't own a gun, that didn't mean she couldn't find a way to access one.

It would be interesting to see what came of the polygraph tests. Even better, it once again put him in close proximity with the beautiful Sally-Ann Li. His gut tightened with anticipation.

Sally-Ann smoothed her hands over her pale sky-blue, pinstriped suit and tried to ignore her disquiet. She glanced across at her father who sat, unmoving, in the hard plastic chair opposite. He'd been silent on the way over, not even answering her direct questions. She couldn't imagine how difficult this was—heading over to face an interrogation in the bowels of the City of Sydney Police Station. She worried he wouldn't be able to withstand the pressure of the examiner and that even though he was being truthful, the results wouldn't reflect that. She didn't know which one of them was more nervous. The thought sent another wave of tension coursing through her.

Janice also sat in the waiting room, which came as a surprise. Sally-Ann hadn't given any thought to the fact the police might have Doug's second wife in their sights. She hadn't seen the woman since she'd run off with Aimee's husband, but it was obvious time had treated Janice well. The woman didn't look a day older or a pound heavier than she had five years earlier. She wore a low-cut, formfitting red dress that hugged her curves and emphasized her bountiful chest. Sally-Ann wondered if the nurse had worn the dress for the benefit of the good-looking detective. Her lips tightened at the thought.

"Mr Li?"

The arrival of Detective Shepherd in the waiting room cut through her thoughts. Her heart skipped a beat at the sight of the tall, broad-shouldered police officer and she was immediately annoyed at her reaction. She'd been around plenty of good-looking men before. She worked in a law firm that employed more than one hundred lawyers and a good number of those were attractive males. *What was it about this man that made her heart beat faster?*

At the sound of his name, her father looked up. Even from across the room, she saw his face lose color. She immediately came to her feet and strode over to where he sat. She glared at the detective.

"I'd like to reiterate what I told you earlier: My father is here against my advice."

The detective regarded her lazily. "Yes, I believe you already made that quite clear when you called the other day. I'm assuming your position hasn't changed?"

The sparkle of humor in his eyes infuriated her. He was playing with her! She and her father were suspects in a murder investigation and the detective in charge was *playing* with her! It was too much!

Anger heated her cheeks. She opened her mouth to give him a piece of her mind, but he cut her off before she could utter another word.

"Mr Li, if you're still willing to participate in the polygraph test, I'll ask you to come with me."

With a determined expression, her father looked from the detective to her and back again. Sally-Ann recovered her composure enough to give him a reassuring hug. "Are you sure you want to do this, Dad?" she whispered in his ear. He nodded in acknowledgment and then pulled away and followed James out of the room.

With nothing left to do, Sally-Ann returned to her seat. Janice regarded her with interest.

"Hello, Sally-Ann. It's been a long time," the woman in the blood-red dress said in a conversational tone.

Sally-Ann stared at her. Was the woman actually trying to be friendly? That's what it seemed like. Was she out of her mind? She'd run off with the husband of Sally-Ann's sister while that very sister was lying paralyzed in a hospital bed! Friendly! What planet was she from? She certainly didn't even have a toehold in the world Sally-Ann inhabited.

It took all of her self-control, but she managed to ignore the urge to once again give Janice Carter a piece of her mind by pretending to be immersed in the emails on her phone. From the corner of her eye, she noticed Janice's lips tighten at her lack of response, but after a moment, the woman looked away and also pulled out her phone. The two of them sat in silence.

After what felt like a lifetime, James reappeared with her father following close behind. He was pale and trembling. Alarmed, Sally-Ann jumped to her feet.

"We're all done," the detective said to her.

"How did he do?" she asked, her heart beating hard.

James pulled her aside and his voice lowered. "I'm afraid he failed."

Sally-Ann's hand came up to her mouth. She gasped in shock. "No! There must be some mistake. He couldn't have failed. Did you properly calibrate the machine? There must be some explanation. My father didn't have anything to do with Doug's murder."

The detective held her gaze, his eyes hard. "There's nothing wrong with the machine, Ms Li. What I want to know is, is he lying to cover up for himself, or for you?"

Another wave of shock rippled through her, followed quickly by anger beyond belief. "How dare you!" she hissed. "I've already told you I had nothing to do with Doug's death and neither did my father. You're wasting time and other precious resources looking at any of my family. Why don't you put the same energy into finding the real killer?"

His gaze didn't waver and his expression remained unchanged. It was as if she hadn't spoken.

"Are you sure you don't want to take the test and set the record straight?" he drawled. Without giving her a chance to answer, he strode over to where Janice sat and invited her to take the polygraph. A moment later, the two of them disappeared down the hall.

Hours later, James sat down in a deck chair on his balcony and stared off into the night. A warm breeze drifted in across the harbor, bringing with it the salty tang of summer. What his one-bedroom bachelor pad lacked in size it made up for in location. His condo was on the top floor of a small complex wedged between two other much larger buildings. It was in shadow most of the day, but he had a decent view of the harbor. The sight of the wide expanse of blue water, the twinkling lights on the foreshore mansions, the sailing boats and other watercraft never failed to soothe him after a long day.

He leaned over and reached for the scotch glass he'd set near his deck chair. He took a sip of the single malt and relished its smooth burn, willing his mind to switch off for even a few minutes and give him a moment of rest.

Ever since two of his suspects had taken the polygraph test, he'd been tense and out of sorts. Both Chao Li and Janice Carter had failed. He already knew Janice had lied about at least part of what she'd told him and when he'd confronted her about that lie after the results of the polygraph became known, she admitted she'd gotten confused over the dates and her shifts. It turned out she wasn't at work that night and couldn't tell him where she'd been—just another suspect without an alibi.

Then there was Sally-Ann's father. James had watched the test from behind a two-way glass partition and had been surprised at the man's nervousness. It wasn't unusual for people to feel uncomfortable—after all, the only reason they were there was because they were considered suspects in some form of criminal behavior—but Chao's reaction seemed more severe than the average person's. The few times James had witnessed such an extreme reaction had been with a suspect who'd ultimately been found guilty.

Then there was Sally-Ann. *Where did she fit in?* She'd refused to take the polygraph. In itself, he didn't read too much into that. She was a defense lawyer. Her instinctive reaction was to withhold information from the police. It wasn't the defense team's job to make out the case for the prosecution. He understood her innate reaction not to make things easier for him.

But was that all there was to it? Was it merely a professional instinct that had kicked in and made her refuse to take the test, or was there something more sinister behind it? She was certainly bright enough to plan a murder. She also owned a high-powered motorbike and could handle a gun. The fact she didn't own a gun didn't mean anything. By her own admission, she had free access to her father's collection—and according to the Firearms Registry, he owned five guns in total, including the same type of gun used in the murder. She also had no alibi.

Then there was the business card. She'd appeared genuinely surprised and confused about the presence of her card at the crime scene. In ordinary circumstances, he'd probably believe her protestations. But coupled with everything else, it was another piece of circumstantial evidence that pointed toward her guilt—or at least to the fact she was present at the scene.

He needed to ask Chao Li to hand over his nine millimeter for testing and hope his daughter didn't insist on a warrant. If it came down to it, James probably had enough evidence against the father and the daughter to get one, but it meant further delays and time was of the essence. It had been five days since the murder and the case was going cold.

If Chao refused to hand the gun over voluntarily, James would be forced to wonder what the man had to hide. In his experience, people with nothing to hide were more than happy to cooperate with the police, particularly when they were investigating something as serious as murder and yet, so far, the Li family hadn't been too forthcoming on the cooperation front. Was it the defense lawyer thing that held them back, or something else?

He was determined to find out.

Sally-Ann paced the small confines of her parents' front room and tried not to let her frustration and growing concern show. She still couldn't believe her father had failed the polygraph. Had he lied to her when he'd assured her he'd played no part in Doug's murder?

"Sally-Ann!" her mother said sternly. "Please, stop pacing! You're making me nervous."

With an effort, Sally-Ann slowed her footsteps and then threw herself down on the couch. Her father stared back at her from his position in his favorite armchair, a worried frown lining his face.

"I'm sorry, daughter. I don't know what you want me to say."

"Oh, Dad! I told you not to take that polygraph!"

His jaw set into a stubborn line she'd seen far too many times. "I did nothing wrong, Sally-Ann! I have nothing to hide!"

"Then how did you fail the test? I don't understand!"

He ran a hand through his short hair, setting it on end. "I got nervous!" he said. "I haven't been inside a police station since we were in China. When I got into that small room—the walls were padded and it was so confining—I felt like I was suffocating! I thought I could handle it, but... I couldn't. I felt dizzy and couldn't breathe properly. The man administering the test tried to calm me down. He asked me if I was sure I wanted to take the test, seeing as how nervous I was and I still told him yes."

"Why didn't you just decline and leave, Dad? They couldn't force you to take the test."

"I know, but I wanted to do it. I wanted to clear my name. I thought I'd be okay. But not long after the questions started, I began to have flashbacks to the time in China—interrogations, torture, escaping in the middle of the night. Taking nothing, stealing away like we had something to hide. I did nothing wrong then, either, but I was made to feel I had. No one would believe me. I had no choice but to flee."

His voice hitched and Sally-Ann saw the devastation in his face. Her heart went out to him and to her mother and to what the two of them had endured, but that didn't help now. The fact was, her father had failed the lie detector test. The detective had even more reason to believe he was involved in Doug's murder and that was troubling, to say the least.

Aware that her increasing anxiety was only going to make her parents more distressed, she drew in a deep breath and made an effort to calm down. When she felt more in control, she stood and walked over to where her father sat and kneeled beside him. She reached for his soft, worn hands and squeezed them in an attempt to reassure him.

"It's all right, Dad. This isn't China. The police won't arrest you without any evidence. You say you had nothing to do with Doug's murder and I believe you. Don't worry about the polygraph. Like I said, the results can't be used as evidence. The police use it as a tool in their investigation and the fact that you failed will pique their interest in you, but they still have to find proof that you murdered Doug and we both know that won't be forthcoming."

Her father gave her a weak smile and she could tell he was grateful for her efforts. "Thank you, Sal. I appreciate your attempt to make me feel better. I should have listened to you in the first place and refused to take the test. Now look what a mess I've made of things. That detective—"

"Is only doing his job, Dad, and he'll continue to do so. He's trying to solve a murder investigation. It's only natural he look at the people surrounding Doug, me included. I'm on the suspect list, too, remember?"

Her father looked even more troubled. "I wish the police would just find the real killer and leave us all alone." He looked up at Sally-Ann. "That detective seems like a smart man. Why can't he find the person responsible?"

Sally-Ann averted her gaze, uncomfortable discussing James Shepherd with her father. "I don't know, Dad, but at least you can rest easy knowing that the police in Australia have to follow the rules and Detective Shepherd strikes me as someone who respects the rules."

She risked a glance in her father's direction and noticed his gaze had sharpened. "What is it, Dad?"

"You seem rather taken with this detective. I saw the way you looked at each other back there. What's going on between the two of you?"

Heat crept up Sally-Ann's neck and spread across her cheeks. She turned her face away in an effort to avoid her father's gaze.

"N-nothing, Dad," she stammered. "I don't know what you're talking about."

She felt the weight of his gaze, but was determined not to look at him. If she did, she was certain her face would betray her.

"Stay away from him, daughter." Her father's voice held a stern warning.

"Dad!" she protested. "There's nothing going on between me and Detective Shepherd! Whatever you think you saw, you imagined."

Her father threw her a hard stare. "I know what I saw, Sally-Ann, and it frightened me. Police officers are bad news. I don't care what country they come from. They're all the same. They're power hungry and they enjoy exerting their authority over others. You won't ever convince me there's an officer alive on this planet who can be trusted."

Sally-Ann's heart sank. She'd always known about her father's attitude toward members of law enforcement, but to hear him state it so plainly in that moment was like a dagger to her heart. Not that she'd developed any tender feelings toward the good-looking detective, but in the dark and lonely hours of the night, she'd allowed herself the temptation of fantasizing just what it might be like to spend time with him, get to know him, be held in his strong protective arms…

She made an impatient sound in the back of her throat and thrust the images from her mind. Her mother had drawn closer, a worried expression darkening her face.

"Sally-Ann, it isn't true, is it? You don't have something going on with this police officer, do you?"

Sally-Ann shook her head and got to her feet. She went over to her mother, who barely came up to her shoulder—and Sally-Ann wasn't tall—and hugged her.

"No, Mom. There's nothing going on between me and Detective Shepherd. I'm not sure what Dad thought he saw, but I assure you, it was nothing. I was there as Dad's lawyer. I was making sure Detective Shepherd knew that and didn't overstep his boundaries or violate any of Dad's rights."

"I thought you said he was a man who played by the rules?" her father interjected.

Sally-Ann opened her mouth to respond and then closed it. She drew in a slow breath and acknowledged her father's question with a nod. She chose her words with care.

"I did, Dad, and I still believe that's the case. Despite your instinctive distrust of anyone connected with law enforcement, I think Detective Shepherd is a good man."

The sound of her father's cell phone ringing caught everyone's attention. He fumbled around in the pocket of his shirt and eventually produced the handset. He answered the call. For a few moments, he listened and then he said, "Hold on a minute."

With his hand over the mouthpiece, he shot a panicked look in Sally-Ann's direction. "It's him! The detective! He wants my gun. The Glock."

Sally-Ann thought fast. "Tell him to speak to your lawyer."

Her father nodded and removed his hand from the mouthpiece. "I think you should speak to my lawyer."

There was a moment's silence while her father listened to the caller on the other end of the line and then her father said, "Hold on. She's right here. I'll put her on." He handed the phone to Sally-Ann.

Her heart skipped a beat and then took off at a gallop. She drew in a surreptitious breath and went into lawyer mode.

"This is Sally-Ann Li. How can I help you?"

The deep rumble of Detective James Shepherd's voice caressed her eardrum. She tried not to think about how good his voice sounded. Once again, he asked for her father's nine millimeter Glock.

"Do you have a warrant?" she asked.

"Do I need one?" he replied.

Sally placed her hand over the mouthpiece and turned back to her father. "Are you *sure* your gun wasn't used in Doug's murder, Dad?" she whispered.

His face filled with indignation. "Why do you keep asking me this, daughter? Of *course* I'm sure! I had nothing to do with that business!"

"Okay," she said and brought the phone back to her ear.

"Are you still there, Detective?"

"Yes, Ms Li. I'm still here," came the bemused reply.

"I've spoken to my father. He's happy to give you access to his gun without a warrant. I'll bring the gun to you."

"Thank you, Ms Li. That's mighty accommodating. I look forward to seeing you."

Sally-Ann gritted her teeth against his condescending tone and with a brief word of farewell, she ended the call.

CHAPTER 10

James studied the papers spread over his desk and tried to make sense of them. He'd summarized what he knew about each of the suspects and had added the latest information about the polygraph tests. Both Chao Li and Janice had motive. They also either owned or had access to a motorbike that fit the description of the one seen leaving the crime scene. Neither of them had a substantial alibi and both Li and Carter had failed the polygraph.

Chao could shoot and owned a number of guns, including one that took the same type of ammunition that was used to murder Douglas Hanley. Janice Carter didn't own a gun and told them she didn't know how to use one, but that didn't mean she hadn't arranged for someone else to do the shooting—someone else who knew how to shoot and happened to own or have access to a motorbike—or who had borrowed hers.

Then there was Sally-Ann. Just the thought of her made his gut tighten and his pulse skip a beat.

The truth was, he didn't want to think of her as a suspect in a murder investigation. She was the hottest woman he'd ever set eyes on and something about her drew him—as if they had an indefinable connection. He couldn't explain it, but he was almost sure she felt it, too, despite the fact she'd fought it as much as he did.

If only they'd met under different circumstances...

But the facts couldn't be ignored. Sally-Ann was just as likely a suspect as the other two. She owned a motorbike, had access to a gun, had means and motive and quite possibly, opportunity. He'd made inquires of the man who managed the bar on Bathurst Street. He confirmed Doug was a regular there. Which meant Janice would have almost certainly known where to find him. And if Doug had passed that information on to Aimee Li who in turn passed it on to her family...

He groaned aloud in frustration, feeling like he was going around in circles. Despite the circumstantial evidence, they had nothing definite tying any of their suspects to the crime. It was really pissing him off and meant that the next time Maureen Hanley called for her regular update, he'd have nothing to add.

That thought made him groan again. He understood the need for Doug's mother to be kept informed of the progress made in her son's murder investigation, but she'd become a monstrous pain in the ass with her constant phone calls and requests for information. If only she was just as forthcoming when the questions were directed at her.

He'd made a point of asking her about Janice Carter and why she hadn't mentioned at their first meeting that her son had a second wife. The woman had prevaricated for a moment or two, but eventually conceded Janice's existence. She also admitted the two of them had recently parted, but hastened to add it was probably only temporary: Doug loved Janice with all his heart.

When James asked her about the split, she agreed there had been tension between Doug and Janice over Janice's desire for kids. When he asked if she'd ever seen her son and Janice arguing, she denied that things had ever gone that far and reminded him it was the Asian woman who had the real gripe against her son and it should be Aimee Li and her family that he was looking at.

It irked James that Maureen seemed so certain of the Li family's guilt. Was it because she was racist, like Aimee Li had said, or was Doug's mother on the right track? She'd been wrong about the last call on her son's cell phone, but was she wrong about all of it? He wished he knew.

The phone at his elbow rang and he absently picked up the receiver. Recognizing the voice on the other end of the line, he swallowed a groan.

"Maureen, how are you doing?" he asked, keeping his irritation from his tone.

"Detective Shepherd, what's going on? It's been more than a week since my darling Douglas was mowed down in that alleyway like a stray dog. Have you made any progress finding his killer? Have you made any arrests?"

James gritted his teeth and remained calm. "No, Maureen. I'm sorry. My colleague and I are working as hard as we can. Unfortunately, we have no one definite in our sights. We—"

"I've already told you, Detective! It's that Li woman, for sure. She might not have pulled the actual trigger, but you mark my words, Aimee Li's had it in for my son ever since the accident. If it wasn't her, it was that sister of hers. Have you spoken to Sally-Ann?"

"Yes, Maureen, I've interviewed all four members of the Li family, just like I've spoken to other witnesses and persons of interest."

"And what, Detective? What do you have to show for it?"

Her demanding tone irritated him no end and he forced himself to count to ten before responding. He wanted to tell her to back off and give everyone a break. But he couldn't, of course. She was the grieving mother. She deserved to be the first to know if there were any new developments. She wasn't the first relative to hound the police for information. James understood their need. It made them feel connected somehow to their loved one. He got that. He really did. He'd probably be the same way if anything ever happened to someone he cared about deeply.

He thought of his sister and was relieved she'd finally agreed to return home. His condo felt empty without her, but it was for the best. She needed the safety and security of two loving parents who were prepared and capable of looking after her. While he loved her and wouldn't want to see her come to any harm, he was rarely home and when he was, he was often distant and distracted, his head filled with his latest investigation.

No, it was better for everyone that Lizzie had returned home, where she belonged. She'd promised to make a bigger effort with their step-mom and had reluctantly agreed that Anita cared more for her than Lizzie had admitted.

"Detective? Are you still there?"

Maureen's strident tone grated against his ear and he forced himself to refocus. "Yes, Maureen, I'm still here, but I'm going to have to cut this short. I'm waiting for the arrival of another witness. I—"

"Who?" she demanded.

"I'm sorry, Maureen. I can't tell you who, but I assure you, Detective Wang and I are working around the clock on this. We'll find your son's killer. I promise."

As the words fell out of his mouth, James compressed his lips and shook his head. *What the hell was he doing?* It was a rookie mistake to make promises he might not be able to keep and Maureen Hanley wasn't the kind of person who forgot. He suppressed another groan and hurriedly ended the call. He'd no sooner placed the phone back on his desk when it rang again. With an impatient oath, he picked it up. "Detective Shepherd."

"Detective, I have Sally-Ann Li downstairs. She says you're expecting her."

James' belly somersaulted in anticipation. *She*

was here. While he'd used the arrival of a witness as an excuse with Maureen, for a moment he'd forgotten Sally-Ann was on her way. Now she was waiting for him downstairs.

After thanking the receptionist, he hung up the phone and pushed away from his desk. Wang glanced up from his computer screen.

"Where are you off to?"

"Downstairs. Sally-Ann Li offered to bring her father's Glock in for testing."

"Do you have a warrant?"

"Didn't need one. Old man Li handed it in voluntarily."

Wang's eyebrows rose in surprise. "I thought you said he failed the polygraph?"

"He did, but he must be confident his gun wasn't used in the crime."

"Either that or he's just plain stupid."

James shook his head. "None of the members of the Li family strike me as stupid."

Wang nodded slowly. "You're right. The gun must be clean."

"Yeah, well I guess we're about to find out. I'll be back in a minute."

He bounced down the stairs and into the waiting room. The sound of his boots was muted by the carpeted treads. She stood with her back to him, small and petite in another costly suit. This one was black and would have looked severe on some women, but Sally-Ann had teamed it with a soft pink blouse that peaked out over the collar of her jacket. The suit reflected the color of her long, glossy hair. Once again, it hung loose down her back.

"Ms Li," he called.

She turned on her four-inch heel and strode toward him. In her hands, she held a leather gun case.

"Detective Shepherd. I brought the gun."

He nodded and glanced at the case in her hands. "Let's go upstairs. I'll log it in." He turned and retraced his steps. She followed in silence. He took her into a vacant interview room and then left her briefly while he found the required forms.

"Okay, I've filled in the details of the gun and its owner and that it was surrendered voluntarily. It matches the description of the gun listed in your father's name in the Firearms Registry. That's a good thing."

She stared at him. "My father's a good man and an honest, law-abiding citizen. He has a license for each and every one of the firearms in his possession."

James held her gaze and nodded. "And yet he failed a polygraph that specifically asked him questions about his ex-son-in-law's murder. How do you figure?"

Anger flashed in her beautiful brown eyes and her lips tightened. Her gaze lowered to the scarred Formica table that stood between them. She was silent for a long moment, as if debating how best to respond to his question. At last, she looked up at him with a quiet sigh.

"You must understand. My father has an intense distrust of the police and anyone connected to law enforcement. Being in a police station, near police officers made him extremely nervous.

Unfortunately, it affected his results."

"I already ran his name through our data base. He doesn't have a criminal record. Why's he so nervous of the police?"

Once again, she took her time answering. When she did, there was a sad expression in her eyes, along with a new intensity.

"What I'm about to tell you has been kept a secret for sixteen years. Can I trust you to keep it to yourself?"

He held her gaze. "Yes, of course, within reason. If it has anything directly to do with the murder investigation, I can't promise I'll stay silent. But I'm an officer of the law. I know how to keep my mouth shut."

She stared at him a moment longer, before dropping her gaze. She sighed quietly.

"Sixteen years ago, my father took his wife and daughters and fled China, fearing for his life. He'd been falsely accused of treason by the Chinese authorities. False evidence was brought forward and they were convinced he was selling state secrets to the US. Until then, my father was a lawyer of some renown in Beijing. He had several international clients, mostly property developers, but he did not betray his country.

"Anyway, the Chinese government was convinced the property deals were nothing more than a cover for his real work—espionage—and they arrested him. Dad's certain they were also targeting him because he had the audacity to go against the one-child policy that was in force before I was born. Anyway, he was interrogated for ten days straight, tortured and God knows what else. I was thirteen at the time. We were all terrified. We didn't know if we were ever going to see him again."

She drifted off, as if caught up in memories. When she spoke again, her voice was soft and husky with emotion.

"And then one night, he arrived on our doorstep, thin and pale and disheveled and barely able to speak. Even now, he rarely talks about it and never in any great detail. Suffice it to say, he fled with us to Australia in the hope of escaping the Chinese authorities and the punishment they had in store for him. He managed to evade them, but he's been looking over his shoulder ever since, convinced they're still searching for him."

James shot her a look of disbelief. "After sixteen years? I doubt it."

Sally-Ann shrugged. "I agree. It's a long shot. Still, it's what he believes."

"And hence his fear of the police," James finished.

"Yes. He told me that when the examiner started asking him questions, he had flashbacks to the time when he was interrogated by the authorities in China. Unfortunately, it affected his results."

"Do you think it might help if he re-sat the test?" James offered.

Sally-Ann shook her head. "No, I don't think so. He came home pretty upset. I think the whole incident shook him up. I don't want to put him through that again." She paused and then added, "But I'll do it."

James blinked in surprise. "You'll sit the test?"

Her gaze remained steady on his. "Yes."

"But what about—?"

"Forget about that. I know my father's innocent and *I* sure as hell had nothing to do with what happened to Doug. We're not trying to hide anything. Have the examiner ask me whatever questions he likes. If this is what it takes to prove the members of the Li family are innocent, I'll take the damn test." Her eyes hardened. "Set up a time."

James stared back at her. "Are you sure?"

A long moment passed between them. James' pulse jumped and blood rushed to his groin. The moment seemed to stretch forever and then Sally-Ann nervously licked her lips and looked away. The moment was gone.

Afraid his body would betray him, James pushed away from the table with the excuse he needed to make contact with the company that administered the polygraph tests. He hurried from the room. After making the call, he took a moment to collect himself before returning to the interview room. Sally-Ann sat where he'd left her. She had her phone out and was scrolling through something on the screen.

He cleared his throat. "The company can do it either tomorrow or the day after. What times do you have free?"

She looked up and then returned her attention to her phone. She checked her calendar and together, they set a date and time for the test. After securing the gun in the evidence room and seeing her out of the police station, James returned to his desk.

"How did you do with the Li woman?" Wang asked, glancing up as James pulled out his chair and took a seat.

"Fine. I logged the gun in as evidence and will put a call in to ballistics. Hopefully they'll test it today or tomorrow."

"What made her convince her father to hand it over?"

James leaned back in his chair and stacked his hands behind his head. He blew his breath out on a sigh.

"Her father failed the polygraph yesterday. According to Sally-Ann, it was because he has an extraordinary fear of the police. She told me he fled China after being wrongly accused of treason. It happened sixteen years ago, but he still thinks they're looking for him. Being inside the station answering questions, apparently brought the whole thing back. He freaked out. Sally-Ann says it was why he failed the test. His fear skewed the results."

Wang sat forward in his seat and narrowed his eyes in concentration. "Do you believe her? About the China thing? It sounds pretty farfetched."

James nodded. "Yeah, I think I do. Of course, there's no way to check their story, but who would make up such a thing? And we don't have any real evidence that either member of the Li family is involved in this crime. It would certainly explain why the father failed the polygraph."

"What about the lawyer? Is she still refusing to take one?"

"As a matter of fact, she's changed her mind. We've arranged for her to take a test tomorrow afternoon. She's confident she'll pass and that it will help remove suspicion from her family."

"Fair enough," Wang said and returned his attention to the screen in front of him.

James called someone in ballistics and received an assurance the gun would be tested as soon as possible. After finishing up some reports, he returned a couple of calls and then logged off.

"I think I'll head home," he said to Wang.

His colleague merely nodded in response. James wondered what had the man so engrossed. With a shrug of dismissal and a murmured farewell, James left the squad room.

———————

Hung waited for the door to close behind his colleague before he pulled his mouse close and opened his mail program. It took a moment for the new messages to load and he anxiously scanned the heading of each one. Ten emails in, he found it.

Clicking on the email, he read the brief text and then opened the attachment. His heart thumped in anticipation. The colored photos were much clearer than the black-and-white 5 x 8s he'd been given prior to his departure for Australia. There were photos of the two girls together and separately. There were a large number of photos of Lihua Zhang at home, at the market, and even more of Yu Zhang. Some had been taken from a distance. Many were close up. It was obvious the Zhang family had been under surveillance for some time before Yu's arrest.

One thing was clear: Yu and Lihua Zhang were Chao and Fen Li. Sally-Ann's account solidified it all. They looked slightly younger in the photos, but there was no doubt: *He'd found them.*

Sally-Ann doodled on the legal pad in front of her and tried to concentrate on her work. A pile of witness statements that comprised the brief of evidence against her fifteen-year-old client were spread out across her desk. Bradley Nguyen had been charged with armed robbery. He'd sworn to her he was innocent.

The police had supplied her with a grainy copy of CCTV footage taken inside the 7-Eleven. Even she couldn't tell who the perpetrator was. For the most part, the offender had his back to the camera and his face was shrouded by the hood of his jacket. The height and build were close, but Bradley was an average-sized teenager. A lot of boys his age fit those stats.

A fortnight earlier, she'd entered a not guilty plea before the court and at that time, the trial had been set down for the next month. She was going for a defense of mistaken identity and just hoped Bradley's alibi witnesses would hold up. If they didn't and the police witnesses stuck to their stories, it might not go so well for him. With his history of two previous convictions for armed robbery, if he was found guilty, he was looking at doing serious time.

Her thoughts turned to the polygraph test she'd agreed to take. It was scheduled for later that afternoon. She still wasn't sure that she'd made the right decision. She'd always advised her clients against sitting the tests and there were good reasons for that. Now she was battling flashbacks of her own, to the nightmare days of her teenage years when she was often the brunt of unfounded accusations and no matter how long and how loudly she protested, she usually wasn't believed.

Did she really want to put herself through what would be as good as an interrogation when she didn't have to? Even the thought of it had her heart pumping harder. She could almost feel her blood pressure rising. The examiner would ask her in as many ways as he could think of whether she or any of her family members had anything to do with the murder of Douglas Hanley and she would have to repeatedly answer in the negative. At the same time, she'd have to ensure her heart rate didn't increase and that she didn't break out in a sweat and any number of other indicators they looked for when determining guilt.

Then again, she had nothing to hide. She was innocent of any wrongdoing. This wasn't high school. Surely the truth would win out. She'd become a lawyer to make her family proud and because she believed in their system of justice. She believed in giving people the benefit of the doubt. Innocent until proven guilty. That premise underpinned the very foundations of their criminal justice system. It was the only way it could be.

No, she'd take the damn polygraph and be done with it. She might have been angry at Doug for the past five years for what he'd done to her sister, but the results would prove she had nothing to do with his murder. The ballistics tests on the gun would come back negative. The nightmare would be over.

CHAPTER 11

Hung Wang eyed the naked buttocks of the sweet young thing he'd arranged to meet in his apartment and his cock hardened. He was on his lunch break, but this wouldn't take long. It never did. The girl was barely legal, but what did he care? In fact, he preferred them young.

Money had already exchanged hands. Two hundred dollars and she was all his for an hour. She'd do anything he wanted. The thought of what was to come sent a surge of excitement rushing through him. He undid the button on his suit pants, lowered his zipper and shucked them off, along with his underwear. His cock stood to attention, short and thick. He strode over to the bed.

The girl was on her hands and knees as he'd instructed. Coming up behind her, he grabbed her hips and hauled her toward him. He rubbed the tip of his cock up and down the crack between her sweet cheeks and then slid it lower toward her slit. She pushed back against him and moaned.

Of course, it was all for show. It was the only downside to fucking prostitutes. It never meant anything to them. *He* never meant anything to them. It pissed him off, even though the more logical part of his brain accepted that to the girl on the bed, this was nothing more than a job.

Without warning, he slapped her buttocks—hard. She cried out in surprise and alarm. He chuckled. He loved it when he caught them unawares. It always made the final moment so much more pleasurable...

She twisted her neck until she was looking at him. "What the hell? Would you just get on with it, Mister?"

His laughter deepened. Oh, yes, he was going to enjoy this hour of entertainment. He moved over to the closet and pushed clothes belonging to the real Hung Wang out of the way. Leaning down, he pulled out a black leather riding crop he kept there for just this purpose and brought it back to the bed. This time, he climbed on the mattress.

He ran the crop up and down the spine of the woman beside him, teasing her. He flicked at her tits, ran it across her mouth and forced it between her teeth.

"Suck it," he ordered.

She threw him a look that he'd seen many times before, but it was followed quickly by a look of resignation. He'd paid her well for her time. For the next hour, she was his. She opened her mouth and sucked on the leather as if it were his cock.

When he couldn't stand it a moment longer, he removed the crop and replaced it with the real thing.

Her lips closed around him and he groaned in delight. She sucked and licked and squeezed and it was so agonizingly good, he almost gave up on his other plans. He'd let her suck him for as long as he could stand and then he'd blow hard in her mouth. It was a tantalizing proposition… But no, he wanted more from her than that.

Pulling away, he reached down the side of the bed for the restraints he'd hidden there before he'd left for work that morning. Turning her on her back, he took both of her hands and pulled them above her head. She started in surprise, but didn't struggle as he secured both of her wrists to the wrought iron headboard. He slid his way back down her body, his cock still standing to attention. Once again, he was tempted to end this way sooner than he'd planned, but knowing the enjoyment that lay ahead for him, he resisted the urge and picked up the riding crop.

Her eyes flared wide. He pushed her legs apart and flicked at her bush with the whip. He moved lower, caressing the soft folds of her pussy and then thrust the crop inside. She yelped in alarm and the first trace of fear flittered across her face. He smiled. It was good. It was so good.

He pushed the crop in and out, his actions quick and rough.

"Hey!" she shouted. "That hurts!" She pulled against the restraints, but to no avail. His smile widened.

"Relax. I'm just having a bit of fun. You like to have fun, don't you?"

He slowed down his movements to something that resembled a caress. Some of the tension went out of her. He removed the crop and then positioned himself between her thighs. Taking hold of her hips, he rammed his cock in hard. She gasped, but otherwise remained compliant. He tightened his hold on her hips and fucked her hard.

The pressure built in his balls and his cock. She felt so good around his flesh. Knowing he was close, he once again reached for the crop. Her eyes were closed. He sniggered and in time with the rhythm of his hips, he brought the leather down.

Her eyes flew open and she screamed in pain, but it didn't halt his progress. Across her tits, across her ribs, her belly, her face... Anywhere he could reach. He whipped her in time with the pounding of his cock and his arm danced in a frenzy of movement as he reached the pinnacle and with a shout of triumph, toppled over the other side.

Slowly, his breathing quieted and he climbed off the girl on the bed. Red welts striped every inch of pale skin above her thighs. Tears glittered in her eyes. Her look was full of despair and hate.

"Why did you have to go and do that?" she whimpered. "You hurt me."

He leaned over and released the restraints and then shrugged. "Pain is merely a state of mind. You'll be fine."

She scooted to the far side of the bed and

began to pull on her clothes. He did the same. When she was dressed, she went over to the dresser to collect her handbag. She riffled through it and then turned to him, anger glittering in her eyes.

"Where is it?"

He stared at her calmly and smiled. "Oh, you mean, this?" He waggled the fifty-dollar bills he'd given her before the fun had started.

Her eyes narrowed. "That's mine."

He chuckled at her show of courage and secretly admired her spirit. She was a feisty one, for sure.

"If you want it that badly, why don't you come and get it?" he goaded.

She stepped toward him, one step, two. When she was a mere yard away from him, he pulled his service revolver from behind his back and shoved it in her face.

"Are you sure you want that money, little girl?" he sneered.

She cried out in fear and helplessness. Tears glittered in her eyes. Up close and dressed in a hot pink mid-riff top and black mini skirt, she looked even younger than he'd supposed.

She stared at him and slowly shook her head. "What's your problem, mister? You've had your bit of fun. Now, give me my money, or I'll go to the cops."

He laughed out loud, long and joyous. She stared at him, wary and confused.

"Don't think I won't do it!" she cried. "I know people. Just watch me."

He only laughed harder and then, just as quickly as it started, his laughter stopped. With his free hand, he reached into his back pocket and pulled out his police credentials. He waved them in her face.

"Oh, so you know people, do you? Well, guess what? So do I."

Her eyes widened in surprise and then fresh fear filled her face, along with disappointment.

"You're a shit, do you know that?" she cried. "A total shit!" Flinging her handbag over her shoulder, she stumbled from the room. Hung's laughter followed her down the stairs.

James wiped his palms down the sides of his suit pants and tried to calm his nerves. In a few short minutes, provided she kept their appointment, Sally-Ann Li would once again be in the police station asking for him. This time, it was to take a polygraph test.

He was still surprised that she'd changed her mind. Innocent or guilty, she was a defense lawyer and in his experience, very few of them offered up their clients to the police to undergo such testing. Still, if she passed, it would go some way to removing her from the suspect list—or at least to be pushed a fair way lower on it then she was now. The polygraph results might not be admissible as evidence, but unless the person sitting the test was highly skilled in deceit, the test tended to point to the truth of guilt or innocence.

Her explanation about why her father had failed the test seemed reasonable and though he had no way of proving if her story was correct, he believed her. There was a simplicity and honesty to her that spoke to him, and the vulnerability she'd displayed when he spoke about the difficulties he guessed she'd experienced in high school resonated with him. It was stupid. He barely knew her and yet he was drawn to her in a way he couldn't explain or describe. She insisted she had nothing to do with the murder of Douglas Hanley and it startled him to realize how much he hoped that was right. In the next hour or so, he'd discover if she told the truth.

The gun had been sent to ballistics. He was still waiting on the report. He wouldn't be surprised with a negative result. Still, it was the only nine millimeter handgun Chao Li owned and a failure to match the bullet casing found at the scene would also go some way to removing him and his daughter from suspicion.

The phone on his desk rang and he picked it up and listened while the receptionist downstairs informed him that Sally-Ann Li had arrived. James ignored the leap in his pulse and detoured to the interview room where the expert administering the polygraph test had set up his equipment.

"Ms Li is waiting downstairs. Are you ready for her?"

The man nodded. He was short and portly with thinning gray hair, but Reginald Peters was the best in the business as far as polygraph examinations were concerned. He'd been administering the test for more years than James could remember. He trusted the man implicitly and regarded his results with a great deal of respect.

"Send her up," Reginald said.

James went down the stairs and keyed in the security code that would allow him to enter the public waiting area. Sally-Ann was seated in one of the hard plastic chairs that were lined up along one wall of the room. She looked up as he entered and for a long moment, their gazes held.

A thousand butterflies swarmed in his gut and just as many thoughts rushed through his mind. Every time he saw her, he was reminded all over again of her stunning beauty. She was dressed in yet another classically tailored suit and this time, her blouse was green. It was late in the afternoon and presumably she'd spent a long day in court or hunched over her desk, but she looked as clean and fresh and unwrinkled as if she'd just stepped out of her dressing room. He looked down at his charcoal-gray suit and blue-and-white polka dot tie and wished he could say the same thing about himself. He wondered how she saw him...

He'd been at work since early that morning. He'd collided with Wang in the tearoom and had ended up wearing a fair portion of his coffee. He hoped the stain on his jacket wasn't visible. He was only relieved the brown liquid had missed his white shirt.

Without waiting for him to acknowledge her, Sally-Ann stood and came toward him, sending his thoughts about his spoiled suit scattering like dandelion seeds on the wind. She held out her hand.

"Detective Shepherd. We meet again."

They exchanged handshakes and James' mind snagged on the soft warmth of her hand. Surprisingly, it felt a little damp. *Was she really that nervous?* He cleared his throat in an effort to regain some focus. "Thank you for coming in, Ms Li. I wasn't sure you'd show."

She arched one perfectly shaped, dark eyebrow and looked at him dubiously. "Really? I told you I would. I'm a woman of my word, but you wouldn't know that because you don't know very much about me at all. Right now you have me pegged as a murderer."

To his consternation, he blushed. *Dammit! How had she gotten under his skin like that? Made him feel like an awkward school boy?* He was only doing his job. He ignored her comment and turned on his heel and headed back up the stairs, not waiting to see if she followed. She'd been upstairs before. She knew the way.

Sally-Ann followed James up the stairs and surreptitiously wiped her damp palms against her skirt. She tried to focus on his broad shoulders and taut bottom in an effort to distract herself from the reason she was there. She'd put on a show of bravado for the detective, but nothing could take away from the fact she'd agreed to take a polygraph test. She was sure it would clear her name and it was for this reason only she'd agreed to it, but right here, right now she wasn't sure it was a good idea. She was a suspect in a murder investigation. *Did it get any more serious?*

Her heart thumped and adrenaline surged through her veins. A faint headache caused a dull throbbing behind her eyes. She drew in a deep breath in an effort to slow her heart rate and get control over herself. If she didn't calm down, she'd fail the test, just like her father had. That wouldn't look good to the detective, despite any explanation she might offer.

She forced herself to quit second-guessing her decision and concentrated on the reason why she was there. She was going to be asked about Doug and his murder. She could handle that. She didn't have anything to do with Doug's death and didn't know anyone who did. A wave of helpless anger washed over her as she thought of the man who'd ruined her sister's life. Okay, she hadn't murdered the man, but she was only a little bit sorry he was dead.

James led her into a small room with padded walls and no windows. One wall was made up of thick two-way glass. A middle-aged man with a large belly stood as she entered and greeted her with a friendly smile.

"Ms Li, I'm Reginald Peters. I'm from Australian Polygraph Services. I'll be administering your test."

James looked from Sally-Ann to the technician. "I guess I'll leave you to it."

James closed the door behind him and Sally-Ann

immediately felt like the walls were closing in. She pushed the feeling away and forced herself to breathe normally. She knew all about polygraphs, even though this was the first time she'd sat one. She knew they weren't so much a detector of lies as a record of autonomous bodily reactions to stress. The stronger the reaction, the more likely the subject wasn't telling the truth. If she didn't get control of herself, she'd fail the test.

The stern talking to had an effect and as she moved further into the room, she felt much calmer.

The examiner shot her a look. "Are you all right, Ms Li?" he asked.

"Y-yes, I'm fine. And please, call me Sally-Ann," she replied.

He asked her to take a seat and then sat opposite, in front of a laptop and a small box-like contraption with cables extruding from it that sat on the desk. In calm tones, he explained how the test worked.

"Do you have any questions?" he asked when he was finished.

"N-no," she stammered, wishing he'd just get on with it.

"Very well, then. Let's get you hooked up."

With that, he connected various wires to her fingers. Another one was strapped around her chest. A blood pressure cuff was placed around her upper arm.

"There, that should do it," he said and then returned to his seat. He tapped on the keyboard of the computer and a moment later, glanced across at her. "Are you ready?"

Sally-Ann drew in a surreptitious breath. She eased it out and nodded. "Yes."

"Very well, then. I'll start with some straightforward questions so we can establish a baseline. Answer as truthfully as you can. Then I'm going to ask you something and I want you to lie. That also helps establish parameters from within we conduct the test. Do you understand?"

She threw him a smile that felt more like a grimace. "Yes. Please, let's just get on with it."

"All right, then."

The man cleared his throat and began asking questions. Like he'd promised, the questions started out easy. She was asked to give her name, address and occupation. She was asked about the home where she'd grown up in and where she'd attended school.

Her heart skipped a beat, but she forged on and answered honestly. Then the examiner asked if she was married and then nodded in her direction.

She interpreted his action as meaning this was the question where she was meant to lie and told him, yes, she was very happily married. He looked down at the data recording on the paper in front of him and nodded.

"You're doing very well, Ms Li. I think we have enough to establish baseline data. Now the test can begin."

Immediately, her belly tightened with nerves, but with a concerted effort she ignored them. This wasn't about her. It was about Doug. Nothing more. The questions became increasingly pointed and every now and then, a question that appeared so random as to not have any connection to anything was tossed at her. Then Doug and his murder was raised again.

At the thought of what he'd done to sweet Aimee, she clenched her fists and then once again forced herself to relax. She counted ten beats of her heart before she answered. Yes, she knew Douglas Hanley. No, she didn't have anything to do with his murder. Yes, she'd been angry at what he'd done to her sister. No, she never wanted to see him dead.

The questions went on and on and she forced herself to breathe slowly and evenly and answer each as concisely and truthfully as she could. Though the experience was so much worse than she'd imagined, she was determined to see it through to the end. She'd done nothing wrong. She had nothing to hide. She'd stand her ground and prove her innocence if it was the last thing she did.

At last, the technician fell silent and Sally-Ann let out a sigh of relief. *It was over.* She felt like she'd been put through the wringer. She pushed away from her chair and reached out toward the desk to steady herself, not sure if her legs would support her.

"Are you all right, Ms Li?" The technician's brow furrowed with concern.

All out of answers, Sally-Ann gave him a jerky nod of acknowledgment, collected her handbag and hastened from the room.

———————

James stared at the results in front of him and couldn't believe his eyes. Sally-Ann had left the police station without saying good-bye and now he understood why: Her test results were inconclusive. They neither confirmed nor denied her guilt.

"Don't look so concerned, James," Reginald chuckled. "The results aren't quite as straightforward as they appear."

James looked up at the examiner and frowned. "What do you mean?"

Reginald moved closer and propped a hip against James' desk. "Have you ever heard the term 'guilt grabber'?"

James shrugged. "It's someone who feels pangs of conscience about doing the wrong thing even when they haven't done anything, isn't it?"

"Yes. And I think Ms Li is a classic case. She passed the questions that directly related to the victim, but when I asked her if she'd ever hurt someone, her responses went through the roof. If you ask me, I don't think she's ever hurt someone, but she might have thought about it at some stage and that's enough to spark the feelings of guilt that were evidenced when she answered that question. There were a few other similar questions and I'm fairly confident when I tell you I think she flunked the test because she has a highly developed sense of right and wrong and she failed those questions not because she's actually guilty of doing anything wrong, but because she feels guilty at the mere thought of having thought about doing something wrong. Do you understand what I'm saying?"

He paused until James nodded, then continued: "And who knows? Maybe there was a time in her past when she did think about hurting someone? It could have been anything, not just something as serious as murder. She'd still exhibit the same guilt, the same reactions."

James nodded and tried not to show his relief. "So, you don't think she murdered Douglas Hanley?"

Reginald shook his head. "No, I don't."

After seeing the man out of the station, James returned to his desk. He contemplated what Reginald had said and wondered if Sally-Ann's responses had been connected to her childhood. She hadn't told him in any detail about her high school years spent in a foreign country, but he'd read between the lines.

Had those years of torment affected her results? Or was she merely a guilt grabber, like Reginald suggested? Either way, she was now a long way down his suspect list and for that, he was grateful. *He should inform her of the results.* It was only right. Besides, it would give him a chance to see her again. The thought made his heart jolt. In less than two weeks, this woman filled his thoughts and dreams more often than he cared to admit.

With his mind made up, he reached over and opened a file that lay on his desk. He flipped through the pages until he found the notes he'd made during his interview with Sally-Ann. He scanned through them until he found what he was looking for: her address. With his phone, he took a picture of the details. He closed the file and set it to one side. He shut down his computer and pushed away from his desk. After collecting his jacket from the locker room, he left.

It was a little after eight and the sun had barely sunk below the horizon. A warm breeze lifted his hair and brought with it the spicy smells of curry and meat and other tantalizing aromas that emanated from the numerous restaurants that lined King Street. In fact, the street was often referred to as "Eat Street" by the media.

His belly rumbled. He'd skipped lunch and had made do with coffee and a doughnut for breakfast, but right now he was on a mission to question Sally-Ann before the evening was over. Dinner would have to wait.

She lived in the inner west suburb of Newtown, less than two miles from the city. It was a popular area with young professionals and had an exuberant vibe that was contagious. Music blared from the occasional bar and people laughed and joked as they passed him on the crowded street. There was a relaxed air, even though many of the passersby were likely on their way home from work. It was a refreshing change from the hustle and bustle and stress and strain often exhibited by the crowds downtown.

He'd taken the train from the city, leaving his car at work. Inner city parking was often hard to come by and having been born and bred in the inner west, he was familiar with the narrow side streets where most of the housing in Newtown was situated. Sydney's public transport system was a cheap and reliable way of getting around and

Sally-Ann's digs were only a short walk from the station.

He came to a cross street and turned right. The street where she lived was old and narrow and was bordered on both sides by a row of original terrace houses. Many had been repainted in modern colors and tidied up with smart front fences and neat gardens. This part of Newtown had once been a far less desirable place to live, but with its proximity to the city, over the past decade or so developers had seen the potential and had moved in with money to burn. The stylish townhouse terraces he saw today were a result, and as familiar as he was with the local real estate, he knew they didn't come cheap.

He reached number ninety-six and his belly clenched with nerves. What would she think of him arriving on her doorstep without being invited...? It was one thing to speak to her inside the busy confines of the squad room, but this was quite different.

Being outside her house, asking to be invited in... It put things on a different level, a more personal level.

From the moment he'd set eyes on her he felt like he'd been sucker punched. There was something about her that touched him deep inside. But he was investigating her for murder. On some level he knew it wasn't wise to speak with her outside of his working hours, but the truth was, he wanted to spend more time with her. He wanted get to know her better. But most of all, he wanted to talk to her about what had happened during the polygraph test. Was it simply that she was a guilt grabber, like Reginald had suggested, or was there something more sinister behind her failed responses? He was determined to find out.

With a deep breath, he filled his lungs and slowly eased out the air. Squaring his shoulders, he flipped the steel latch on the gate and let himself into the yard. A handful of long strides later and he stood on her small front porch. With a quick look around him, and before his courage gave out, he rapped on the door.

CHAPTER 12

Sally-Ann refilled her wine glass and settled back against the couch. She was still annoyed that she'd voluntarily submitted to the polygraph test. There was an old saying that a lawyer who represented herself had a fool for a client and never had that rang more true. The test hadn't gone well and she'd been too upset with herself afterwards to return to work. Instead she'd called and offered her secretary some excuse she could barely remember and had come straight home, via the liquor store. She was already on her third glass.

A knock sounded at the door. She frowned. It was only a little after eight, but she didn't often get unannounced visitors. Her family usually called ahead of time to check if she were home and to let her know they were on their way. She worked long hours in the city. She often didn't get home until late and when she was in the middle of a trial, her hours were even more erratic. They'd learned the hard way not to turn up announced.

Tonight had been different. After the debacle of her polygraph test, she'd left the police station in a flurry of panic, wanting nothing more than to get away from the place. She hadn't even waited to find James and say good-bye. She wondered what he thought when he realized she'd left without speaking to him.

By now, he'd probably have the results from the examiner. No doubt they hadn't been good. Her face flamed at the thought that after looking over the results he might be even more convinced of her guilt.

"Dammit!" she groaned and buried her face in her hands. Why, oh why, had she agreed to do it? She'd broken her own rule and look what happened. She was even worse off than before. How was she going to explain her results to the detective? She'd already been forced to explain away her dad's.

She groaned again and reached for her glass, taking a healthy sip. The knock on the door came again, reminding her abruptly that someone was waiting on the other side. She stood with glass in hand and made her way across the polished floorboards that continued down the hall. From force of habit, she looked through the peephole and groaned a third time.

He was there. The detective. He was standing on her porch on the other side of the door. And he looked none too happy. A jumble of thoughts rushed through her mind. Her heart took off at a gallop. She moved abruptly and wine sloshed over her hand. She cursed under her breath.

What should she do? Should she answer the door? She had all the lights off in the house, barring a small lamp that burned in the living room. She'd been hiding out in the dark, drowning her sorrows. Her car was parked out back. He might not know for sure that she was home. *Could she just ignore him and pretend she wasn't there?*

The knock came a third time and this time, he called out her name. She bit her lip, still undecided and then shook her head and forced herself to come to her senses. *What was she, a child?* So, she'd failed a lie detector test. It wasn't the end of the world. With her mind made up, she thrust back her shoulders, drew in a fortifying breath and pulled open the door.

With one sweep of his long dark lashes, his gaze raked over her from head to toe. He paused briefly at the half-full wine glass in her hand and a slight smile of amusement tugged up the corners of his mouth. She cursed the fact her heart did a little somersault at the sheer sexiness of his good humor.

"I take it you've come to gloat," she muttered sourly.

One dark eyebrow rose in response. "And why would I be here to do that?"

"Because I failed the polygraph. I was so sure it would remove me from suspicion and instead..." Her voice hitched a little and she defiantly took another sip of wine.

His smile disappeared and there was a glimmer of sympathy in his eyes that made her heart clench.

"I'm not here to gloat," he said quietly. "I'm here to talk about what happened and to offer my support."

She narrowed her eyes at him suspiciously. "And why would you want to do that? You're hell bent on pinning Doug's murder on me or a member of my family. Why would you care how I feel?"

He gave her a measured look and remained silent. She looked for answers in his solemn gaze. After a long moment, he blew his breath out on a sigh.

"Can I come in?"

They were ordinary words, said without inflection, but her heart flip-flopped and then took off at a run. He looked so dark and handsome in his tailored suit and expensive tie. His boots were polished to a shine and gleamed in the light that bounced off the front porch. A whiff of expensive cologne drifted past her nostrils and tickled her senses. She was close enough to see the scattering of freckles across his nose.

Did she want this man inside her home? Could she trust herself to remain on guard with the enemy so close at hand? Was he the enemy?

Her sadly neglected libido urged her to open the door wide and let him in. She blushed at the thought and was immediately irritated with herself. She shifted from herself to him and wondered what was going through his mind. *Did he like what he saw when he looked at her?*

No. He'd come there to discuss the case and, in particular, her epic polygraph failure. He wasn't there for personal reasons, no matter how much she might wish that were true.

She thought of how things might have been if they'd met under different circumstances...and then swallowed a sigh. Stepping back, she pulled the door wider to allow him to enter. She indicated the way forward with her hand. She'd let him have his say and then send him on his way.

He walked ahead of her, toward the kitchen. She switched on the hallway light so that he could see where he was going and then hurried ahead of him. She flicked the switch for the kitchen and the room was flooded with light. He entered right behind her and she noticed with pride how he looked around with what appeared to be genuine appreciation at the quaint fixtures and fittings.

She'd purchased the terrace house a few years earlier, after saving every penny for years and had renovated the Victorian semi to better reflect the era in which it had first come to life. The high ceilings and ornate cornices had been freshened up with white paint. The walls were a deep heritage green color that went well with the polished timber floorboards and picture rails.

The kitchen appliances were all new, but were of vintage design that was in keeping with the age and style of the house. A tall crystal vase of fresh oriental lilies, her favorite, sat on the dark timber kitchen table and filled the room with their heavy scent. And then James sneezed.

"I hope you're not allergic?" she muttered.

"No, not at all. Just a little something that tickled my nose."

"Probably dust," she offered with a wry smile. "I'm afraid I haven't had time to do a proper cleaning around here for weeks."

"It's fine. Don't worry about it."

He moved further into the kitchen and all of a sudden, the size and breadth of him seemed to fill the room. She rounded the counter in an effort to put some distance between them and to catch her breath.

"W-would you like a cup of tea or coffee? Or... Or m-maybe something stronger?" she stammered, noticing his gaze on the wine glass still in her hand. She hastily set it down on the counter.

"Thanks," he eventually responded. "Coffee would be great."

Grateful for an excuse to turn her back on him, she busied herself getting coffee things, including setting the kettle to boil. She pulled milk from the fridge, banging her hip on the door in the process. Swallowing a curse, she found the sugar bowl in the pantry and set them both out on the counter.

Bemused, James watched her. "Thanks, but I take mine black."

She frowned at him in mock annoyance and tried to hold back a smile. "Really? After all that trouble? You could have said so before."

"Hey, I'm sorry. You didn't give me a chance." He laughed and the rich sound of it touched her somewhere deep inside. She shivered from the deliciousness of it as her nipples puckered in response.

She'd long since ditched her jacket and the

blouse she wore was made from some kind of flimsy synthetic material and lace. The thin fabric did nothing to conceal her reaction to him. His gaze zeroed in on her chest. Her cheeks burned with the knowledge he was fully aware of her body's betrayal.

A long second passed between them. He stared at her and she couldn't look away. His green eyes darkened to the color of a deep pond surrounded by forest and his lips parted on a silent breath. The air was suddenly charged between them. She tried to breathe, but could only manage the tiniest gasp. *What did he think about her obvious response to him?*

The noise from the road outside her door dissolved into nothingness. She could hear nothing over the rush of blood in her ears that mimicked the beat of her heart. And then he blinked and looked away and the moment was over. She felt strangely bereft and was immediately irritated with her reaction.

The water in the kettle came to a boil and she hurriedly made him a cup of coffee. Wanting nothing more than for him to say his piece and leave, she thrust the cup toward him and then leaned back against the counter with her arms crossed defensively over her chest.

"Why are you here, Detective?" She narrowed her gaze on him and tapped her foot, waiting for his reply.

He chuckled. "Are you really in that big a hurry to get rid of me?"

"Yes," she snapped. "As a matter of fact, I am."

His expression sobered. "Don't you want to know how you did on the polygraph?"

She tensed, but refused to back down. "I know how it went. I blew it, didn't I? You don't have to tell me. I can see it written all over your face."

"You didn't blow it, Sally-Ann."

She stared at him in amazement. He must be playing with her. There was no way she passed that test.

She narrowed her eyes in suspicion. "What are you talking about?"

He shrugged. "The test results were inconclusive."

Anger at him and at herself for wanting so much to believe she'd passed, surged through her. She took a step toward him, her hands clenched into fists.

"Inconclusive?" she scoffed. "Right. So the whole sorry exercise was for nothing. My results neither condemn nor exonerate me. Great." She turned away in disgust, still annoyed by the fact she'd agreed to sit the damn test at all—and that she'd let him in.

"What happened in there, Sally-Ann?"

The words were spoken so softly, so tenderly, tears rushed to her eyes. She ducked her head and blinked them back, unwilling to let him see how much his kindness affected her.

"Talk to me, Sally-Ann."

There it was again—that kindness and compassion she'd sensed in him right from the start. Knowing he was waiting for an answer, she kept her face averted and stammered out a reply.

"W-why do you think something happened?"

He reached for his cup and took a sip. She watched while he carefully set the cup back down. It felt like an eon passed before he spoke again.

"You're a smart, confident professional. You know the rules as well as I do. No one agrees to sit a polygraph test without knowing the outcome. You were sure the test would come out favorably, that it would eliminate any suspicion of your guilt. Reality was, in fact, while the results didn't strengthen our case against you, they definitely didn't absolve you from any guilt. The woman I know wouldn't have submitted to such a test if she weren't certain she'd pass... And yet you didn't pass conclusively and I came here to find out why."

To her consternation, he moved around the counter until they were standing close. Too close. She tried to move back, but she came up against the cupboard. His gaze was steady and probing.

Her heart skipped a beat. She wanted to look away. He moved until their clothes brushed and then reached out and with the tip of one finger, tilted her chin up, holding her head in place. She couldn't have looked away if she wanted to.

"I'll ask you again," he murmured and his voice was husky and low. "What happened in there, Sally-Ann?"

His finger was warm on her skin. His cologne filled her nostrils. A hint of five o'clock shadow darkened his cheeks. He was standing way too close.

The thoughts tumbled through her head like a group of preschoolers bouncing up and down on a trampoline, and all the time, his eyes remained locked on hers. Finally, finding her wits, she batted his hand away and made her escape.

She strode around to the other side of the counter. Her face felt flushed. Her breathing was too fast. She drew in some deep breaths and did her best to get her pulse rate under control.

There was no escaping it: She had to answer him. *But what could she say?* Only her sister knew the truth. There was that occasion more than a week ago when he'd made reference to high school and she'd been surprised at his level of insight, but they were almost strangers. She couldn't bare her soul to someone she hardly knew. Then again, from the first moment they'd met, she'd felt a connection to this man, like they'd known each other from another lifetime. It was strange and unexplainable, but she couldn't deny it. And from the way he looked at her, she was sure he felt it, too.

Blindly, she reached for the glass of wine she'd deposited on the counter and emptied the contents in one gulp. When she'd finished, she set the glass down and swiped the back of her hand across her mouth. She threw him a look of defiance.

"You're right. Something *did* happen in that examination room and it wasn't pretty. Are you sure you want to hear about it?"

His gaze remained steady on hers. "Yes."

She looked around for the bottle of wine,

feeling the need for the additional courage the alcohol could give and remembered she'd left it by the couch in the living room. Picking up her empty glass she suggested he bring his coffee and follow her. She refilled her glass from the bottle and took a seat in front of the seventy-inch, flat screen TV that was mounted on her wall.

"I take it you like watching television," he remarked dryly as he took a seat on the matching couch opposite.

"I like watching old movies on Netflix," she replied, refusing to apologize for the fact her TV took up almost a third of the wall space. "It's how I unwind."

He merely nodded. "I prefer the cinema, myself."

"Yes, but they don't play old black-and-white films at the movies," she protested without heat.

"You're right," he agreed and sipped his coffee.

Knowing she couldn't avoid the moment forever, she gulped another mouthful of wine and then set it down on the side table next to her chair. Finally, she cleared her throat.

"Do you remember when you asked me how it was in high school?"

"Yes. You said you arrived in Australia when you were thirteen. I have a younger sister. She's seventeen. She's going through some tough times. I couldn't help but wonder if you'd found it tough going, too."

She compressed her lips and nodded. "Let's just say I know all about school yard bullies."

"Did you ever seek any help from teachers or the school counselor?"

"No. That would only have made things worse."

"So you kept the torment to yourself," he said gently.

Sally-Ann took a steadying breath and shrugged. "Not quite. I told my sister. She was also newly arrived in a foreign country. I thought she might understand."

"And did she?"

"Yes, but it was different for her. She was older, more certain about who she was. I'd just hit puberty. It was a tough time."

"Tell me about it," he encouraged softly, leaning forward.

She closed her eyes and drew in another fortifying breath, praying silently for courage. She'd kept the secret torment of her high school years buried deep for so long, she wasn't sure where to start, but something inside her urged her to confide in this kind man who sat so patiently across from her. His concern appeared genuine, his compassion and understanding so real.

Could she trust him with her innermost secrets? With the demons that continued to haunt her, even now? What would he think of her after she told him about it? She didn't know, but she wanted to take the chance, she wanted to find the comfort and release that she instinctively knew, baring her soul to him, would bring.

"From the very first day at Leichardt High, I was treated like an outcast. I'm not sure why. There were plenty of kids there from different cultural backgrounds, but I guess most of them had been born in Australia though their parents might have come from overseas. They spoke English without an accent. They were familiar with the Australian ways. They fit in. I didn't. Right from the start, I was a target for the mean girls, the scapegoat for anything that went wrong."

James regarded her in silence. "How so?" he asked softly.

Chapter 13

Sally-Ann stared at him and for the first time in her adult life, wanted to share the torment of her childhood. She drew in a breath and mentally prepared herself for what was to come.

"For a start, I was Asian," she said. "While Leichardt was and still is a multicultural suburb, it was largely populated with Italian immigrants. We were Chinese without much English. We stood out. On top of that, I was smart. Really smart. Together that was a lethal combination that attracted the bullies in droves."

James' eyes filled with anger, but when he spoke, it was sympathy that laced his tone. "Kids can be hurtful."

She grimaced. "And teenage girls the worst of all."

He nodded in agreement. "Oh, yeah."

"It wasn't one thing in particular," she continued. "It was more a daily assault. The sly comments about my intelligence; the scorn at my stilted English; the accusations if anything went missing. They did it on purpose. Stole things from other unsuspecting students and then blamed it on me." She shook her head slowly back and forth. "It didn't matter whether I defended myself with sound arguments or chose to remain silent, the outcome was always the same: tried, convicted and sentenced in the blink of an eye."

Her voice had turned husky with emotion as the memories surfaced again. "That was the reason I became a lawyer," she continued softly. "I wanted to champion the vulnerable of our society, those without a voice."

"So you became a child advocate," he said gently.

She shot him a small, proud smile. "Yes, I did."

"You showed the bullies," he said and his eyes shone with admiration.

Her smile widened. "Yes, I did."

"Did you ever think about getting back at them in other ways?"

She regarded him warily. "What do you mean?"

James cleared his throat. "Reginald told me he asked if you'd ever hurt anyone before. It was one of the questions you failed when you answered no."

Sally-Ann bit her lip, unsure how to respond. There were many nights she'd spent as a teenager dreaming up ways to torture her classmates, humiliate them, hurt them the same way they'd hurt her, but she'd never gone through with it. She could never hurt someone for the fun of it. Should she come clean to James? Would it help him accept her polygraph results?

"Have you ever heard of the term 'guilt grabber'?" he asked before she could formulate a response.

She frowned and shook her head. "No. What is it?"

"It's a 'who,' actually."

He went on to explain to her the meaning behind the odd phrase. She nodded in understanding. That made so much sense.

"That's me," she said. "I'm one of those people. I've never done anything to hurt another person, at least, not intentionally, but there were plenty of times back in high school when I thought about it."

James nodded. "That's what Reginald thought. He was the one who suggested that might be the reason for your inconclusive results—that knowing you'd thought about hurting people was enough to trigger a guilty response when you were asked the question. Sometimes people are too honest to pass a lie detector test."

He gave her a lopsided smile and her belly somersaulted with nerves. She averted her gaze and fell silent. James took another sip from his coffee cup. Sally-Ann sipped at her wine. She was feeling so much better, so much more relaxed and she had James to thank for it. He'd accepted her revelations without any qualms and even appeared proud of her achievements. It made her feel good about herself and about the woman she'd become. It made her want to get to know the man who'd brought out that in her.

"Tell me about yourself," she said.

He shrugged and set his coffee cup aside. "There's not much to tell."

"Come on," she teased. "Fair's fair. I've revealed the tragedy of my high school years. The least you can do is tell me a little about yours."

He sat forward on the sofa and rested his elbows on his knees. "All right, but I assure you my story is nowhere near as interesting as yours."

She shot him an encouraging smile. "Please, tell me. I'd really like to hear it."

He gave her a long look that sent her pulse racing. Heat crept up her neck and spread across her cheeks. She averted her gaze and picked at a loose thread in her blouse. To her relief, he began to speak.

"I was born and bred in Sydney to working-class parents. I was good at school and even better at football, but I wasn't that interested in either. I had a few good mates, but it wasn't all smooth sailing."

"How so?" she asked, curious. She couldn't imagine he'd suffered like she had.

"My parents worked hard, but we weren't well off. We always had enough to eat, but there was never anything for extras. When I was fifteen, all I wanted was a pair of Nikes. All my friends had them, but we couldn't afford them. I knew that, but it didn't stop me from asking for them. Mom told me we didn't have enough money for shoes like that and Dad told me to forget about it." He gave a self-deprecating laugh. "Easier said than done when you're fifteen."

"What happened?" she asked.

James sighed. "I got a part-time job at

McDonalds and started saving. I was making a little over seven dollars an hour. I worked out how long it would take me to save the money and I couldn't wait for the day."

She smiled, imagining a young James saving his hard-earned cash. "Did you buy them?"

He shook his head. "I used to keep my money in a Milo tin beneath my bed. I'd pull it out at least once a week and count it and work out how much more I needed. Then one day, I took it to school and showed all my mates. I was so proud of the money I'd managed to save."

His voice drifted off, as if he were lost in memories. "What happened?" Sally-Ann prompted him quietly.

James sighed again. "Somewhere between third period and lunch, the money disappeared. I don't know how. I'd left the tin in my locker. Not many people were even aware it was there. But, when I went to the locker at lunch time, my locker door was half-open and the money was gone."

Her heart went out to him. "Oh, James! How terrible! What did you do?"

"I asked everyone if they'd seen anything, but of course, nobody had. The money was gone."

"You poor thing! After all your hard work!"

He nodded. "Yes, but really, it served me right. I took the money to school to brag about how much I'd saved. I shouldn't have been so proud."

She gasped in outrage. "You had every right to feel that way! You'd worked hard for that money!"

He gave her a small smile. "Yes, well, that's nice of you to see it that way. Lucky for me, my parents were also kind. They were upset the money had been stolen, but they never once reprimanded me for taking it to school. They understood how hard I'd worked to get it and how proud I was of what I'd achieved."

"So, you didn't get the Nike shoes," she said softly.

He shot her a lopsided smile that emphasized his good looks. Her heart skipped a beat.

"I haven't finished yet," he murmured and followed it with a wink.

This time, her belly somersaulted with nerves and excitement. *Could he get any sexier?* She still couldn't quite believe he was sitting on her couch and they were sharing stories about their pasts. This man, this compassionate, understanding man who could have walked off the set of a movie, was in her house, listening to her tales of woe and responding in kind. *How had she gotten so lucky?*

Then again, he was a detective investigating her and her family for murder. Perhaps things weren't so rosy, after all. The thought dimmed her excitement and along with that, her smile.

"So, what happened?" she asked a little tersely.

He looked at her with surprise, but continued. "The day I turned sixteen, my mom came into my room early that morning and brought in my present. It was wrapped in colored paper and there was also a card. When I opened the box, I found a pair of brand new Nikes."

Despite herself, Sally-Ann smiled with joy. "She bought them for you!"

James nodded. "She'd also been saving." His

voice was thick with emotion. Her heart clenched. She wanted to move closer to him, to touch him, to squeeze his hand.

"Mom had saved up and bought me a pair of Nikes. They were white and red high tops, just like the ones I'd wanted. I was so proud that day when I wore them to school. I felt like I was walking on air. I couldn't wait for everyone to see them. For once, I had shoes that were every bit as good as what everyone else wore."

"That's a lovely story," she said softly, pleased that he hadn't suffered like she had. "I mean, it wasn't good that someone stole your money, but it worked out all right in the end."

"Yes, except that isn't the end of the story. I wore those shoes to school feeling so happy and proud and a group of senior boys met me on the way in and accused me of stealing them. They knew my folks were poor; too poor to afford shoes like that. Soon, it was all around school that I'd stolen the Nikes. Even my mates weren't sure who to believe. I never wore those shoes again."

Sally-Ann brought a hand up to her mouth, horrified at the image of a young James being unjustly accused and not being able to take pleasure in the shoes he'd wanted for so long. It was like her high school days all over again. She bit her lip against a surge of emotion.

"No wonder you understood when I told you about my experience," she said quietly.

He looked up at her. "Yes."

"Did that have anything to do with you becoming a police officer?"

"I don't know. I didn't make a conscious decision like you did to champion the cause of others more vulnerable in our community, but I think it had some bearing on my choice of career. I was determined to be the kind of cop who investigated all angles, who didn't jump to conclusions, who did what had to be done to find the evidence that supported the solving of the crime. I like to think I'm still that kind of cop."

She stared at him and he stared right back. Once again, the air between them became charged. Her heart thumped hard against her ribs and her mouth went dry. She wanted to kiss him, to ease his pain. She wanted to reassure him he was a good man and a good cop.

Without thinking, she stood and came over to where he sat. Bending low, she framed his face with her hands and pressed her lips to his. For an instant, he tensed in surprise and then his mouth relaxed beneath hers. Pliant and warm and tasting faintly of coffee, he kissed her back.

Heat ignited inside her and tingled all the way to her core. The kiss deepened. Tongues tangled. And then he was pulling away and she was left gasping for breath.

"I'm sorry, Sally-Ann. I can't do this. The investigation..."

She stared at him aghast, reeling with embarrassment. Then anger set in. "Hang on, you can't seriously still believe I'm a suspect?"

He shrugged helplessly. His eyes pleaded with her to understand. "Well, no, not really. You're a long way down the list."

She stepped back and glared at him. "A long way down the list! You're the one who just told me your examiner believed I'd failed the polygraph because I'm too honest. What does that tell you about me? I didn't kill Doug and neither did my father. Now, if you don't believe that, I have nothing more to say to you."

"We should get the report back from ballistics tomorrow," he muttered, avoiding her eye.

She continued to glare at him. "Good. The bullet that killed Doug won't match my father's gun and that will prove he had nothing to do with this. The sooner you get that report, the better. Now, I think you should leave."

James stood and she was forced to look up as he reached his full height. "I'm sorry, Sally-Ann, but I have to do my job. Please try to understand."

Without another word, he turned and walked out of the room. The front door closed with a decisive click. Sally-Ann swiped at the tears that had gathered in her eyes and told herself not to be stupid. Detective James Shepherd wasn't worthy of her tears. And that was that.

She flipped through the pile of photos with increasing desperation. There were ones from when Doug was little—barely three or four. Then came the ones as a teenager, a young adult and finally the wedding photos. Of course, she had no photos of the first wedding. *Why would she?*

As she studied the pictures, her hand trembled and tears ran down her cheeks. He looked so happy. They both did. She recalled it like it had been yesterday. It had been a beautiful day. And now he was dead and she'd killed him.

Was he even now looking down on her, hating her for what she'd done, or had he found forgiveness in his heart? Was that even possible? Was *anyone* capable of forgiving such a monstrous deed—and after they had died?

She thought of Doug's first wife, Aimee, and truly didn't know...

CHAPTER 14

James rubbed at his eyes with the balls of his hands and sighed at the thought of the long day that stretched ahead of him. He'd left Sally-Ann's place feeling out of sorts. He'd spent a restless night pacing the floor of his living room. He wanted to believe in her innocence. The explanation Reginald had offered made sense and Sally-Ann's recount of her teenage years seemed to support that, but was it enough to remove her completely from suspicion? Her father had also failed the test and though she'd offered James an explanation, it now seemed so lame... Convenient. He didn't know what to believe and it was tearing him up inside.

He liked her more than he wanted to admit. If she weren't a part of his investigation, he'd already have asked her out and from the kiss she gave him the night before he was almost certain she would have said yes.

His mind cast back to that sweet moment in time. The kiss had taken him by surprise, but the feel of her soft, warm lips on his had sent a hot and urgent rush of need surging through him, it had taken all his self-control to pull back.

Still, he was glad he had. As much as he wanted to taste and touch every inch of her, she was involved in a murder investigation. Until he was certain she was in the clear, he had to stay the hell away from her for his own sanity and for the sake of his career. If she were charged with murder and it was discovered he was fraternizing with her... Things wouldn't go well for him. He'd worked far too hard and was much too passionate about his job to throw it all away over a woman, even a woman as lovely and desirable as Sally-Ann Li.

"That ballistics report just came in."

James blinked and focused on his partner. Wang sat at the desk across from him. "Excuse me?" he asked.

"The ballistics report on that nine millimeter came back. Apparently the gun was fired recently, but the striations on the bullets don't match. Chao Li's in the clear, or at least, his gun wasn't the one used in the shooting."

James absorbed the information in silence. It didn't come as a surprise that the gun had been used recently. Sally-Ann's father had admitted he liked to shoot. It was the reason he collected firearms. Besides, James' gut had never been keen on Chao Li as the perpetrator.

His gaze strayed to the whiteboard and snagged on the name of Janice Carter. She'd also failed the polygraph. If anything, she'd been even more nervous than the Li family. At the time, he'd thought it a little strange, but now that the results were in, he couldn't help but wonder what she was hiding. The evidence against her wasn't as strong as the evidence against Sally-Ann, but Janice had failed the polygraph and that counted.

"We need to look harder at Carter," he said to Wang.

His colleague nodded thoughtfully. "It's true, she didn't do herself any favors by failing the lie detector test and she owns a motorbike that matches the description of the one given by our eyewitness. Then again, so does Sally-Ann Li... And Ms Li's polygraph results leave a lot to be desired."

Wang shot him a pointed look and James averted his gaze. "Reginald was of the opinion that Sally-Ann was a guilt grabber."

"Oh, so you mean she's too honest to pass the test. *Really?*" Wang drawled.

James went on the defensive. "Hey, Reginald is the best in the business. He conducted the examination. I hold his opinion in high esteem. Besides, Sally-Ann also told me she'd been bullied at school and that being in the examination room, having questions fired at her, caused her to have flashbacks to bad times at school. She was sure that also contributed to her inconclusive results."

Wang looked at him dubiously. "And you believed her?"

James nodded. "Yes, I did."

"And what of her father? Didn't he also have a sad tale to tell?"

James shifted a little uncomfortably under the directness of his partner's gaze, but refused to look away. "Yes."

Wang merely chuckled and shook his head dismissively. "That's right. The 'fleeing from Chinese authorities' story. I wonder how long it took for them to come up with that. Still, it's had the desired effect. You're no longer looking at Chao as the murderer and the way you're defending the daughter..."

James opened his mouth to protest and then closed it again. It was true. He didn't think Chao Li was responsible for the death of Douglas Hanley and he was less and less inclined to think Sally-Ann had done it, either. Now all he had to do was find the real perpetrator to prove it. And, knowing that's what he did best, he wouldn't rest until he was sure he had the right person behind bars.

"Who do *you* think did it?" James asked.

Wang took his time replying. Leaning back against his chair, he stacked his hands behind his head and stared at the whiteboard, as if for inspiration.

"Let's go over what we know," Wang eventually replied. "None of our four suspects have alibis, or at least, none that would hold up under pressure. All four have motive. One owns the same type of gun used in the crime, but tests prove this gun isn't the one we're looking for. Two of our suspects are confident in their use of firearms, but this doesn't mean the other two couldn't arrange for someone else to fire the shot. Aimee Li didn't sit the polygraph test, but from what I understand, she's been pretty much eliminated as a suspect, right?"

"Right," James agreed. "I just can't see her being the one to orchestrate this. She was upset at the news of Douglas Hanley's death and even though her alibi's weak, her motive for killing him is even weaker. Coupled with the fact she's in a wheelchair and would have to arrange the hit with someone who agreed to take out her ex and then escape on a motorbike, I pretty much ruled her out."

Wang nodded. "So that leaves us with three. Two of the three failed the polygraph. One was inconclusive. The Li family members have provided explanations for their unfavorable results; albeit their explanations are a little hard to believe. What did Janice Carter say about her results?"

James grimaced. "I haven't had a chance to speak with her about them. She's on my list of people to follow up today."

"It will be interesting to hear what she says."

"You can come with me, if you'd like. I'm heading out shortly. I called ahead to the hospital. She's on a day off today. She lives in Granville, not far from Maureen Hanley. I'm hoping to surprise her at home."

"Good. I think I'll stay here and catch up on some paperwork, but let me know how you do."

James pushed away from his desk and shrugged into his jacket. "I will," he said. Picking up his keys, he headed for the exit.

———

Hung Wang waited for the door to close behind his colleague before he straightened in his chair and pulled his keyboard toward him. Anger pulsed through him as he recalled the sad story the Li family had hatched to explain their arrival in Australia: being wrongly accused, hunted by the Chinese authorities, fearing for their lives. It made him furious to hear the lies they were spreading—and to his partner, no less.

The truth was, they were traitors to their country, speaking out about their government and leader, selling secrets to China's enemies in the West. Hung knew all about it. He'd memorized the list of offenses Chao and Fen Li had committed against the state. He'd pored over every page of the thick dossier he'd been given in an effort to aid his cause. Now, he'd finally found them. Finally, he could bring them to justice, return to his home country a hero. Make contact with his son.

He'd emailed his contact in China and was awaiting further instructions. The end was almost in sight. He couldn't wait...

James checked the address on the screen of his inbuilt GPS and pulled the squad car over to the curb. Climbing out of the vehicle, he made his way toward a dingy-looking two-story apartment block that was squeezed beside another similarly ugly building.

Janice lived in an older part of the suburb

where gentrification had yet to arrive. The buildings were *circa* 1970s and were grubby from accumulated dirt and grime. The pavement that ran along the front of them was cracked and stained. Wooden paling fences that had once been painted were now broken and peeling. Boards were missing in places. Garden beds were nothing more than dirt and dead weeds and contributed to the overall feeling of neglect. It surprised him to discover Janice lived in such a place. She seemed to put so much stock in her appearance. Obviously that sense of pride didn't extend to her current place of abode.

He climbed the single flight of stained and crumbling concrete steps and walked along the balcony until he found Janice's front door. He rapped on the wooden panel. Peeling paint fell off under his fingers. The door opened almost immediately and Janice stood in the opening.

"I thought I told you—"

She broke off when she spied him. Her eyes widened in surprise. Her hand went to her hair, which was not quite as perfect as it had been the other times he'd seen her. Granted, she was on a day off. It wasn't a crime to relax her standards when on her own time.

"Janice, I was wondering if I could take a moment or two of your time."

She recovered quickly and offered him a wide smile. "Of course, Detective. I'm sorry. You took me by surprise."

"Yes, well, I happened to be in the neighborhood," he lied. "I thought we might talk about your polygraph results."

A little of the color disappeared from her cheeks and her smile became more forced, but she nodded and opened the door wider. "Come in."

He followed behind her down a dimly lit corridor that ended in a kitchen that was tired and dated. A pile of dirty dishes filled the sink. Food scraps, a half-empty bottle of milk and cereal boxes lined the cracked countertop. A modest flat screen TV stood in the corner of the adjoining living room, the channel tuned to one of the morning shows. A man sat with his back to them on the couch. Janice shot a nervous look in his direction and then once again returned her attention to James.

"So, Detective, can I get you a coffee?"

"No, thanks."

"Perhaps you'd prefer tea?"

"No, I'm good, thanks. Let's talk about your results."

She licked her lips nervously and sent another glance in the direction of the couch. James immediately understood.

"Is there somewhere a little more private you'd rather talk?"

"Y-yes. Let's go through to the bedroom."

Ordinarily, James might have baulked at interviewing a witness, especially a female one, in her bedroom, but apart from the bathroom, it appeared to be the only other room where they could hold a private conversation. He followed her back down the hallway and then into another room.

She flicked on the light and the room was bathed in a soft golden glow. Even so, the romantic lighting didn't hide the fact the bed was unmade, closet doors yawned open and the floor was littered with shoes and clothes. Janice Carter might look like a million dollars, but the truth was, in her private life she was a slob.

Still, none of that mattered to him. He couldn't care less how she lived. The only thing that interested him was why she'd failed the polygraph. He told her as much.

She sat down on the bed and put her face in her hands. Quiet sobs escaped through the gaps between her fingers. "I don't know what happened, Detective. Truly, I don't."

"You failed the polygraph, Janice. It's obvious you know more than what you've told me. Now, are you going to be straight with me, or do I have to take you downtown?"

She took a deep shuddering breath and looked up at him. Her mascara had smudged, leaving black trails on her cheeks. Her eyelashes were clotted together with tears. She opened her mouth and James nodded encouragingly.

"I don't know anything about it!" she wailed. "I don't know who killed Doug! I loved him! I wanted to carry his babies! I could never do anything to hurt him and I don't know who did!"

James tightened his lips on a surge of impatience. She was lying and they both knew it. Those questions, and more, had been put to her during the lie detector test and she'd lied then, too. Still, without any direct evidence tying her to the crime, there was nothing he could do. Swallowing a curse of frustration, he tossed one of his business cards in her direction and followed it with a gruff order to call him when she was ready to tell the truth. With that, he left the room.

The TV was still blaring in the living room. The man who'd been sitting on the couch now stood in the kitchen, a coffee cup in his hand. He looked up as James passed by the door. Their eyes locked. James started in surprise. Adrenaline surged through his veins. *What the hell was Todd Flanagan doing in Janice Carter's kitchen?*

The thought had no sooner formed in James' mind when the ex-con made a sudden move. He dashed toward the exit and then realized James was blocking the way. His gaze darted around the room, panic in his eyes. The only way out was through the doorway where James stood.

"Well, what do you know?" James drawled, strolling further into the room. "The police have been looking everywhere for you, Todd. You're a hard bastard to find." He chuckled without humor. "Fancy finding you here! This must be my lucky day. Detective Wang's going to be thrilled. Ever since you skipped bail, he's been hell-bent on finding you. I can't wait to make the call."

"Fuck off, pig. You don't have nothin' on me," Flanagan spat.

"Now, now, now, Todd. Manners, please! If that were true, we wouldn't have half of the New South Wales Police Force looking for you. You're on everyone's wanted list, including mine. That happens when you shoot a man in cold blood."

Todd's eyes narrowed in an angry sneer. "I didn't shoot no one. You can't prove that I did."

"Tell it to a judge, Flanagan. You're coming with me."

James closed the distance between them. He braced himself for a struggle, but the man put up no resistance when James spun him around and clamped handcuffs around his wrists. They passed a wide-eyed Janice on their way out.

"You ought to be more careful about who you keep company with, Janice. You're really dragging the bottom with this one."

She looked at him with a fearful expression on her face, but remained silent. James sighed inwardly. There was so much more behind her beautiful façade. He hoped she'd be forthcoming with more information the next time they met. For now, he had Todd Flanagan to deal with.

He hustled the man out of the door and secured him in the back of the squad car. Flanagan cursed him the whole time, but James ignored him. Climbing behind the wheel, he took out his phone and related what had happened to Wang. After receiving his colleague's congratulations, he ended the call and started the ignition.

"I wanna do a deal."

James looked in the rearview mirror at his prisoner and frowned. "I beg your pardon?"

"I said, I wanna do a deal. I have some information. About that guy who was murdered the other night in the city."

James stilled. He'd found Flanagan in Janice

Carter's apartment. Janice was one of his suspects. *Was it possible Flanagan knew something about the murder?* His heart picked up its pace, but he forced himself to speak calmly. It wouldn't do to let his prisoner know how important the information might be to him.

"Wait until we get to the station," he replied casually. "You can tell me everything you know. Then we'll see about a deal."

And with that, he pulled out into the traffic.

CHAPTER 15

James entered the police station through the back door and walked Flanagan past the cells and into an interview room. Still handcuffed, he gave the man an order to stay put and went to find Wang. His colleague was still at his desk, hunched over his computer. He looked up as James approached.

"I can't believe you found him! Good on you for recognizing the bastard!" Wang beamed.

James accepted the praise without comment. "Flanagan's ugly mug has been on every wanted poster around. It wasn't too hard to recognize him."

"Still, if it had been a rookie or someone less observant who did that house call... It was a lucky break—that's for sure. The guys who are investigating the homicide involving Flanagan will be thrilled."

"Yeah. I'll put a call in to them as soon as I'm finished with him."

Wang frowned. "What do you need him for?"

James compressed his lips and grimaced. "He said he had information about Doug Hanley's murder. In the same breath, he asked to do a deal. I don't know if he's bullshitting, or if he has some genuine information, but I can't overlook the fact he was found in Janice Carter's kitchen."

Wang nodded thoughtfully. "Do you think he's telling the truth?"

"Who knows? But I certainly want to ask him a few questions."

"What did you tell him?"

"I told him I'd hear what he had to say before we talked about any kind of deal."

"Good. Do you want me to sit in with you?"

"Can you spare the time?"

"Of course. Give me a minute. I'll see you in there. Which room?"

James told him and grabbed a fresh notepad off his desk before heading back to the interview room. Flanagan sat where he'd left him. If anything, he looked even more disgruntled.

"I want to talk to someone who's got the authority to do a deal," he snarled the moment James entered the room.

"Steady on, Flanagan. I haven't even taken a seat. Besides, I already told you. There'll be no talk of a deal until after I hear what you have to say. Your information might not be as valuable to me as you think."

"Oh, it's valuable, all right," the man replied.

James held his gaze. "That's for me to decide. Oh, here's Detective Wang. He's been working with me on the Hanley homicide. He thought he might listen in to what you have to say."

After closing the door, Wang took the seat beside James. He acknowledged Flanagan with a curt nod. They went through the preliminaries of advising the prisoner of the fact the interview would be recorded and obtained his personal details, including his full name, address and date of birth.

When it was done, James tugged the notepad toward him. "All right, Todd. Start talking."

The prisoner looked down at his lap. He fidgeted with his fingers, scratched at a scab on his arm, ran a hand through his greasy hair and at last looked at the detectives.

"I think Janice was the one who killed that guy in Bathurst Street."

"What makes you think that?" James asked in a bored tone.

"Because she asked me to do it for her—and I refused."

That got their attention. Both James and Wang came alert. James sat up straighter in his seat. Wang frowned hard at Flanagan. Still, they didn't want to tip the man off about the importance of his information. James doodled on the blank page in front of him and casually asked Todd another question.

"Right. So she just called you up out of the blue and asked you to murder her estranged husband."

Flanagan glared at him. "No, asshole, she didn't just call me up."

"Watch your language, Flanagan," Wang warned.

James shot the man a hard stare. "All right, then. Tell us what happened. But first of all, tell us about Janice Carter. How long have you known her?"

Flanagan lowered his gaze to the Formica desk that separated them. A moment passed and then he began to speak.

"I've known Janice all my life. She's my younger sister."

Despite his desire to remain calm and disinterested, James was sure his surprise was all over his face. Flanagan looked nothing like the glamorous nurse and apart from the physical differences, they didn't even share a last name.

Flanagan eyed him churlishly. "I know what you're thinkin'. We don't look nothin' alike. I should have been a bit more specific. She's my half-sister. We share the same mother, but we have different fathers. Mine pissed off years before Janice came along. Mom hooked up with Jan's dad when I was twelve. Jan was born a couple of years later. She was such a beautiful baby. All that blond hair. And she loved me, she really loved me. In her eyes, I couldn't do no wrong.

"Then I started spendin' time on the streets. Things weren't so good at home. My step-father worshipped the ground his little girl walked on. Me, he didn't think so kindly about. I dropped out of school and started hangin' around a fast crowd. Before I knew it, I was in trouble with the cops. I guess things just went from bad to worse and I started spendin' time in jail. Jan eventually grew up and realized her older brother wasn't the saint she thought him to be, but she never gave up on me.

"She'd visit me in jail whenever she could. The other inmates were jealous. They wouldn't believe I had a sister as hot as she was. Don't worry, I used to milk it for all it was worth. I'd get ciggies and shit from the commisary. The blokes were willin' to trade just about anything for a few minutes with Jan, up close."

"She didn't mind the attention?" James asked curiously. The woman hadn't appeared shy, but being the center of attention from a roomful of criminals or guards was another matter. Flanagan brushed away his question.

"Of course not! Did you get a look at her? Jan's always been a looker and she loves the attention. She spends a fortune on her appearance." He looked down at his old, stained clothes and chuckled. "She didn't take after her older brother, that's for sure."

"Tell us why you think she shot Douglas Hanley," Wang said.

The humor faded from Flanagan's face and his eyes became shadowed with concern. "It's not that I want to rat on her...but I'm in a spot of trouble. If I get convicted of that other homicide, I'm lookin' at doin' twelve to fifteen. That's a lot of time in the slammer. I don't think I could do that much time. It has a way of wearin' you down, gettin' to you until you don't feel human anymore. You know what I mean?"

He directed the question to Wang, but it was James who answered. "No, Flanagan, we don't know what you mean. We make it our business to abide by the law and stay out of jail. Unlike you. Now, tell us why you think your sister murdered her estranged husband."

Flanagan's jaw tightened and a stubborn look filled his eyes. James cursed silently under his breath and hoped he hadn't blown their chance to find out what the prisoner knew. To James' relief, a moment later, Flanagan once again started to speak.

"Jan came to me a couple of months ago. She was mad as hell at Doug. They'd been havin' some marriage problems for a while, but I'd never seen her like this."

"What kind of problems?" James asked in an effort to establish how close Flanagan was to his sister.

"She wanted a baby. She'd been married to Doug for three or four years and nothin'. She told me one night that Doug had some problems with his fertility, but she was certain they could work things out. She mentioned IVF and sperm donors, but to be honest, I tuned out after that. But I do know that Doug wasn't keen on outside interference and it caused problems between them."

"Is that why they split up?" James asked.

"Probably. I dunno. I was doin' a stint in jail for armed robbery when that happened. She only told me things hadn't worked out."

"How did it come about that she asked you to murder Doug?" Wang asked.

"I got out on parole and went to live with her. It

seemed like every minute of every day she was carryin' on about her ex. In the end, I got sick of it. I asked her why the hell she didn't get rid of him. I wasn't fully serious, but she took a likin' to the idea. That's when she asked me if I'd do it."

"Why you?" Wang asked.

Flanagan shrugged. "I dunno. I guess she thought she could trust me and it wasn't like I was above breakin' the law. I'd never killed anyone before, but I was far from an angel. She'd visited me enough times in prison to know that. First she asked if I knew someone who could do it. Eventually, the conversation worked around to the point where she asked me if *I'd* do it."

"What did you say?" James asked.

"I told her she was fuckin' crazy. Why would I go and do somethin' like that? I might have done some stupid shit in my day, but I never killed no one. Besides, she was the one with the beef against Doug. I never had nothin' against him. He was a bit of a schmuck, but that didn't mean I wanted to see him dead."

"How did she react?" James asked.

"She didn't like it. Not one bit. But there was no changin' my mind. I had enough goin' on without takin' on somethin' like that."

"Why should we believe you, Flanagan?" James demanded. "We both know you'd be prepared to say anything to save your ass."

Todd blustered for a moment and then ceased. He stared at James. "You don't have to believe me. I got it all on tape."

James sat forward. "What do you mean?"

"My phone. I recorded one of our conversations. A bit of insurance. Bein' asked to top someone is pretty serious shit. I didn't want it to come back and bite me. Lucky I was thinkin' so clearly at the time."

"Where's your phone?" Wang demanded.

Flanagan felt around in the pocket of his shirt and pulled out an iPhone. He handed it across the table to James' colleague. "Here."

Wang took the phone and then frowned. "What's your password?"

"12345678"

Wang shot the man a look of disgust. "You're joking?"

"No, mate. Why would I be jokin'?"

James merely shook his head in silence and waited while his partner played with the phone. A few minutes later, Wang started the recording. Janice could be heard talking to her brother and as Todd had said, she asked him several times if he'd murder her estranged husband. To Todd's credit, he repeatedly refused her request. When it was over, James looked at Wang. His colleague nodded. It was damning stuff.

"Does your sister know how to use a firearm?" James asked.

"Nope. She wouldn't know one end of a gun from the other."

"Could she have found someone to show her?" Wang asked.

Flanagan shrugged. "Maybe. She's a very resourceful woman, but I don't see her bein' the shooter."

"Then what do you think happened?" James asked.

Flanagan stared at him for a while and then lowered his gaze. "I think when I turned her down, she found someone else to do it."

The rumble of the engine of a powerful motorbike finally registered on her thoughts. Coming out of her comfortable chair, she went to the front window and peered out. The familiar figure striding up her garden path sent a shiver of apprehension down her spine. The man was dangerous. Of course, that was the reason she'd contacted him in the first place.

His knock on the front door came loud and sharp. It was a "don't fuck with me" kind of knock. She'd heard it once before. Knowing that he wouldn't go away until she spoke to him, she drew in a fortifying breath and pulled open the door.

"What is it?" she asked, pleased with the haughtiness in her tone. There was no hint of the fear she felt inside.

"I want more money. Another twenty grand."

She gasped. "That's outrageous! I already paid you that much and you didn't deserve it. Why would I give you any more?"

His eyes turned mean and narrowed on a glare. "Because you know what I'll do if you don't."

Her belly quivered with nerves, but she held her ground. "You know, I'm getting a little sick and tired of your endless threats. You've been paid good money for what little service you gave me. Now, it's time you went on your way. Please don't bother me again."

She went to close the door, but his hand came up and stopped the action. Anger and something much more sinister glinted in his eyes. He moved closer until his face was up close to hers.

"You've got it all wrong, lady. You're not the one who calls the shots and you certainly don't tell me how and when this thing ends. You're the one who contacted me, remember? One word from me, and the cops will be all over you and it won't end until you're in jail. Don't forget that."

She forced a laugh and waved away his threats, as if they meant nothing. Inside, she trembled with fear. He danced on the dark side of life. If anyone could make good on their threats, it was him.

How could she have been so stupid? She should never have tracked him down, told him of her plan. Now she was stuck with the fact he knew enough to land her in jail and there was nothing she could do about it.

Except pay him what he demanded...

She gritted her teeth in silent protest. She refused to pay him another cent. But what if she didn't have a choice? Was she brave enough to call his bluff? The truth was, she didn't know, but right now, she didn't have enough money to give him what he wanted and the knowledge terrified her. Still, there was no point showing him her fear. He was like a wild animal. The moment he sensed her distress, he'd go in for the kill. No, it was best she play it cool, like she usually did.

"Like I said, Viktor, you've been paid well for the little that you did. There will be no more money from me. Tell who you like. It's no concern of mine. Do you really think the police will believe you over me?" She let out a peal of raucous laughter, knowing how it would grate upon his nerves. Hopefully it would be enough to send him packing, never to return.

His face went puce with anger and spittle flew from his mouth. "You haven't seen the last of me, you bitch! Just you wait! You'll regret the day you laughed at me. No one laughs at Viktor Popov and gets away with it!"

He turned on his heel and stormed down the path. She watched from the safety of her doorway as he threw a leg over his Harley and went roaring off down the street. With a shaky sigh of relief, she closed and locked the door, taking care to ensure the deadbolt was in place.

Phew! It was over. Now she could go back to her TV program in peace. Reaching for her cup of hot chocolate, she took a sip and sighed with pleasure. It was nice to be able to take comfort from the little things in life once again.

CHAPTER 16

Sally-Ann twirled a piece of her long straight hair around her finger and tried to concentrate on the statements spread across her desk. The day had been slow and though she had plenty of work to do, her mind kept straying to the good-looking detective and to the even nicer kiss they'd shared.

She probably shouldn't have done it, but she wasn't sorry she had. He was the lead detective in the murder investigation of her ex-brother-in-law's murder, but she was innocent of any wrongdoing and eventually, James would realize that, too. Then she wouldn't be involved in his investigation at all and they'd be free to explore their feelings. And she was certain he had as many feelings for her as she did for him.

She felt it in the way he looked at her and in the way he said her name and she'd definitely felt it in his warm, soft lips and the way he'd returned her kiss. No, she had no qualms about the knowledge that at some point, he'd exonerate her as a suspect and then they'd be free to get to know each other better.

She allowed herself a few moments of daydreaming and then reality raised its ugly head. He was a police officer. Not in her wildest dreams could she imagine any scenario where her parents would accept him as her boyfriend. Forget the murder investigation. Convincing her parents that he could be trusted—though he was a cop—would be the hardest task of all.

Was she up to the battle? Was he? Hell, she didn't know the answer to either of those questions and it was doing her head in.

The phone on her desk buzzed and she distractedly picked it up. "Yes, Barbara?"

"Sally-Ann," her secretary said, "I have Detective James Shepherd on line three. Will you take the call?"

Sally-Ann's heart leaped with excitement and she forcefully told herself to calm down. She hadn't spoken to him since he'd left her place the night before. *What should she say? How should she act? Should she mention the kiss, or ignore it?* Indecision gnawed at her temples and she groaned in exasperation and eventually answered the call.

"Detective Shepherd, what can I do for you?" *There, that was the way to do it. Play it cool.*

"Ms Li, we've had an interesting development."

Ms Li. He was playing it as formal as she. That was fine. She could go with that. She cleared her throat. "Oh?"

"Yes. We've spoken to a witness who claims to

have knowledge of the person who killed your ex-brother-in-law. We're still checking out his story, but it appears you and your family might be off the hook. On top of that, the ballistics tests on your father's gun came back negative."

"So, we're in the clear?" She could hardly keep the elation from her voice.

"Yes. It seems that way."

"What about my business card? I thought you were convinced that placed me at the scene."

"Yes, well, as much as I hate to say it, the existence of your business card appears to be nothing more than a coincidence."

"That's great. Thank you for passing on the news. My parents will be over the moon and so will my sister. We've all been so worried even though we knew it wasn't us. My father was convinced the police wouldn't do their job properly and would point the finger at one of us—being immigrants. I'll be pleased to tell him that isn't true."

"Yes. I'm… I'm pleased, too."

The admission was voiced quietly, almost uncertainly, as if he were feeling his way. Sally-Ann's stomach somersaulted with nerves. *Was she brave enough to ask the next question? What if he backed away, refused to acknowledge the special something that was between them? Would it crush her?* Probably. But if she didn't ask, she'd never know. With her mind made up, she took a breath and blurted it out before she lost courage.

"Would you like to come over for dinner?"

There was silence on the other end of the phone and it seemed to last forever. Just when she didn't think she could bear it another second, he answered.

"Thank you. That would be nice."

James hung up the phone and stared at it with something akin to disbelief. Had he really just accepted a dinner invitation from Sally-Ann Li? What was he thinking? She might not be on his suspect list anymore, but she was still on the periphery of his investigation. *Wasn't she?*

The evidence against Janice was rather damning, particularly the recording, but their chief witness was an ex-con with a record as long as his arm who by his own admission didn't want to be sent back to jail. They still hadn't sorted out any kind of deal and James had made no promises there. He'd made it clear to the man that there'd be no deal if his information didn't pan out.

Still, James was relieved the information pointed in this direction. The thought of spending an evening with Sally-Ann, a Sally-Ann who could rest a little easier about spending time with a cop, had his belly twisting with excitement and anticipation. He tried to focus away from the investigation and concentrate on what bottle of wine he would bring to impress her.

He recalled the red she'd been drinking when he arrived at her home the previous night. He wondered if she also liked white and then wondered if she liked sweet or dry. It was probably best to play it safe and choose a nice Cabernet Sauvignon. Not too sweet, not too dry. In fact, it was probably just right.

But first, he still had to deal with Janice Carter before heading out. A squad car had been sent around to her place to pick her up and bring her to the station. The day was almost over, but he wanted to question her about what her brother had told them. If it were true, she'd be charged with Doug's murder and James' work would be almost done. It was a nice thought. And with that arrest, he'd be able to get Maureen Hanley off his back.

His cell phone rang in his pocket and he pulled it out and answered. "Detective Shepherd."

"James, it's Lachlan."

James nodded, recognizing the voice of one of the patrolmen who'd been sent to collect Janice. "Lachie, how did you do?"

"Not good, I'm afraid. She wasn't there. I called the hospital too, but they said she's not rostered on until tomorrow. They don't know where she is."

James bit down on a sigh of disappointment, but managed to end the call on a cheery note.

"Don't worry about it, Lachie. Hopefully she's just running errands. Her brother's locked up tight for the night and won't be making any phone calls. Stay at your post and arrest her as soon as she shows. We need to get to her before she becomes aware that her brother squealed."

"No problem, James."

"Thanks. I'm going to call it a night, but contact me if you find her."

"I will."

James ended the call and dropped the phone back in his pocket. Logging off his computer, he bid a hasty farewell to Wang and made a beeline for the exit.

———

Sally-Ann picked up the vase of flowers and repositioned them on the table for what seemed like the hundredth time. She couldn't believe how nervous she was about seeing James again. She'd left work early, and spent all afternoon preparing dinner, wondering what they'd say to each other and whether he'd kiss her hello.

Did she want him to? Of course she did! The not knowing was twisting her stomach into knots and then a knock came at the door and her belly went into a nosedive. Tucking her hair behind her ears, she patted it in place, straightened her light summer dress and then headed down the hallway to open the door.

He looked just as gorgeous as he always did. His navy-blue suit was a little bit wrinkled and his red-and-white striped tie was slightly askew, but the sight of him still managed to snatch her breath and send her heart racing.

"H-hi," she stammered. Heat enveloped her cheeks. She stared somewhere in the direction of his lapels, too uncertain and embarrassed to meet his gaze.

He stepped forward and pecked her on the cheek. The simple act was carried out so naturally that it was enough to steady her nerves.

"You look beautiful," he said. "Thank you for inviting me to dinner."

She smiled shyly. "Thank you for coming. You look good, too. I hope you like curry."

He nodded and sighed with exaggerated happiness.

"Shall we?" she asked.

He shot her a slow and sexy smile that curled her toes and then followed her into the house. Sally-Ann led the way into the kitchen that was filled with the aroma of hot and spicy curry.

"This is for you," James said, handing her the bottle of red wine.

She smiled with pleasure. He must have remembered that she drank red wine. She thanked him and absently noted the label and realized he'd spent a fortune. "You shouldn't have," she protested.

"I wanted to," he replied. "I just hope it goes with curry." He grinned and immediately her body responded.

Her heart skipped a beat and then took off running. Desire ignited in her depths. He was much too nice and much too sexy for her peace of mind. How could she concentrate on continuing to prepare dinner with a man like James Shepherd in her house?

"We should open it," she managed and turned

away from him to hunt for a corkscrew in one of the kitchen drawers. Finally, her fingers closed around it and she withdrew it in triumph.

"Here, let me," he said, reaching for the opener.

Their fingers brushed and Sally-Ann stifled a gasp. Heat spread from her hand, up her arm and traveled across her face. Her skin tingled from his touch. Blindly, she opened cupboards looking for wine glasses. She took the moment to draw in a couple of breaths and get herself under control. She turned back to him with a bright smile on her face and two glasses in her hand.

"Here we go," she said and placed the glasses on the counter in front of him.

He poured them each a glass and then handed one to her. Once again, their fingers touched and once again, her body reacted. Not wanting to reveal her emotional turmoil, she kept her gaze averted and took a sip of wine. It was rich and warm and mellow. The woody and earthy scents of it filled her nostrils. She breathed it in and sighed. "This is delicious."

He sipped from his glass and then nodded. "You're right. It's very nice."

"Thank you again for bringing the wine. I appreciate it."

"My pleasure. Besides, it's the least I could do after you offered to cook for me. I can't remember the last time a woman cooked for me."

His gaze captured hers and though her heart beat a frantic rhythm against her chest, she couldn't look away. The green of his eyes was mesmerizing. The promise of passion almost stole her breath. He set his glass down on the counter without breaking eye contact. As if it were the most natural thing in the world, he closed the distance between them and drew her into his arms.

Her chest brushed against his and her nipples tightened in response. Heat exploded through her. Without conscious thought, she put her arms around his neck and tilted her head up to receive his kiss. His lips were warm and pliant and moved with grace and ease over hers. He tasted of wine and warm male. The stubble of his whiskers scraped her cheeks.

He angled his head to deepen the kiss and when his tongue probed her lips, she opened them and welcomed him in. He groaned under his breath and pulled her more tightly against him, until every inch of her was pressed against the long, hard length of him.

The kiss continued. They couldn't get enough. Sally-Ann's hands roamed over his chest and shoulders. His hands learned the shape and feel of her butt. His erection pressed against her belly, leaving no doubt that he was enjoying this as much as she was.... And then he murmured something about the curry and that brought her back to reality with a jolt.

Pulling her mouth from his, she stared up at him, her breath coming fast. She blinked and tried to remember what it was that had broken them apart. *The curry.* Right. It was in a pot on the stove. She needed to turn off the heat.

With a murmur of apology, she pushed away from him. His arms dropped and she stepped out of his embrace and moved over to the stove. From a distant part of her mind, she realized the curry was almost done. Flicking the switch, she turned off the power and then turned back to him, her head still full of him and their kiss.

"Wow," she stated softly.

His answering smile was filled with just as much wonder. "You're right. That was wow and I'm nowhere near finished. What about you?"

She nodded in agreement and smiled. In two swift strides, he was by her side and once again took her in his arms. Their lips met and joined. Mouths opened, tongues danced. Need burned hot and bright. Without warning, James bent and lifted her in his arms. He strode toward the kitchen table and put her down on the sturdy wood. Leaning across her, he lifted the vase of flowers and set them out of the way. Then he kissed her over and over...and this time it was different.

The mindless passion of a few moments earlier had relented to a softer, more tender kind of attention. He kissed her eyelids, her cheeks, her nose. He nuzzled her neck and nibbled on her earlobes and breathed in her sweet scent. And then his hands moved to cup her breasts and stroke her nipples through the thin fabric of her summer dress. She thrust her chest forward so that her breast filled his hand and moaned with the sheer ecstasy of it.

"You're so beautiful," he whispered between kisses.

She burned from the inside out. Everywhere he touched, he left a trail of fire. She dropped her head backward and let him have free access to wherever he chose and gasped in delight as he took advantage of her unspoken offer. His hand stroked up her bare leg, across her small calf muscle to her slim thigh...and higher. When his fingers scraped the lace of her panties, she cried out.

Framing his face with both hands, she kissed him hard on the mouth. Without releasing him, she lay back down on the table, bringing him with her. He took hold of her hips and dragged her toward him. Spreading her legs wide, he positioned himself between them. Once again, his fingers found her secret place and this time, they slipped inside her panties and stroked her warm, slick flesh. Her legs closed involuntarily as she tried to capture and hold his hand in place, but he gently spread them open again and began a rhythmic stroking that drove her insane.

Over and over, his finger glided over her sensitive flesh. At the same time, he reached behind her and unzipped her dress. His hand slipped beneath her bra and stroked her nipple. It puckered under his ministrations and elicited another moan. Never before had she been touched so thoroughly by a man. His eyes were glazed with desire. His face was tense with need. He withdrew his hand from between her legs and she murmured in protest.

"I want to see you naked. I need to taste your skin," he said.

Heat spiraled low inside her and blossomed into a fire in her core. Driving her crazy with need, he slowly removed her dress, lifting it over her head. Her bra quickly followed. Finally, she lay spread before him on the table, clad only in her panties and a moment later, even those were gone. He stared down at her, as if in a daze, his face filled with wonder.

Impatiently, she reached for him, needing to feel the weight of him against her, but he brushed her hands away.

"Patience, sweetheart. I haven't finished with you, yet."

With that, he knelt on the floor in front of her and buried his face between her thighs. His tongue replaced his finger and he stroked her up and down. He probed into the soft crevices and then thrust his tongue inside her. She gasped and fisted her hands, holding them straight by her sides as he turned her world upside down.

There was nothing and no one but him and the pleasure he gave her. The pressure inside her continued to build until she knew for a certainty that she couldn't hold it back a moment longer.

"James!" she gasped.

He lifted his head and smiled at her. "Come for me, Sal. I want to taste you on my lips."

His words sent her teetering on the edge then free-falling over the other side. She gasped and cried out, her inner muscles clenching and releasing over and over from the power of her orgasm. Moments later, she felt the amazing aftershocks in the trembles and shaking of her legs. It felt like a long time later when she finally drifted back to earth.

"How was that?" he asked softly, a tender smile playing around his lips.

"That was...amazing," she said.

"Good. I'm glad."

"Now it's your turn," she said and did her best not to blush.

He chuckled. "Don't you worry, I'm not going to miss out."

With that, he reached into the back pocket of his pants and pulled out his wallet. She saw the flash of plastic and realized he'd retrieved a condom. She sighed silently in relief. At least one of them had thought about acting responsibly.

She struggled to come upright, but he gently pushed her back down. "Oh, no. I want you just like that, all flushed and relaxed from your orgasm, spread before me like a feast."

A fresh wave of tenderness and desire went through her, rekindling the flame that had yet to go out. He'd already gotten rid of his jacket and within moments, his shirt and tie and pants had disappeared. Just as quickly, he shucked off his underwear and sheathed himself with the condom.

His cock jutted out thick and proud from the juncture of his thighs. Warmth spread through her at the sight of it. He stared down at her wordlessly, his eyes dark with desire, need glittering in their depths. Once again, he held her by the hips and dragged her toward him. The table was just the right height.

He probed her slick entrance with his cock and her legs fell wider apart. Holding her gaze, his hands tightened around her hips and with a single hard thrust, he pushed himself all the way inside. She gasped from the welcome impact.

He remained perfectly still, as if relishing the sensation of being surrounded by her wetness and warmth. And then he began to move. In and out, his cock glided inside her, filling her, stretching her wide. His face was a mask of concentration, like he was lost in another world. The knowledge that she had that kind of power over him filled her with awe.

The desire he'd reignited inside her caught fire and soared as he moved faster. She stretched her arms toward him, but he held himself out of reach. Over and over, he pounded inside her and each time, her need grew. The familiar pressure between her legs continued to build, increasing with the pace of his thrusts. His hands tightened almost painfully on her hips as he became lost in a frenzy of need.

Her breath came fast, her fingers clenched and once again she was within reach. And then he surged forward and cried out. The relief and ecstasy on his face tipped her over the edge. Her body shuddered and clenched and quivered on another orgasm as he reached his climax. With a final groan, he collapsed against her, his head cushioned on her chest.

It was a long moment later that he stirred and pulled away. A tender smile filled with wonder broke slowly across his face.

"*That* was amazing."

CHAPTER 17

James was swimming in a pool of contentment. The sun was pleasantly warm on his face. The air around him was filled with the scent of lilies. He remembered seeing some in a vase on Sally-Ann's table and all of a sudden, the night before came back to him in a rush. He blinked and slowly became aware of the soft and regular breathing of the woman beside him. The sheets were tangled around their feet.

Sally-Ann lay on her back with her eyes closed. One arm was flung above her head, the other nestled against her side. Her small round breasts sat high on her chest, her nipples a soft, dusky pink. Her ribs expanded and fell with each breath. His gaze moved lower, across the smooth tanned skin of her belly.

He remembered making love to every inch of her throughout the long hours of the night. First on the kitchen table and later, in the shower and finally, he'd woken some time in the early hours and loved her again on the bed. He was crazed for the feel of her. He needed to have her close. The speed and ferocity of his developing feelings would have scared him if he'd taken the time to contemplate what was happening between them.

They'd shared stories about their childhood. He'd heard all about her life in China, before it had all turned so bad. He'd told her about Lizzie and the difficulties she was experiencing. They both agreed those teen years were a rough time in anyone's life, particularly when Lizzie had lost her biological mother. It was natural for her to lash out at the substitute. James assured her Anita was anything but the wicked step-mother and Sally-Ann was confident that, provided James and the other adults in Lizzie's life continued to love and support her, she'd eventually realize they wanted what was best for her and the defiance would die a natural death.

James felt the same way, but it was good to have his thoughts on the subject reinforced by someone he cared about. And he did care. The knowledge filled him with surprise.

Twenty-four hours earlier Sally-Ann had been a suspect in a murder investigation. Now that she was as good as cleared, he'd allowed his burgeoning feelings free rein. And she'd responded in kind. He still marveled at the way she'd returned kiss for kiss, stroke for stroke, orgasm for orgasm. It had never been that way for him before and he instinctively knew it wouldn't be like that with anyone else. He only hoped she felt the same way.

The sound of a knock on the front door jarred his senses and interrupted the pleasant flow of his thoughts. Sally-Ann mumbled in her sleep and pulled the sheet up over her head. He frowned and peered at the clock that stood on the nightstand. It was barely seven. *Who would come calling so early?*

The knock came again and he cursed quietly under his breath. It was probably a delivery guy. Striding down the hall naked, he found his boxers on the floor in the kitchen and hurriedly pulled them on. Not bothering with a shirt, he headed toward the entrance and opened the front door.

Chao Li stood before him.

Sally-Ann's father blinked and his eyes widened in shock. James tried to think of something to say, but came up empty. There was no way to explain away what was obvious to both of them: James had spent the night.

"D-detective Shepherd! What are you doing here?"

James returned Chao's affronted gaze steadily, refusing to feel guilty. He and Sally-Ann were both consenting adults, after all. "I'm visiting with your daughter," he replied.

Chao's face flushed with anger. "Visiting!" he spat. "Please, don't treat me like I'm stupid."

"Then don't ask stupid quest—"

"Dad! What are you doing here?"

James was cut off by the arrival of Sally-Ann. She was dressed in pajamas and a short cotton housecoat. She stared at her father in horror and he looked just as distressed.

"I came to tell you about the arrest of Janice Carter. It was all over the morning news. But I guess you already know about it, seeing as you're keeping company with the lead detective."

The anger in his voice was palpable. He shot his daughter a searing look that spoke volumes. Sally-Ann flushed with embarrassment. James cursed under his breath that the news of Janice's arrest had become public knowledge. Lachlan must have located her last night. He wondered how the media had gotten wind of it so soon and then dismissed the thought. The how and the why no longer mattered. The damage was done.

"Look, Mr Li, Sally-Ann and I—"

"How could you, Sal?" her father interrupted, pushing his way past both of them and heading down the hall toward the kitchen.

Sally-Ann shot James a look that told him she didn't know what to say and then hurried after her father.

"Dad, please, let me explain," he heard her say. He sighed and closed the door and strode in the direction of the voices that were now raised in argument. He rounded the opening into the kitchen and saw the two of them facing off.

"How *could* you, Sally-Ann?" her father repeated, his fury emanating off him in waves.

James picked up his shirt from underneath the table and hastily pulled it on. He located his pants nearby. Once he was fully dressed, he felt more comfortable fronting up to Sally-Ann's angry dad.

"Look, Mr Li," he said in a placating tone.

Chao shot a lethal glare in his direction and

then returned his attention to his daughter. "A police officer, Sally-Ann! Of all the men for you to bring home! A *police* officer!"

Anger stirred in James' stomach. He sympathized with Chao's tumultuous past, but this had gone on long enough. "Mr Li, it might have escaped your notice, but Sally-Ann is an adult. She's old enough to choose who she spends her time with."

Chao rounded on him, his cheeks flushed with anger. "Don't you dare lecture me on what I should or should not say to my daughter! This is between me and Sally-Ann. It has nothing to do with you!"

James held his gaze. "You're being unreasonable. Leave her alone. She hasn't done anything wrong. And this has everything to do with me. You're judging me solely on my occupation. You don't even know me. It's not like I'm going to harm her. I—" He broke off and stared at Sally-Ann. She looked at him like she was waiting for him to finish. He squared his shoulders and stared her father in the eye. "I care for your daughter, Mr Li. I care for her very much."

Sally-Ann's eyes widened in surprise and tears shone in their depths. "And I care for him, too, Daddy. I didn't mean for this to happen. It...just did."

Chao rounded on her, his face filled with despair. "After everything I told you! Haven't you learned anything?"

"This isn't China, Daddy. Things are different here. Police officers are trustworthy. They're the good guys. Please, Daddy. Try and understand."

Chao shook his head with disgust, then gave his daughter another long look. James could see the struggle on the man's face as he tried to come to terms with the fact his daughter was seeing a cop. With a snort of annoyance and disgust, Chao threw a final glare in James' direction and stormed out of the room. The resounding bang of the front door echoed his abrupt departure from his daughter's home.

James looked at Sally-Ann. He wasn't sure what to say. Their relationship was so new, so fragile, he didn't know if it could withstand such an attack.

"I'm sorry," she murmured, wringing her hands.

His heart melted. He moved closer and took her in his arms, pressing a soft kiss against her hair. "Don't be sorry. It isn't your fault and it really isn't your father's fault, either. From what I've been told, he's been through a lot at the hands of the Chinese Police. I understand how he feels. If I'd been persecuted like he was, I wouldn't want my daughter dating a police officer, either."

She tightened her arms around his waist in response. When she spoke, her voice was muffled against his shirt.

"We would all have been murdered if Dad hadn't arranged for us to flee the country. We arrived with nothing but the clothes we were wearing. We couldn't even keep our names; Dad said it was too dangerous. For years, he constantly looked over his shoulder, convinced the Chinese government would find us. It's probably only been in the last year or so that he's relaxed his vigilance."

"So he accepts the Chinese authorities might have given up?"

She looked up at him and shook her head. "No, but he's not quite as paranoid—that they're lurking around every corner—as he used to be. I don't think he'll ever get to the point where he accepts they've given up. He says they won't. I'm sure he truly believes that. It's the reason he started collecting firearms. They made him feel safer."

"And now I have one of them," James said.

"Yes, the Glock's his favorite. He likes the way it feels in his hand." She pulled out of his arms. "Seeing as the tests came back negative, do you think we could have it back?"

He nodded. "I'm sure you can."

"Good. Dad will be glad to have it returned to him."

A moment of silence fell between them. James opened his mouth to speak and then closed it and then opened it again. *Dammit, he had to know.*

"Did you mean it when you said you care for me?" he blurted.

She eyed him warily. "Did you?"

He held her gaze. "Yes."

The tension around her mouth eased a little and the beginnings of a smile flowered upon her lips. "Really?"

"Yes, really. It sounds crazy, but right from the moment I met you I felt connected to you in a strange and exciting way. I've never felt like this with anyone. I hope you feel the same."

"Yes," she cried and leaped into his arms. With her legs around his hips, she clung to his shoulders. At the same time, she pressed kisses against his lips.

The kiss quickly became more urgent and a rush of blood surged to his cock. With his hands supporting her bottom, he pressed her close, relishing the feel of her soft body pressed to his. Finally, she broke off the kiss. She threw him a look that made his heart race. "Do we have time?" she asked.

He kissed her hard on the mouth. "Plenty of time. Just watch me."

James stared at Janice across the same table he'd been seated at with her brother only the day before. The night in the cells hadn't appeared to soften her attitude any, if the glare she bestowed on him the moment he stepped into the room was anything to go by. Wang had beaten him into work and warned him the prisoner was spoiling for a fight. He wasn't wrong.

"What the hell are you doing, dragging me in off the street? I already told you everything I know," the nurse spat, her eyes shooting fire.

James remained calm and collected. "We both know that's not true, Janice. Besides, we've come into some new information that implicates you fairly and squarely in the murder of Douglas Hanley."

Her eyes lost some of their defiance and took on a more cautious look. "What kind of new information?"

"It has to do with your brother, Todd. Remember him? We met in your kitchen yesterday. He and I had a nice little chat."

She paled and much of her bravado dissolved. "You're lying. Todd would never rat me out."

"That's where you're wrong. Oh, sure, your brother is rather fond of you, but that didn't stop him from trying to negotiate a deal to save his ass. He told us some very interesting information. Like how you asked him to kill your estranged husband."

"The bastard! I'll kill him!"

James shot her a look that spoke volumes. Janice turned all shades of crimson. "I-I didn't mean that literally! It was a figure of speech. I wouldn't really kill him. He's my brother! I love him."

"Like you loved Doug?"

"It wasn't like that!" Janice protested, looking around in a panic. "I don't know what Todd told you, but the thing is, I changed my mind."

James leveled her with his stare. "See, Todd didn't actually have to tell us anything. He had the whole conversation with you recorded. We listened while you harangued him over and over to murder your estranged husband."

This time, her face lost so much color, James was concerned she might be about to faint. He leaned forward in concern, but Janice waved him away. She held a fist up to her mouth and gulped in breaths and eventually appeared to get control over herself.

"Why don't you start at the beginning, Janice?" he said quietly. "And this time, tell me the truth."

She eyeballed him for a second or two then lowered her gaze. Her shoulders slumped in defeat. "Okay, you're right. I did ask Todd to kill my husband."

James' heart leaped with excitement. He very nearly had this case sewn shut. "Why?" he asked, forcibly maintaining an outer calm.

"Because I was mad at him!" Janice exploded. "For years I'd wanted a baby. He knew that. And then he eventually confessed to being infertile!"

"I understand why you'd be angry," James mused.

"Too right, I was! I was mad as hell. The bastard should have told me before we got married! But I was determined to have a baby so I started looking into IVF. There were sperm donors we could use. A baby wasn't beyond reach."

She shook her head, then her mouth tightened with anger. "Doug refused to discuss it," she continued. "Our arguments became increasingly nasty. And then he told me he was glad he couldn't have children because that meant he couldn't have them with me. He said it to hurt me and it had the desired effect."

She paused, as if to gather herself. Tears glinted in her eyes and then clung to her thick eyelashes. James averted his gaze and let her finish.

"I was devastated," she said in a voice that was husky with remembered pain. "I screamed and shouted and called him awful names. I was furious and hurt and shattered all at the same time. I saw my dream of having a baby die right in front of me and he didn't care. That last night, before he left, I was a mess. I'd been drinking and I was still hurting. Our argument turned physical. I punched him in the shoulder a couple of times. I slapped him across the face."

"How did he react?"

"He just took it. He didn't even fight back. I ended up on the floor, collapsed into a heap of anguish and pain. In the end, he simply stepped over me and walked out."

"Where did he go?"

Defiantly, she swiped at the tears in her eyes and her lip curled up in disdain. "He went home to his mother's to sulk and lick his wounds. He knew he'd find a sympathetic ear. She always took his side over mine. Over anyone's. You should have heard her talk about poor Aimee. I felt sorry for the woman. Maureen didn't take too kindly to me either, but she was even worse when it came to Doug's first wife. It was clear she hated everything about Aimee, or at least about the fact she was Asian. It was really nasty stuff. Most of the time, I tried not to listen."

"So you and Doug parted ways and you were left to stew over the fact he'd reneged on his deal. Is that right?"

"I was furious and I had every right to be! Doug had promised we'd have children and then when it came down to it, first he admits he deceived me into thinking it was possible for him to be a father and then he admitted he didn't want kids at all, especially with me! I was entitled to feel angry."

James regarded her steadily. While he felt some sympathy for her plight, the fact was, she'd planned and carried out the murder of her husband. Whether she pulled the trigger or had someone else do it made no difference. The law simply wasn't on her side and that's the way it had to be.

As if sensing his waning support, she blew her breath out on a sigh. When she spoke again, her voice was calmer. "Todd was staying with me not long after the break-up and he took the brunt of my rants. It was Todd who suggested I get rid of Doug."

James nodded. This information was consistent with what Todd had said.

"At first I was taken aback, I mean, I wasn't a criminal. I've barely had a parking ticket and here we were talking about killing someone! It was insane. And yet, I couldn't get it out of my mind. The more I thought about it, the more I liked the idea. 'Hell hath no fury,' right? Besides, it would serve Doug right for deceiving me and for entering into a marriage contract under false pretenses." She pouted.

"I'm not sure that I'd put it quite as strongly as that," James murmured.

"Well, whatever he did, it was a low act and it left me feeling pissed. I wanted to hurt him like he'd hurt me. I wanted to get back at him."

"So you told Todd to kill him for you. Whose gun did he use?"

Janice shook her head, her eyes wide with panic. "No! No! It wasn't like that. See, when it came down to it, Todd wasn't too keen on the idea. He'd just come out of jail. Said he'd never killed anyone and had no intention of going down that path, even for me. If he broke his parole with another offense, he'd be right back in there again. And a murder meant he'd never see the light of day again. He found me a gun, but I looked at it and got scared. It seemed so…lethal."

She paused as if to gather her thoughts. "After a while, I came to my senses and saw how ridiculous my plan was. Killing Doug wouldn't achieve anything, except maybe land both my brother and me in jail. So, I let it go. I changed my mind. I gave the gun back to Todd and told him to get rid of it. There's no way in the world I killed my husband."

She stared at James so earnestly he was almost tempted to believe her, but the circumstantial evidence and her brother's testimony fit too well, and she owned a motorbike. Her brother had somehow procured a gun—probably not a difficult feat given the people he knew on the street—and she'd found Doug in his usual haunt and had mowed him down in the alleyway. She'd made her escape on the bike, thinking she'd gotten away with it. And she almost had.

With a sigh of resignation, he packed up his notepad and pen and stared across at Janice. "You've done a good job of convincing me. The only thing you forgot to do was tell the truth." He sighed again. "Janice Carter, you're going to be charged with the murder of Douglas Hanley."

Fear flooded her features. "No! You can't do this! I didn't do it! It wasn't me! I swear! I changed my mind! You have to believe me!"

"Unfortunately, Janice, you've told one lie too many, including those you told during the polygraph. Now, I suggest you engage the services of a lawyer and try telling your story to him. You want to hope like hell he can come up with a suitable defense because from where I'm sitting, you're all out of options."

With that, he pushed away from the table and stood, intent on bringing the interview to an end. Janice's eyes turned wild with panic and desperation. She reached across and grabbed his arm, halting his progress.

"Please, Detective! You have to believe me!" she begged.

He shook her off. "I don't have to believe anything."

"I'll take the polygraph test again! I swear this time I'll tell the truth! You'll see, I'll pass this time. I swear to God, everything I've told you today has been the honest truth."

James hesitated. She seemed so genuinely distressed over the fact he didn't believe her. In fact, she was almost in tears. An air of desperation surrounded her as she collapsed back into her chair.

James stared at her and felt himself weakening. Despite everything, there was something about her story that rang true. It was possible that she'd hatched up the plan and then changed her mind. The only thing was, Doug had turned up dead.

Was it possible that someone else had wanted him killed?

It seemed more and more unlikely that it was a member of the Li family. He'd been so convinced it was Janice, but now...he wasn't so sure. What harm could it do for her to do the polygraph test again?

"All right," he heard himself saying. "I'll organize another test. In the meantime, you're spending a bit more time in here. Got it?"

She nodded. "When can I see my lawyer?"

"Whenever he can get here. I'll bring you in a phone. You can call him."

James left Janice in the interview room and found the cordless phone they kept in the squad room for just that reason. He spied Wang hunched over his computer. Returning to the interview room, he gave the phone to Janice. "Five minutes. Then it's back to the cells."

She shot him a surly look, but didn't offer a reply. After ordering a constable to stand guard outside the interview room, he returned to his desk. Wang glanced up as James sat down.

"How did you do with Carter? Did you get her to confess?"

"No. In fact, she claims it wasn't her."

"Don't they all," Wang scoffed.

James nodded slowly and then added, "The thing is, I almost believe her. I've agreed to let her re-sit the polygraph. We'll see what that brings."

Wang shot him a sly look. "Are you sure you aren't being taken in by those baby blues and big tits?"

James narrowed his eyes in irritation and refrained from providing his colleague with an answer.

Wang shook his head. "Well, if it's not Carter, then who? I thought you'd as much as eliminated the other two suspects?"

"I did." James blew his breath out on a heavy sigh. "We must be missing something. There's someone else we haven't thought of. There has to be."

The phone on Wang's desk rang and he leaned over and answered it. After listening in silence for a moment, he put his hand over the mouth piece and said to James, "It's Maureen Hanley. She's on line two. She's asking for you."

James groaned. His day just took another turn for the worse. It had been three days since she'd called him. He guessed he ought to be grateful she'd slowed things down. For a while there, she'd been calling constantly for updates. Still, there was no avoiding her. Part of the job was keeping the victim's next of kin informed of any progress. No doubt she'd heard about Janice's arrest. He wondered what she made of it. All of a sudden, he was curious to find out. He headed to his desk and picked up the phone.

"Maureen, it's lovely to hear from you. I hope you've been keeping well."

As he expected, Maureen expressed surprise over Janice's arrest. "I was sure it was that Asian woman, or at least a member of her family. They're not like us, those foreigners. And to think my poor misguided boy actually *married* one!

They should all go back to where they come from. That's what *I* think."

James bit his tongue in an effort to hold back an icy blast of anger. Her racist attitude was appalling and yet she was totally oblivious. No doubt she'd be completely unrepentant if he took her to task for it—and what good would it do, anyway? It wasn't like he was going to change her mind. Her low opinion of people who hadn't been born in her country—and in particular, Asian immigrants—appeared to be firmly entrenched. He had neither the time nor the inclination to try and persuade her otherwise.

"And now you think Janice is behind all this," Maureen continued without pause. "I would never believe her capable of it. I mean, we didn't always see eye to eye—to tell you the truth, I didn't think any woman was good enough for my son—but I never imagined she'd kill him. Are you *sure* it was her?"

"No, Maureen, we're not sure," James replied through gritted teeth.

"But they said on the news she'd been arrested. Doesn't that mean you think she did it?"

"You shouldn't believe everything you hear, Maureen. We're merely following a line of inquiry."

But I heard it on the radio early this morning. I—"

"Sometimes the media get it wrong. Yes, it's true that Janice was arrested, but she's only one of a number of people we're looking at."

"Oh, I see."

The woman sounded disappointed. James

could understand her reaction. It must be tough to cling to the hope that the police would find her son's killer. She probably watched enough crime shows on TV to know the longer it took, the colder the trail became and the less likely they were to find the perpetrator. So far, it appeared none of his leads had panned out.

He thought of Sally-Ann and felt a surge of gratitude. He wouldn't pretend he wasn't happy that she was as good as off the suspect list. Now that he knew her better, he was certain there was no way she was involved in this. No, there was someone else out there who knew all about Douglas Hanley's murder. All James had to do was find him.

CHAPTER 18

Hung Wang scanned through the pile of new emails in his inbox. There were the usual messages from the police union, the boss, a few jokes forwarded from other colleagues. He never responded in kind. No doubt they included him because they thought he was the Hung Wang who now lay in a shallow grave in thick bushland west of the city.

Getting the man's passwords on the pretext of helping him with some home computer glitches had been a stroke of luck. And finding the notebook with all his work and personal codes and login information had provided the icing on the cake.

It had become obvious after reading through the real Hung Wang's emails and listening to his phone messages that the man had been much more sociable than he was. Over the years, his failure to respond to invitations and engage in kind with his colleagues had the desired effect. Gradually, the invitations petered out and the jokes were a lot less frequent, too. And that's exactly how he'd wanted it to be.

He wasn't sure how well his colleagues knew the real Hung Wang, but in the early days especially, he'd kept a low profile, relieved that his physical appearance was so like the man he'd replaced. He continued to worry about other ways of being recognized. It wouldn't do for someone to wonder why he didn't seem like his usual self or to ask too many questions. It had worked well for the past sixteen years.

He kept scrolling through his emails and spied the one he was looking for. Adrenaline surged through him. With a quick check to ensure no one was watching, he opened the message and read its contents. The message was brief:

Eliminate them all.

The words, so sweet and succinct, sent anticipation rushing through his veins. Finally, after sixteen long years, the end was in sight. All that time away from his home country and everything familiar and good. His only child would now be grown. *Would the boy even know him?* If his bitch of an ex-wife had followed through with her threat to alienate their boy from him, the answer was probably not. The knowledge pained him.

Still, that was in the future. For now, he had the Li family to deal with. After all the pain and torment Chao Li had caused him, he was looking forward to finally bringing about the man's death. He'd make sure it was slow and painful. He couldn't wait to put his plan into action. But first, he was going to take the time to let them know he was onto them. To turn the screw a bit.

The thought of the fear that this knowledge would instill in Chao's heart filled him with glee. Finally, the man would know what it felt like to have his world ripped apart. He'd experienced a taste of it in a dark prison cell more than sixteen years earlier. Now he was about to experience it all over again, only this time, it would be worse. Far worse.

With a surge of anticipation, Hung drew a blank sheet of paper toward him and carefully composed the note. He'd learned the words by heart and they flowed from his fingers and onto the page like a dam that had just been released. The letter would alert them to his plan, but he didn't care about that. They'd be dead before they had too much time to contemplate what the threats meant or organize an escape. He'd been searching for them for more than a decade and a half. He wasn't about to let them slip through his fingers again. No, not this time. Never again. Life was sweet. Life was good. It was the beginning of the end.

A one-way ticket to the People's Republic of China had already arrived in his inbox. It was a flight he'd waited years to take. A flight that would bring an end to the pretending and take him back to where he belonged. It couldn't come soon enough.

The phone near his elbow rang and he distractedly picked it up. The receptionist downstairs told him a man by the name of Viktor Popov was in the waiting room. The man was insisting on speaking with the detectives handling the Hanley case. Wang took down the details and promised the girl he'd send someone down right away. He hung up the phone just as James came into the room. Relieved, he shoved the piece of paper in James' direction.

"There's a guy downstairs who wants to talk to you," Wang said.

James halted near his desk. "What does he want?"

"He said he wants to talk to the detective in charge of the Hanley murder."

James' eyebrows rose in surprise. "Who is it?"

"Viktor Popov. His details are all written down there." Wang indicated the piece of paper. James picked it up and read it.

"Viktor Popov. Why does that name sound familiar?"

Wang shrugged, already losing interest in the conversation. He wished James would go away so he could concentrate on more important matters. Like delivering his letter. To his relief, his partner turned away, frowning down at the paper he'd just been given. As soon as James had disappeared back down the stairs, Wang sprang into action. Quickly, he dug out an envelope from a drawer in his desk. Folding the letter twice, he slipped it into the envelope and then licked the seal closed. Stuffing the envelope into the inside pocket of his suit jacket, he logged off, pushed away from his desk and left.

James eyed the burly bald man who sat across from him and tried to work out why he looked so familiar. He hadn't bothered to run a check on Popov's name before he brought the man into a vacant interview room, but he wouldn't be surprised to find the man's name in their system. There was something about him and the way he looked at James that made him think he was familiar with the inside of a jail. Still, the man claimed to know who killed Aimee's ex-husband and after discovering late yesterday that Janice Carter had passed her second polygraph, James was definitely open to suggestions. It was now nearly two weeks since the murder and he was running out of answers.

"So, Mr Popov, you claim to have information regarding the murder of Douglas Hanley. Is that correct?"

"Correct."

The man's voice was little more than a growl. James wondered if he was always that cheery.

"So, tell me what you know."

Thirty minutes later, James was reeling in shock. Viktor Popov swore that he'd been asked by Maureen Hanley to shoot her son. He was meant to make it look like it had been done by the woman's ex-daughter-in-law.

"She has two," James said. "Was she specific about which one?"

"The Asian one. She wanted me to drop the business card of the woman's sister near the crime scene. She was hoping the police would find it and link her to the murder."

James scrawled some notes on the blank

notepad in front of him and tried not to let the witness notice his shock. Nobody but the people involved in the murder could have known about the business card he'd found at the scene. Now it seemed Popov not only knew about it, but knew how it came to be there. It was a plant. *Could Popov be telling the truth?*

Then again, perhaps the man was lying. It wouldn't be the first time a witness had come forward and refrained from telling the truth. *But what did he have to gain?* Unlike Todd Flanagan, so far, the man had asked for nothing. *Could* he be telling the truth? Could Maureen Hanley be responsible for murdering her son? If so, she'd very nearly gotten away with murder.

James cleared his throat. "So, you're telling me the victim's mother contacted you and offered you money to murder her son?"

"Yes."

"How much did she offer to pay you?"

"Twenty-thousand dollars."

"How did she know where to find you and that you'd be willing to take on the job?"

Popov sighed. "She told me she'd seen me on TV. A couple of months ago, a lawyer by the name of Sally-Ann Li represented my son. He was given three years in jail. To say I was furious with that bitch was an understatement. She didn't even try to get him off! So what if he had a criminal record? That didn't mean he was guilty this time! I'm certain she was convinced he'd done it all along. She never even put up a fight. I could have smashed her face in."

James curbed his impatience. "What does this have to do with Maureen Hanley?"

Popov glared at him. "Hold your horses. I'm getting there. See, the thing is, Maureen saw me talking to the media afterwards. I got a bit heated about my son being sent to jail. The poor kid's only sixteen! Sixteen! Fuck! I told the reporters I blamed Sally-Ann Li for putting him there."

James tensed. At last, he was beginning to see. "So, Maureen Hanley contacted you, knowing you had a gripe against the sister of her former daughter-in-law and asked you to do her a favor. Did she tell you about her connection to your son's lawyer?"

Popov smiled with satisfaction. "Oh, yeah. She told me all right. She thought it would sweeten the deal."

"And did it?"

"It sure did. I wanted that lawyer bitch to pay."

"So it was *you* who shot and killed Douglas Hanley."

"No."

James started in surprise. "No?"

"No."

"But you just said—"

"What I said was that Maureen Hanley asked me to shoot her son. I didn't say I did it."

James frowned, his patience at an end. "Listen, Mr Popov, you'd better stop talking in riddles or I'll charge you with obstruction as well as the murder of Douglas Hanley right here and now. Did you kill Maureen Hanley's son, or not?"

"No, I didn't. I took the money and told her she

could consider it done, but I had no intention of murdering that bastard, even as payback for my son. What do you think I am? Stupid?"

James shook his head, confused. "So, who killed him?"

"I don't know. I guess you'll have to ask Maureen."

Sally-Ann spooned coffee into her mug and filled it from the instant hot water faucet. The staff tearoom was empty. Most people had already finished their morning break. She thought about the night before and the way she and James had made love. No wonder she was tired and sore. They'd been insatiable. Even now, the memory of their night together made her blush.

And then she remembered the arrival of her father and how angry and hurt he'd been that he'd found her with James—a police detective. She understood his reaction and she was truly sorry for the hurt she'd caused, but the truth was, she was an adult. She was entitled to make her own choices in life, including choosing the men she'd spend her time with.

With a sigh, she picked up her cup and headed back to her office. She should call her dad and apologize and hope that he'd be able to get past his anger and disappointment and see things from her point of view. Determined to do what she could to smooth things over, she set her mug down on her desk and seated herself. Pulling the phone toward her, she went to dial her father's number. Before she could do so, her secretary buzzed.

"Sally-Ann, I have your father out here. He'd like to see you. He says it's urgent."

Sally-Ann bit her lip in indecision. She considered saying she was busy with a client and then finally decided now was as good a time as any to clear the air.

"Thank you, Barbara. Could you please send him in?" She pushed away from her desk. Before she could stand, the door opened and her father rushed in.

"Sally-Ann! Thank goodness! I wasn't sure if you were in!"

She frowned at the panic in his voice and the perspiration that had popped out on his brow. "What it is, Dad? What's the matter?"

"They've found us, Sal! Oh, God! They've found us! What are we going to *do*?"

Sally-Ann shook her head in confusion. "Who's found us, Dad? What are you talking about?"

"*This!*" He shoved a piece of paper toward her. She took it and scanned the writing. It was a letter of some sort. A threatening letter.

I know who you are and I know where you live.

Those last words on the page slowly sank in. She looked back at her father.

"Where did you get this?"

"It was in my letterbox, right outside the house. Someone knows, Sal! Someone knows where we live!"

She looked at the words again and was filled with a growing disquiet. For all her father's paranoia, she'd always put a level of stock in his concerns.

"This came with it."

She looked up. Her father held out two more sheets of paper. One of them was a recent colored photograph of her and her father standing outside his house. The other was a black-and-white picture of their family, dated sixteen years ago. Dread formed an icy block in her belly.

"See! I told you! They know, Sal. They *know!* They know who we are! Oh, God! They've found us! It's exactly what I've feared all these years. What are we going to do? Where are we going to hide?" he wailed.

At the distress in her father's voice, Sally-Ann came out of her daze. With a shake of her head, she cleared her throat and took control.

"We're going to call James," she said. "He'll know what to do."

"No!" her father cried. "No police! He's one of them! He's probably behind this!"

"Don't be silly, Dad," she snapped. "There's no way James is involved in this."

Her father remained unmoved. "But he knows, doesn't he? He knows more than he should. You told him about us, about China, didn't you?"

She ignored the stab of guilt. "Yes, I did, Dad. I had to. How else could I explain the failed polygraph?"

"Oh, daughter! How *could* you! We've been so careful all these years! What are we going to *do?*" he wailed.

Sally-Ann stood her ground. "It's not him, Dad. I'm sure of it. He'd never do something like this." As she said the words, she prayed silently they were true. To accept otherwise was unthinkable. She leaned over her desk and picked up the phone. "I'm going to call him, Dad."

Amid further protests, she dialed James' number and listened while the call went through to voicemail. She left a message for him to call her as soon as possible. Whatever her father said, she refused to believe James was responsible. No way. Not now, not ever. She hoped her faith in him wouldn't prove to be their downfall.

James made his way up Maureen Hanley's driveway and climbed the steps to her front door. They'd been blessed with another fine summer day. The sky was clear and blue and the sun was bright and high in the sky. He wished for a moment that he had the luxury of a day off where he could spend it relaxing on the beach. With that thought, the urge to light up a cigarette drifted through him, but it wasn't quite as sharp as the last time. He was fifty-eight days in on his quit program and things were starting to look up.

With a sharp rap on the wooden panel, he waited for Maureen to answer. He hadn't called ahead and he was taking a chance that she'd be home. It was nearly lunch time. He seemed to recall her telling him during one of their frequent phone calls that she always ate at home. Something about her many allergies.

The front door opened and Maureen stared at him in surprise. She wore a pair of tailored denim shorts and a white T-shirt. She was of medium height and weight and still had a trim figure. He wondered what she did to stay fit and then shrugged away the thought. How she maintained her fitness was of no real consequence. What concerned him was whether she'd murdered her son.

"Detective, what a surprise! To what do I owe this pleasure?"

"Hello, Maureen. It's good to see you. Do you mind if I come in?"

"No, of course not. Please, follow me."

She led him down a short corridor that ended in an open concept kitchen and living room. It was furnished with pieces that were dated but obviously expensive. He tried to recall what Doug's father had done. Janice had told him the man had passed away the previous year.

"Would you like a cup of tea or coffee, Detective?"

"No, thanks. I'm fine. I'd like to ask you a few questions, if you don't mind."

Maureen frowned, but her smile remained largely in place. "Of course. Ask away."

"Do you know a man by the name of Viktor Popov?"

James watched her closely. Her eyes widened in surprise and then fear chased a shadow across her face. He gazed at her steadily, wondering if she'd tell the truth.

"Popov, did you say? No, I don't think so. Should I?"

"He claims you contracted with him to kill your son."

The room filled with her laughter as she threw back her head and lost herself in mirth. Tears ran down her cheeks. It was a long moment later that she once again was able to speak.

"Oh, Detective! Is that all you've been able to come up with? I know you've been under pressure to find Doug's killer, but really, isn't it a bit much to accuse me, his grieving mother? Perhaps I need to speak with your superior. It sounds like you need some time off. As if I'd ever do anything to hurt my baby. The very idea is ludicrous."

As she spoke, her humor disappeared and was replaced by a hardness in her eyes. James stared at her, taken aback by the transformation. It was like he was seeing her for the first time. His gaze moved around the room and then glanced off a shiny black motorbike helmet. He immediately zeroed in on it and once again addressed Doug's mother.

"Does that belong to you?" He indicated the helmet that sat on a low table on the other side of the room.

Maureen followed the direction of his gaze and nodded. "Yes. Although strictly speaking, I inherited it from my late husband. He loved to ride."

"Did he own a motorbike?" James asked casually.

"Yes, a real beauty. A Yamaha R1. You won't find a finer bike."

"Where is it now?"

"In the garage, of course."

"Do you ride?"

Her eyes narrowed as she appeared to contemplate her response. "Not really. I guess I take it out every now and then. It doesn't do the engine any good to have it sitting around idle for too long."

James' heart picked up its pace and adrenaline surged through his veins. Coupled with Popov's evidence, the bike was just too much of a coincidence. Maureen was about the same size as the person described by the eyewitness. She admitted to owning and riding a bike that also fit the MO. The only thing missing was the gun, but James was prepared to work on that. He pulled out a set of handcuffs and approached her.

"Maureen Hanley, you're under arrest for the murder of Douglas Hanley."

"I'm under arrest! You have to be kidding! What is the meaning of this?" She stepped away from him and before he knew what was happening, she'd opened a drawer in an ornately carved wooden credenza and produced a handgun.

James froze. He'd arrived there without backup. Wang had been caught up elsewhere and James hadn't wanted to wait. Besides, he hadn't thought Maureen Hanley would pose much of a threat. For all her fitness, he loomed over her and outweighed her by at least fifty pounds. But he hadn't been counting on her being armed. There was a chance this might go very wrong.

"Stay where you are!" she ordered and waved the gun in his direction.

After his initial shock, his training kicked in. "Maureen, now listen. Don't do anything stupid. Put the gun down. You need to come down with me to the station where we can talk properly."

"No! I'm not going to jail for anyone and especially not for that ungrateful shit!"

"Who are you talking about?"

"My son, Douglas, of course! First he breaks my heart by marrying that piece of Asian trash and just when I had him back for myself, he gets blinded by a little slut with big tits! Can you believe it? How could he do that to me? His mother? After everything I did for him! He'd be nothing without me! Nothing!"

James watched her closely, waiting for his moment. It came a short time later. In the middle of her rant, she turned to scream abuse at Doug's photo. It hung on the wall behind her. James leaped forward and knocked her to the ground. At the same time, he wrestled the gun from her hand. She kicked and screamed and shouted abuse, but he was deaf to it all. Clamping on the handcuffs, he dragged her to her feet and frog marched her out the door.

On the way to the station, his prisoner continued to hurl abuse from the back seat. He remembered how, from the very first moment, she'd pointed them in Aimee's direction, including being emphatic the last call her son had made had been to Aimee Li's phone. After an examination of the phone, James had been able to prove that was a lie and now he understood her motivation. She'd done everything she could to steer the police and anyone else away from her—and for a while, it had worked.

"Where did you learn to shoot, Maureen?" he asked in a conversational tone.

She stopped her current rant midstream and looked at him in surprise. "I've always known how to shoot. My father used to take me to the rifle range. I was the youngest of five daughters. I was the only one interested in that kind of stuff. I went with my father everywhere and did things a son would have done. He was so proud of me. He's been gone ten years, but I still miss him."

"What do you think he'd say about what you've done?"

Her lips tightened and she fell silent. James glanced at her through the rearview mirror and saw tears pooling in her eyes. So, she felt some remorse, or maybe she was just feeling sorry for herself. Whatever it was, it no longer mattered. This wouldn't be over until she'd confessed on record for all the world to see.

Satisfaction surged through him. Soon, the case would be over and the perpetrator locked up behind bars. It was where she belonged after planning and executing the murder of her son. He supposed he owed Janice an apology and he'd make sure he put in a good word with the homicide team on behalf of her brother.

"Where did you get the gun, Maureen?" he asked quietly, hoping to once again catch her in a moment of weakness.

The woman who sat behind him sighed heavily. "It belonged to my husband."

"Was he licensed to carry such a firearm?"

"Yes, of course he was! Henry Hanley was a fine upstanding citizen! I... I kept the gun when he died. It reminded me of him. He used to love shooting for sport. He said it kept him young."

"You're meant to hand them in when the owner dies," James said in a mild tone.

Maureen shrugged. "No one came and asked for it. Besides, it came in handy."

As she said the words, her eyes widened in fear and color leached from her cheeks. James pulled over to the curb and switched on the recording device he kept in the car.

"Maureen, is there something you'd like to tell me? We can do this here, if you like. I'm recording this conversation. If you feel up to talking, go ahead."

She shook her head helplessly back and forth and the tears overflowed and ran down her cheeks.

"I didn't mean to do it! I was so mad! All his life, I'd helped things run more smoothly. I did his assessments during high school and his papers at college. I bought him his first car. I helped him secure a good job and I gave him the deposit for his first house. Henry always told me I was spoiling the boy; that he'd grow up feeling entitled, but it wasn't like that. At least, not in the beginning."

She sniffed. "Then he went to college and discovered girls. That's how he repaid me for all the things I'd done for him. He married a girl from the Orient! Can you believe it? He knew how I felt about people like that. I always told him they couldn't be trusted. And he goes and brings one home! It was disgraceful!"

With an effort, James held onto his temper. This wasn't about him. He needed to keep her talking.

"Is that why you shot him?"

"Yes! Well, it was one of the reasons. Let's just say, there were a few. He hadn't even left the Asian woman before he was bedding the Carter slut. Here I was rejoicing that things hadn't worked out between him and Aimee and then he tells me he's in love with the rehab nurse!" She shook her head in disgust. "I raised him better than that! He should have never married at all. I was perfectly capable of helping him through life. I'd done it for the first eighteen years or so. I could have done it indefinitely. He didn't need any other women in his life. It was too bad for him he didn't see it like that."

"He took your love for granted," James said, injecting sympathy into his tone.

"You bet he did!" she cried.

The whole sorry story was falling into place. "But then his marriage to Janice failed and all was good in your world," James stated.

"Yes. When he moved back in with me after breaking up with Janice, I could hardly conceal my delight. At last, he'd seen sense and had returned to where he belonged. He was under my roof, next door to my room. He was home where he needed to be. Where *I* needed him to be."

"And when he told you he was going back to Aimee, after all that had happened, you simply couldn't allow it," James guessed.

"Too right, I couldn't! I'd lost him once; I'd lost him twice. I wasn't going to lose him a third time! He'd passed me over two times too many. It wasn't going to happen again."

"Hell hath no fury," James murmured and was struck by the coincidence of how two of the women in Douglas Hanley's life had arrived at the same destination. Only one of them had carried through with their deadly plan.

"So, you came up with the idea to get rid of him. By chance, you saw Viktor Popov on TV. He was angry about Sally-Ann Li and the way she'd represented his son. You knew Sally-Ann was Aimee's sister. You got into contact with Popov and asked him to shoot your son."

Maureen's face twisted in fury. "I paid that thieving bastard twenty thousand dollars! He took the money and then reneged on our deal! When I confronted him and asked for my money back, he laughed in my face! And then he had the nerve to come back a few weeks later and ask for more! He's lucky I didn't put a bullet through *his* head."

James nodded. Her recount was consistent with the statement Popov had provided, although the man had failed to mention he'd come back a second time. No doubt he'd threatened Maureen about going to the police if she didn't come up with the cash. She should have known there was no honor among thieves...

"So you decided to deal with Doug yourself, right?" he asked casually.

"I was left with no other choice. The man I'd paid to do the job had done nothing but steal my money. That's when I knew I had to do the thing myself."

"You knew where to find Doug that night," James stated.

"Of course I did! For the past ten years, his routine's never changed! I knew where to find him and I knew when he'd be leaving for the night. I waited for him in that alleyway and I called to him on his way out. I shot him right in the middle of the forehead. At the time, I was glad. Now, I wish I hadn't done it. I miss him all the time. And he's gone forever. I'll never see him again!"

A sob broke forth and she leaned forward and despite the handcuffs around her wrists, awkwardly buried her face in her hands. James let her cry for a while and then resumed his questioning.

"Did you leave Sally-Ann's business card near the body?"

"Yes." Maureen choked out the word through her sobs.

"You wanted it to look like it had been her, or at least one of the members of her family."

"Yes! I'm sorry! I shouldn't have done it! I just want my son back! I just want him *back!*" Her wail of despair filled the squad car, along with her tortured sobs. In other circumstances, James might have felt sorry for her, but knowing how selfish and cold-hearted she'd been, he felt nothing but disgust. The moment when he formally charged her with the murder of her son couldn't come soon enough.

It was hours later that James eventually had time to check his phone. Maureen Hanley had been formally charged with the murder of her son and had been refused bail. She'd appear in court in the morning and that would be soon enough for James to face her again. He still couldn't believe she'd done it. If it hadn't been for Popov coming forward, she might very well have gotten away with it.

He shook his head at the thought and glanced down at his phone. There were three missed calls from Sally-Ann. He put the phone up to his ear and dialed into his message bank. Each time, she sounded a little more scared as she asked him to call her urgently. Without wasting another moment, he did as she'd asked.

CHAPTER 19

Sally-Ann stared out of her office window and watched the day slowly die. It had been hours since she'd met with her father. She'd left three messages for James, but she hadn't heard from him and with every minute that passed, she became increasingly more concerned that perhaps her father was right.

Was James somehow involved with the threatening letter? When she'd told him about how her family had fled from the Chinese authorities all those years ago, she hadn't dreamed he would use the information against them and yet, how else had the author of the letter become aware of who they really were? Everything inside her rebelled at the thought he might have betrayed her and her family, but she hadn't told anyone else. *What other conclusion could she draw?*

Resting her cheek against the cool glass, she tried to get her head around the possibility that the man she'd spent such a heavenly night with and for whom she was developing real feelings could have behaved so traitorously. She groaned in anguish.

The sound of her cell phone vibrating against her desk interrupted her tormented thoughts. She'd turned the phone to silent during a meeting with a young client earlier that afternoon and hadn't yet switched the ring back on. Abandoning her position near the window, she returned to her desk and picked it up.

James.

He'd given her his personal cell number before he left for work that morning. Had it only been that morning that she'd been deliriously happy and contemplating a future that included him? It seemed almost unbelievable when she considered the dark clouds that had gathered since. She only hoped he could reassure her that he had nothing to do with any of it and dispel her fears.

"James," she said.

"Sally-Ann! I just got your messages. I'm so sorry, I've been flat out at work. You wouldn't believe what happened! Maureen Hanley confessed to murdering Doug. She murdered her own son!"

Forgetting her own troubles momentarily, Sally-Ann gasped in shock. "Are you *sure*? That sounds unbelievable!"

"Yes, almost unbelievable, but it's true. We found a witness who told us she'd contracted him to kill Doug. I confronted her about it and she confessed to doing it herself. We've spent the rest of the day recording her formal interview.

Thankfully for us, she didn't retract any of what she'd said."

Sally-Ann shook her head, still in shock. "I don't believe it. I really don't believe it! Maureen Hanley? I would never have suspected her. She loved Doug almost to the point of obsession."

"Yes, I think that was the problem. She wasn't happy when he married your sister and didn't feel too kindly toward Janice, either. When both of his marriages fell apart and she finally had him back to herself, he started showing signs of reigniting his interest in Aimee. Maureen couldn't handle the thought of losing him a third time—and to your sister, no less. She had less than flattering terms to describe Aimee. It's obvious the woman's unhinged."

"So, who actually shot him? The man she contracted?"

"No. Maureen was almost proud of the fact she shot him herself. The hired killer took her money and then refused to follow through. She decided the only way to see the deed done was to do it herself. Her deceased husband owned a Yamaha R1 motorbike. He also had a nine millimeter Glock. She used both. She went into the city, waited for Doug outside his usual haunt and then shot him dead."

"I still don't believe it! And I know Aimee will struggle with it, too. None of us suspected Doug's mother. Not even once."

"Don't feel too bad about it," James replied. "She wasn't on my radar, either. I'm just glad we caught her and that she'll be forced to face justice. I'll be surprised if she gets less than ten to fifteen, and so she should. She killed her own son in cold blood and all because she was jealous of the fact he chose the company of other women to hers."

"You're right," Sally-Ann murmured. "She's sick. Who does that to a person they care about? Their own flesh and blood?"

James sighed. "It never ceases to amaze me what human beings are capable of. In my line of work, I see the worst of it."

"It must be hard," she said quietly, feeling for him.

"Yeah, sometimes it's a bitch."

Silence fell between them. James was the first to break it. "You sounded worried on the phone. Is something wrong?"

Sally-Ann contemplated whether she should burden him even further with her problems and then pushed the thought aside. She was almost certain he had nothing to do with leaking their whereabouts to whoever had sent the note. She needed to trust him until he proved otherwise.

"My father dropped by my office this morning. He brought a note with him. It was delivered to their house, earlier. It contained a message and some photos that made him think someone knew about his true identity and the life he'd fled from in China. It was threatening." She paused and then added, "Did you tell anyone what I told you about my parents?"

"No, of course not," came the swift denial.

Sally-Ann sighed in relief. "Then who could have sent it? No one else knew."

"I have no idea. Are you sure they really know who he is? Could it have been a fishing expedition?"

"We're pretty sure the person knows. There was a photo taken of my family in China when I was just thirteen. It was outside our house in Beijing. The photo was dated and included with the letter my father received, along with one taken recently. I don't think there's any doubt whoever sent them has made the connection."

"Where's the letter now?"

"I have it in my office."

"All right. I'll come right over. I'm as good as finished here for the day. I'll see you soon."

She ended the call and for the first time since her father had arrived at her place of work that morning, the dread that had been churning in her stomach eased. James was on his way. He'd know what to do. He'd take care of things. He was a cop. He went after the bad guys and locked them up. It's what he did.

———————

James tossed his cell phone into the pocket of his shirt and pushed away from his desk. Following the arrest of Maureen Hanley, a search warrant had been executed on her house. The bike, with the keys still in it, was found in the garage out back, along with a diary Maureen had kept for many years.

Inside it were pages and pages of vicious

ramblings on every girl her son had ever dated, going all the way back to high school. She'd been thrilled when the boating accident that left Aimee in a wheelchair also brought an end to their marriage. And when Janice had walked out after Doug revealed he had no desire for children, she'd celebrated with champagne and flowers. Sally-Ann was right. The woman was sick.

"Good job on that Hanley case," Wang said, interrupting James' thoughts.

"Yeah, we got lucky." James pulled on his jacket and hunted around on his desk for his keys.

"Where are you off to?" Wang asked. "I thought we might go and have a celebratory drink. It's not every day we close a murder investigation so quickly and with a full confession, no less. You did well."

James looked across at Wang where he sat at his desk. "Thanks, but I'm on my way over to see Sally-Ann Li."

His colleague cocked an eyebrow and threw James a knowing grin. "Ah, I see. Like that, is it? No wonder you weren't interested in the buxom Janice."

Heat crept up James' neck and slowly spread across his cheeks. He was annoyed at his reaction. Sally-Ann had been cleared of any wrongdoing. He was an adult and so was she. They were allowed to see whoever they wanted. He stared with defiance in Wang's direction.

"As a matter of fact, it is. I like her and she likes me. We're seeing each other."

Wang laughed. "Good for you! I'm happy for

you. Not only do you close a murder investigation, you also get the girl."

"Yeah, well, thanks." He picked up his keys. "I've got to go. Sally-Ann needs me."

Wang frowned. "Is everything all right?"

"Yeah, it's fine. She's just a little upset about something her father received. I'm going to see if there's anything I can do to reassure her and cheer her up."

Wang grinned and then winked. "A good-looking guy like you, I'm sure you'll think of something."

The phone on James' desk rang. He glanced at it, tempted to ignore it. Sally-Ann needed him and he was as good as finished for the day. The phone continued to ring.

"Are you going to answer that?" Wang asked.

With a muffled curse, James reached over and picked up the receiver. "Detective Shepherd."

He listened while the receptionist downstairs told him there was someone wanting to see him.

"Who is it?"

"I'm afraid he wants to surprise you, Detective. I'll send him up."

James hung up the phone and frowned. *Who could it be?* Obviously a fellow police officer. No one else was allowed upstairs unescorted. He turned and strode toward the door that led to the stairwell. He only made it halfway across the room when the door opened and a familiar face appeared.

"Jett Craigdon! What the hell are you doing here?" James stepped forward and enveloped his former partner with enthusiasm.

Jett grinned. "I was in the neighborhood and thought I'd drop by and say hello."

James laughed. "Man, it's been years! What have you been doing with yourself?"

Jett held up his left hand and wiggled his fingers. Light bounced off a wedding ring. "I went and got myself married. We have a couple of kids and a few months back, moved out into the suburbs. Life's good."

James shook his head in bemusement. "Wow, I'm happy for you. She must be pretty special to take you on."

Jett chuckled. "Oh, yeah. Danielle is more than special. She's the best."

Becoming aware of Wang seated behind them, James turned and introduced Jett. "This is a guy I used to work with years ago," he said. "Jett Craigdon, meet Hung Wang."

Hung nodded in Jett's direction. Jett acknowledged the greeting, frowning slightly. "Hung Wang. I used to work with a Hung Wang a long time ago. I was a rookie police officer and he was a detective."

Hung stared at him in silence for a moment and then a smile split wide his face. "Jett! Hell, I didn't recognize you as that fresh-faced probationary constable from all those years ago! How have you been?"

Jett's frown deepened. "Hung? Are you the Hung I used to know?"

Hung chuckled. "Of course it's me! It must be all these wrinkles and gray hairs that have put you off. I agree, life hasn't treated me as kindly as you.

You're in good shape, buddy. Married life must be agreeing with you."

Jett nodded a little uncertainly. "Yeah, it is. I'm sorry you've been doing it tough. You look...different."

Once again, Hung chuckled. "You're right. I've taken a few knocks over the years and I'm a fair bit older than you. I don't bounce back like I used to."

"Yeah, I guess," Jett replied slowly.

James punched Jett lightly on the arm. "It's so good to see you! How long are you in the city?"

"I've been in court all day giving evidence in a drug trial. I had a few spare minutes and thought I'd call in and see if you were here."

James smiled. "Well, it's been good to see you."

"Yeah," Jett replied. "You, too."

"Listen, mate, I hate to cut this visit short, but I'm on my way out. I'm meeting someone."

"Hey, no problem. I'll catch you later. Here's my card."

"Thanks. It was good to see you. I'll call you." James slipped the card into his wallet. With a final quick handshake, he collected his things and headed for the exit.

———————————

Hung stared at James' retreating back and waited for the door to close behind him. Jett Craigdon hovered near Hung's desk, making him nervous. Of all the luck to run into someone who'd known the real Hung Wang. He'd managed to pull off the subterfuge for sixteen years, and now, on the eve of bringing the whole awful assignment to an end, he was being confronted by someone who could blow his cover apart.

"So, you've worked here all this time?" Jett asked, his tone conversational.

Hung gritted his teeth and answered. "Yes. I enjoy the work and the location. There wasn't any reason to leave."

"Are you still living at Epping?"

"No, I moved closer to the city."

"I bet you're still drinking everyone here under the table, right?" Jett grinned.

Hung forced a laugh. "Of course. I have to uphold my reputation, don't I?"

Jett chuckled. "It sounds like not everything has changed, then." He shook his head, as if beset with memories. Hung was relieved when the man said, "Anyway, I guess I'd better get going. It was good to see you again."

"Yes, you too. Take care of that family of yours."

Jett nodded. "Thanks."

He turned and headed to the door. Hung breathed a surreptitious sigh of relief. Almost instantaneously, he dismissed that worry and was filled with a rush of impatience. His colleague was on his way to see Sally-Ann Li because of something her father had received. *It had to be the letter.*

Hung had driven by the Li family home in the early hours of the morning and had slipped the envelope in their mailbox. Chao must have found the letter and taken it to his daughter. Given that she was a lawyer, that wasn't surprising. The timing was too coincidental for it to be anything else. He hadn't counted on a relationship developing between Sally-Ann and James... Now she'd called James to discuss it, and no doubt ask his advice...

His colleague was smart. He'd immediately try and find out who left the note and photos at the Li home. Hung had been given authority from the top to take action. There was no point in waiting any longer. He needed to act fast. Soon, he'd be on a plane back to China.

After sixteen long years, he'd return a hero. His cousin's oversight would be forgiven. Doors that had once been slammed shut would be opened. He'd return to his rightful place within the People's Liberation Army and his trusted and revered position in the government.

The sweet taste of success flooded his senses and he was filled with a surge of adrenaline. The time had come to destroy the Zhang family. Soon, there would be no trace of them or the identity they'd taken on so many years ago. And that's exactly what they deserved for betraying their glorious homeland.

Shutting down his computer, he opened his briefcase and stowed the final bits and pieces that evidenced his time in the detectives' squad room of the City of Sydney Police. Ever since his discovery of the real identity of Chao and Fen Li, he'd been slowly removing any trace of his presence at the station. When his final act of retribution came to fruition, he'd disappear among the crowds at Mascot Airport, bound for the country of his birth.

His colleagues would wonder about his abrupt disappearance. They'd be even more perplexed when they realized he'd vanished without any trace, like a ghost. Even his apartment was now bare. There was no evidence left to link him to the deaths of the Li family.

The media would have a field day when the bodies were eventually found. He was counting on them to make the connection; linking the death of Douglas Hanley and the arrest of Doug's mother for murder, with the bodies of the Li family. Perhaps they'd even speculate that Maureen Hanley had been the one to organize the hit from her jail cell in a final act of prejudice and hate. Anything for a sensationalized story. Journalists would stop at nothing for a front page opportunity.

With a bit of luck, the deaths of the Li family would be just another unexplainable homicide that would leave detectives scratching their heads and trying their best to link it to Maureen Hanley or the number of other shadowy possibilities that had been unearthed—namely Todd Flanagan and Viktor Popov. There was always the possibility the police might find the note Hung wrote, but he'd been willing to take that risk. Whatever they decided, it wouldn't impact on him. He'd be long gone, never to return.

With a furtive glance around the squad room to ensure he was alone, he pulled out a handkerchief and carefully wiped the monitor, the keyboard, the desk and all the drawers, eliminating every smudge and print that might have been left behind over the course of his time in the squad room. At last, he was satisfied that this part of his life would no longer exist.

And then he pushed away from his desk, picked up his jacket and briefcase. Next he went to the gun room. Ignoring the requirement to sign out his service revolver, he collected the gun and stowed it in the holster on his belt. Without a second glance, he quietly exited the room.

———

James gave his name to the receptionist and was directed to the tenth floor. The elevator whisked him upwards in near silence and after greeting Sally-Ann's secretary, he was quickly shown to her office. She stood as he entered and walked straight into his arms. He pulled her close and pressed a kiss against her hair.

She felt so right, like she belonged there in his embrace. Memories of their night of passion rushed through his mind and he knew he wanted to spend many more nights like that. In fact, he wanted to spend *all* his nights like that, with her. He hoped she felt the same way, but right now, he had to figure out what was going on with her father and the curious letter she'd mentioned.

Gradually, he loosened his hold on her and allowed her to step away. She moved over to her desk and picked up a piece of paper and brought it over to him. He took it out of her hand and read it.

"You said your dad gave you this. Where did he find it?" he asked.

"It was in his mailbox."

"Was there anything else with it?"

She went back to her desk and picked up an envelope. She came back to him and he pulled out two more pieces of paper. They were the photographs she'd mentioned. He turned them over. On the back of the black-and-white one there were Chinese letters and a date stamp. James handed it back to Sally-Ann.

"Can you read this?" he asked.

She looked at the letters in surprise. "I didn't see these earlier."

"What does it say?"

She looked more closely and her lips tightened. Fear shadowed her face. He tensed and his heart skipped a beat.

"What is it?" he asked.

She looked up at him and worry darkened her eyes. "It says Lu, Lihua, Biyu and ChangChang Zhang."

"Who are they?"

"I was born ChangChang Zhang. My sister was first named Biyu and my parents were Lu and Lihua Zhang. When we came to Australia, Dad insisted we change our names. And so we did."

"So this is you and your family in China? Before you arrived here?"

"Yes."

A sense of foreboding trickled through his veins and settled in an icy lump in his gut. Why would someone send such a letter and include the photos unless they were up to no good? And even *if* they were up to no good, why would they send the pictures and give themselves away? They obviously knew about the Li/Zhang family secret, a secret the family thought they'd kept hidden for sixteen years. As far as he knew, he was the only person who'd been let in on their circumstances and their fears—and he sure as hell hadn't said a word.

"Who else did you tell about your past?" he asked.

Anger flashed in her eyes. "No one! What do you take me for? My father's guarded that secret for sixteen years! I only told you because…because I thought I could trust you!"

He held her away gently by the arms in an effort to calm her down. "Hey, I'm sorry. I didn't mean it like that. And of course you can trust me! I haven't breathed a word to anyone!"

She frowned in confusion. "Then if it wasn't you, who was it?"

James opened the letter again and stared at the words that were written there. The tone of the letter was acidic and he surmised it had been written by someone who held a deep-seated anger against the Li family. It went on and on about how they'd betrayed their leader and their country when they'd sold secrets to the West. Finally, it hinted that the game was up and their time on earth was limited. The final sentence chilled James to the bone.

I know who you are and I know where you live.

Something shifted in his memory and he tried to figure out what it was. He continued to stare at the words in the hope that the light bulb would go on. And then it hit him. The handwriting. He'd seen it before. He was certain of it.

He dug into his jacket pocket and pulled out a crumpled piece of paper. Smoothing it out, he saw the name and other details of Viktor Popov written there. He put the paper next to the letter and saw that the samples were the same. He frowned in confusion and disbelief.

"I don't believe it. It can't be," he murmured.

"What is it?" Sally-Ann asked, concern and curiosity clouding her voice.

"This letter. I think it was written by my colleague, Hung Wang."

Sally-Ann's frown deepened. "Do you mean the detective who came with you that day to my sister's place?"

"Yes."

"He's Chinese."

James stared at her. Of course, he'd known Wang was Chinese, but that fact had never seemed significant—or alarming. But accepting that Wang was the one threatening the Li family didn't make sense. The man had lived in Australia for years. It was almost ridiculous to think he was on the Chinese government payroll and even more ludicrous to suggest he'd been charged with the responsibility to hunt them down.

James compared the handwriting again and couldn't disregard the similarities. No matter that it didn't make sense, the evidence dictated otherwise. And then he remembered something else.

"Shit."

Sally-Ann stared at him. "What is it?"

"Wang. It's him."

"Because of the handwriting?"

"Yes, but there's something else. I told him about your father. I told him how he failed the polygraph test but that you'd explained it by telling me how he'd fled from the Chinese police."

Her eyes widened in disbelief and her face flushed with anger. "You said you didn't tell anyone!"

"I'm truly sorry Sally-Ann! I forgot! I wasn't thinking about my partner. He's a cop. I work with him on a daily basis. We tell each other lots of confidential things. I was confident he'd keep it to himself." James shook his head. "No, on second thoughts, it can't be Wang. I'd trust him with my life. He's a good cop."

"How well do you know him?" she asked quietly.

James opened his mouth and then closed it again. He thought about what she'd said and the longer he contemplated it, the more the dread in his gut grew. He realized he didn't know Wang very well at all. He'd worked with the man for six months, but what did he really know about him? He'd seen the family photograph on the man's desk, but he'd never met his wife and son. He didn't even know where they lived.

Aware that Sally-Ann waited for his answer, he finally admitted, "I don't know him very well at all."

"I see."

She said it with such a knowing air, he was forced to issue a protest. "I don't think you do. I've worked with Hung Wang for a long time. I've never had cause to wonder if he's someone he's not. I need to go and talk to him. I'm sure he can sort this out. There must be some explanation. We'll probably be laughing about this later."

Sally-Ann looked unconvinced, but he didn't give her any more time to argue. Kissing her soundly on the mouth, he set her aside and, tucking the letter and photos in his jacket pocket, he left the room.

CHAPTER 20

Hung's step was brisk as he crossed with the traffic lights and blended in with the crowd of pedestrians headed toward the train station. Ever since he'd been given the authority to get rid of the Zhang family, he'd pondered the mechanics of how to make it happen.

Chao and Fen lived together. Doing away with them would be easy, but the daughters posed a problem. They lived in separate residences in different parts of the city. With the older one being bound in a wheelchair, overpowering her wouldn't be difficult. It was the lawyer who most concerned him, particularly now that she'd grown close to his colleague.

It had taken him a little while, but at last he'd come up with a revised plan. He'd leave Aimee until last. Over the past week, he'd been following her. Her routine was more predictable. She always left her office at five. A cab would be waiting for her downstairs. It delivered her to her condo every afternoon except Thursdays. On that day, she went to the market and arrived home much later. The cab driver helped with her bags.

Today was Tuesday. If he managed to get rid of the others this afternoon, he might still have time to break into Aimee's place and lie in wait for her. It would be a simple matter to come up behind her and catch her unaware. She wouldn't even know what had happened when he put a bullet through her brain.

He'd be in and out of her place in a matter of minutes—maybe less—and no one would be the wiser. In anticipation of what was to come, he'd already hacked into the security firm that monitored her building, including the CCTV cameras and he easily unarmed both alarms and security vision. No sense in making it easy for the cops investigating the break-in and murder. By the time they figured it out—*if* they figured it out— he'd be long gone.

But first he had to complete his mission and that meant kidnapping Sally-Ann. He'd send another message to her parents to draw them out and he'd be sure to word it in such a way that there would be no doubt in their minds he meant business. He might even remind Yu Zhang about Hung's ability to torture. Yu knew firsthand how creative he could be.

It was interesting that Yu hadn't recognized him when he'd attended Yu's home. Not his face, of course. His face had always been covered. But it wasn't as easy to disguise one's voice. Hung thought Yu would hear his voice in his nightmares for the rest of his days. Apparently not.

Well, a little reminder of what Hung was capable of wouldn't hurt and he'd warn them against involving Shepherd, too. He didn't need his way-too-smart colleague involved. Then, once he had all three members of the Zhang family together, he could set about eliminating them, like he'd been ordered to do. One by one.

The cell phone in his pocket rang and he hurriedly pulled it out. James Shepherd's number flashed on the screen. *Dammit. Was the man onto him already, or was this just a work-related call?* He needed to play it cool, either way. No sense alarming his partner before he'd managed to get the deed done.

"James, how are you doing?" he responded, forcing a casual tone.

"Good, Hung. I...I was wondering if I could change my mind. I'm hoping you and I can get together this afternoon, go for a drink like you suggested? I got to thinking how we've worked together all these months and yet I barely know anything about you. I'm sorry. I've been remiss. I should have made a bigger effort to get to know you. I apologize and I'd like to make it up to you now."

Hung bit his lip in indecision. The last thing he wanted was to meet with James and lose valuable time. He'd made up his mind that today was the day. Once he'd dealt with the Zhang family, his life would once again be his own. He'd be free of the burden of searching for fugitives who'd remained hidden for so long. He could return to his homeland, reconnect with his family;

get to know his son. Why did his colleague have to choose today of all days to get friendly?

He forced a laugh. "Sorry. Something's come up. Today's not so good for me now. I've made other plans. Besides, what's there to know? I'm a pretty simple man. Let's make it next week?"

"Hey, I don't even know where you were born or where you live. I've never met your wife and son. I don't even know which football team you follow. Come on, let's go for a drink."

"I'm sorry, James. I just don't have the time. Perhaps we can do it another day?"

"Oh, come on, Hung! We just got a confession out of a murderer. Let's go out and celebrate. You suggested it earlier..."

If he hadn't already set plans in motion for the extermination of the Zhang family that afternoon, he might have been tempted. It wasn't often the men he worked with offered to spend time with him outside the office. And then another thought occurred to him. "What about Sally-Ann? I thought you were going over to see her?"

"I did. But she's busy at work. She pretty much blew me off."

Hung frowned. "I thought you said she was upset about something?"

"Yes, well she'd recovered sufficiently by the time I got to her office. I left her there poring over witness statements for her next trial. So, are you going to meet me for a drink?"

Hung shook his head almost regretfully. "I'm sorry, I really can't get away."

"Okay, I guess I'll see you tomorrow."

"We'll catch up another time," Hung promised, knowing it was a lie.

"I'm counting on it."

Hung ended the call and shoved the phone back in his pocket. Hurrying down the steps to the subway, he ran down the last few steps and jumped onto a train just as it began to pull out. He found an empty seat and threw himself down with a sigh. In less than thirty minutes, he'd be outside the Zhang family home. He patted the letter in his jacket pocket. This time, he'd slip it under the front door so that it would be noticed quickly. Then he'd catch a train back to the offices of Sydney Legal and put the second part of his plan into action. A surge of nervous excitement went through him. He couldn't wait.

The phone on Sally-Ann's desk buzzed and her secretary came on the line.

"Sally-Ann, I have the receptionist from downstairs on the line. She says she has James with her. He was wondering if you could meet him in the lobby. Apparently he has something important to tell you."

Sally-Ann frowned. James had left there less than an hour earlier, on his way back to the office. He said he was going to look into Hung Wang's background. *Had he found something relevant? Why didn't he just come upstairs?*

The questions rushed through her mind, but she

told Barbara to let him know she was on her way down. With that, she grabbed her jacket and left. Down in the lobby, she looked around. The occasional person strode into the building. Others spilled forth from the elevators and headed for the street, but James wasn't among them.

Perhaps he'd gone outside? With a shrug, she pushed open the double glass doors that guarded the entry and looked around her. The sun was sinking low and long shadows spilled over the sidewalk. Professionals in suits, and barristers in black robes and wigs, carrying smart briefcases, made their way back from court, followed by their clerks dragging trolleys laden with files. She tried to spot James in the crowd, but came up empty.

"Keep walking, Ms Li and don't try anything stupid. I have a loaded revolver less than an inch away from your spine. One wrong move and you'll end up in a wheelchair, just like your sister."

Sally-Ann froze. At the same time, she became aware of something hard digging into her back. She tried to turn to catch sight of the man who stood close behind her, but only managed to catch a glimpse of black hair and a dark suit.

"Who are you?" she managed, trying hard to keep her fear at bay.

"I'm an old friend of your family, Ms Li. Or should I say, *Ms Zhang*."

She gasped. "You're the one who sent that letter to my father!"

"Yes. And I just delivered another one. By now he should have found and read it. By the time we arrive at our destination, he and your mother should almost be there and that's when the fun will really begin."

He chuckled low in her ear and the sinister undertones sent a shiver down her spine. This was what her father had warned her about. For years, he'd drummed into them the need to keep a low profile, to never get too close to anyone, to keep the secret of their past to themselves. She'd only ever listened with half an ear, convinced her father was being melodramatic or a bit paranoid. Whatever had happened in China had taken place more than a decade and a half ago. As if the men who'd pursued her father in his homeland would still be looking for them now...

But here she was, being prodded forward at gunpoint by a man who most definitely knew who she was—and who intended to even the score against her father. *Who was he and how had he found them? Who was pulling his strings? Was he acting on orders from China or was he a lone wolf, someone with a personal vendetta?*

She clenched her jaw in frustration and wished she'd paid more attention when her father had warned them of the people who could be coming after them. She thought of James and then she thought of Detective Wang. James had left her to do some further investigating into his colleague's background. He seemed convinced something was off.

Wang. Was he the one behind this? Was it him breathing down her neck, forcing her forward at gunpoint? She thought back to the detective she'd met briefly in her sister's place the morning of Doug's death. It seemed so long ago. She kicked herself that she hadn't paid the man enough heed. She'd been too fixated on his partner.

Could it be Wang who was behind her? She decided to test it out.

"I'm not sure how you think you're going to get away with this, Detective Wang. Your colleague is already suspicious. Even now, he's back at the station looking into your background. If anything happens to me or my family, you're going to be the first person he looks at."

She could almost feel the anger as it radiated off the man behind her. His hot breath hissed in her ear. "How clever of you to remember me, *ChangChang*. I guess I'd better move quickly then if I'm to get this done before your cop boyfriend puts it all together." He prodded her hard with the gun. "Now, get a move on!"

A fresh surge of fear flooded through her and she bit her lip against crying out. She tried to eyeball the passersby, pleading with them silently to notice her distress, but most didn't even look in her direction and the few that did shot her no more than the briefest of disinterested looks.

Please, James. Please help me. Please.

James stared at his computer, perplexed. Hung Wang's personnel file filled the screen, but it wasn't the man's address or date of birth that had

James confused. No, it was the photo that all of them had taken when they were employed by the New South Wales Police Service. This one had been taken when Hung had first started at the City of Sydney Police Station. Though there was a definite resemblance, it just didn't look like him. *What the hell was going on and what did it mean?*

The phone in James' pocket vibrated against his chest and he tugged it out and answered the call.

"James, it's Jett. I've been thinking about this all afternoon. It's got me all wound up."

James frowned. "What are you talking about?"

"That detective. The one you introduced as Hung Wang."

James came alert. "What about him?"

"How well do you know him?"

James stilled. The very same question had been voiced by Sally-Ann only an hour earlier. "Why do you ask?"

"I don't know how to say this."

"Jett, for Pete's sake! Just spit it out."

"Look, I don't know who that detective is, but he isn't Hung Wang. At least, not the Hung Wang I knew."

Icy tendrils of dread slid through James' veins. "Why do you say that?"

"Okay, it's been a long time, but I knew the guy fairly well. When you left, I started asking your colleague some questions. He failed to give me the right answers."

"What did you ask him?"

"I talked about how he used to live in Epping. He went along with it. The only thing is, the Hung Wang I knew never lived in Epping."

"Maybe you were mistaken?" James ventured, not wanting to face the truth.

"No, but that doesn't matter. I also asked your partner about his reputation as a drinker. We laughed about it."

"Why does that show he isn't who he says he is?"

"Because the Hung Wang I knew didn't drink. His father was a violent alcoholic. He'd run away from home at fourteen. He never had anything to do with alcohol. He hated the stuff."

James drew in a deep breath and let it out on a heavy sigh. The dread in his gut congealed into a cold, hard mass. He thought back over the past couple of weeks, when the Li family had first hit his radar. Wang had accompanied him on most of the occasions he'd interviewed witnesses, including the members of Sally-Ann's family. His partner had displayed interest in the people, but not to the extent that James considered his interest odd. Then again, he'd been very preoccupied lately, spending hours on his computer...

Could it be Wang behind the threatening letter? Was he a Chinese spy sent to find the fugitive Li family? The idea was preposterous and James would have discounted it out of hand except Wang was Chinese, spoke fluent Mandarin and now, if Jett's accusations were to be believed, he wasn't who he pretended to be.

Who was he and where was the real Hung Wang?

James cleared his throat. "Listen, Jett. I'm in the middle of something right now, but I really appreciate your call. I have your card. I'll get back to you later, okay?"

Without waiting for a response, he ended the call and then opened the camera gallery on his phone. He scrolled through his photos and found the pictures he'd taken of Janice Carter's bike. Wang had been captured in one of the frames, standing near the bike. Working quickly, James scanned the photo into his computer and then activated the face recognition software. It took several minutes, but finally the computer found a match.

With increasing dread, James clicked on the file and opened it to an old black-and-white photo. Wang had been highlighted by the software program as a match. James peered closely at the photo. Though the man was younger, it was definitely Wang.

Looking down at the caption below the picture, James read through the names, searching for Wang's. It wasn't there. He read through the names again and counted along the row of people. Wang stood in the group third from the left. The name in the caption third from the left was Liu Wei and yet, it was clearly the Hung Wang he knew who stared back at the lens.

What was going on?

James scanned the article attached to the photograph and icy terror filled his heart. According to the article, the picture had been taken of representatives of the Chinese government during a visit to Australia sixteen years earlier.

The Li family had fled for their lives around the same time. It was too much of a coincidence. James was certain: Wang was a Chinese spy, left or sent here to hunt down the Li family, just like Chao Li had feared.

And now James had led the man straight to them by telling him about Chao's past.

As the implications formed in his mind, he stared at the screen, aghast. He was the reason Wang had found them! He'd as good as led the man to their door. There was no doubt Wang had written the threatening letter. *Was he even now making plans to have the Li family extradited back to China?*

The thought was terrifying and galvanized James into immediate action. He shot out of his chair and pulled on his jacket. He tugged out his cell phone, intent on calling Sally-Ann to warn her. Before he could put the call through, the phone rang in his hand. He glanced down at the screen, but didn't recognize the number. Tempted to let it go through to voicemail, he let out a sound of irritation and answered the call.

"Detective Shepherd."

"Detective! It's Chao Li. Please! I need your help! He has Sally-Ann! Please, he has my little girl!"

James' blood ran cold. His heart stopped dead and then took off at a gallop. His chest went so tight he could barely breathe. "W-what are you talking about?" he asked, terrified to hear the answer.

"The man who's been looking for me all these years, who sent me that threatening letter. I received another letter from him just now. It had been slipped under my front door. He says he has Sally-Ann and he's threatening to torture her. I think he was one of the men who tortured me back in China. He says if we ever want to see her alive again, we must go to him."

"Who must go to him?" James asked and tried hard to keep the fear from his voice.

"Me and my wife, Fen. He said… He said we were to tell no one, especially you."

James frowned. "He actually mentioned me by name?"

"Yes."

"Fuck." It had to be Wang. He was the only person who knew James' connection to the Li family.

"Did he leave any directions?" he asked, urgency in his voice.

"Yes. He gave me an address in Mascot."

"Near the airport," James guessed. "He's making a getaway."

"He's taking us all back to China!" Chao wailed, his voice filled with panic.

"Listen, calm down, Mr Li. He can't just do that. There's security at the airport… We don't know anything yet."

"Don't tell me to calm down! I knew this would happen! You're the reason it's happening! Sally-Ann entrusted you with our secret and you've betrayed her in the worst possible way!"

"No! I swear it wasn't me," James exclaimed. "I-I didn't mean to share that news with my colleague."

"So, you *did* tell someone! You betrayed my Sally-Ann!"

"Please, Mr Li, let me finish. I... I only told my colleague. At the time, I didn't realize he was with the Chinese government. I-I'm so sorry."

James' announcement was met with silence and then Chao spoke again. "How do I know I can trust you? You're one of them! How do I know you're not in on it, too?"

James bit down hard on a surge of impatience. "You don't," he replied through gritted teeth. "But right now, I'm the only hope you've got. I'm not involved in this, but I think I know who is. You're going to have to trust me."

"Trust you? Ha! You're a police officer! How can I do that?"

"I understand that it's going to be difficult, Mr Li, but what choice do you have? Besides, you called me, didn't you? Even when he told you not to. On some level, you must believe I'm on your side."

"I can tell my daughter cares for you," he said in a tone that was slightly less aggressive. "She's nobody's fool. If she trusts you, I have to accept she sees something in you that I don't."

James drew in a deep breath and eased it out, glad that they seemed to be getting somewhere. "Mr Li, I care for your daughter, too. In fact, I've... I've fallen in love with her." As he said the words, he realized they were true. He just hoped he was given the chance to tell her.

"The thought of your daughter in trouble terrifies me," he said quietly. "I've done some research into one of my colleagues. I'm not sure if you remember Hung Wang, but he was the detective who accompanied me to your home."

"Of course I remember! He was the Chinese officer who spoke Mandarin."

"Yes."

"I knew there was something about him. See! It's like I told you! He's a police officer and he has my baby!"

"Please, Mr Li, you need to let me help you." James heard the desperation in his voice. An eon of time seemed to pass before the man replied.

"I guess have no other choice."

James sighed heavily in relief, but there wasn't a moment to spare. "Where are you supposed to meet?"

Chapter 21

The heel of one of Sally-Ann's sandals caught on an uneven piece of pavement. She tripped and would have fallen if the detective who followed behind her hadn't reached out and hauled her upward. She let out a shriek of alarm, but was grateful for his support, even as the gun remained held in a steady position against her back.

"Don't go trying anything stupid," Wang hissed in her ear. "I could just as easily shoot you here. By the time anyone noticed, I'd be long gone."

Sally-Ann glanced around the almost-deserted parking garage and shuddered. He was right. Though the garage was nearly full of vehicles, there were very few people about and most were too far away to see or hear anything should her captor lose patience and decide to bring things to a sudden end.

She bit down hard on a sob of panic and once again, sent up a silent, desperate prayer for James to find her, though she had no idea how that might come about. He'd left her harboring serious questions about his colleague, but that didn't mean he'd come to the conclusion that Wang was the man behind the threats to her life and others in her family.

She was prodded toward an early model, navy-blue BMW 1-Series Sedan. Wang directed her to move closer. The doors unlocked at her approach and she turned in time to see the detective holding a set of keys in his free hand.

"Get in the driver's seat," he ordered, waving the gun in her face.

She stared at the lethal weapon and tried to hold on to her courage.

What were his plans for her? Would she follow all of his instructions only to be shot down in cold blood? But what choice did she have? Though he wasn't a large man, he had a sinewy strength about him that belied his slight frame. On top of that, he outweighed her by thirty or forty pounds... And then there was the gun. That alone gave him a decided advantage and one she wasn't brave enough to challenge. At least, not until she had nothing left to lose. Thankfully, she hadn't quite gotten to that point, yet.

With the gun still trained on her, she opened the door and climbed behind the wheel. Quickly, Wang got into the passenger seat and ordered her to drive.

"W-where to?" she stammered, switching on the ignition and putting the car into reverse.

"Turn left as you leave the parking garage. I'll direct you as we go."

His voice was emotionless and the coldness of it sent a shiver down her spine. With the gun still pointed at her, she had no choice but to do as he ordered. With dread filling her belly, she pulled out and merged with the heavy afternoon traffic. Another couple of turns and they were headed south-west, away from the city.

With each mile she put behind them, her fears intensified. It was only the feel of her cell phone in the pocket of her jacket that offered her some form of reassurance. At least someone could call her and she might even find the opportunity to make a call. It was also possible that if James eventually realized she was with Wang and that he posed a danger to her, he might be able to triangulate her cell phone signal and find her, or at least narrow down her location.

Those frantic thoughts went through her mind as she did her best to concentrate on the traffic. She clung to the comfort that James was already a little suspicious of his colleague. She prayed he'd found something more to alert him to the fact he needed to locate her—and fast. If he called her office, he'd be told she left more than thirty minutes earlier to meet him. That news should be enough to raise considerable concern. She just hoped he found her in time.

Twenty-five minutes later, Wang ordered her to turn into the driveway of what looked like an abandoned warehouse. The steel-and-aluminum structure was surrounded by a high wire fence with dead grass and straggly weeds lining the perimeter. He demanded she leave the car and open the rusty metal gate. He threw her a key and directed her to fit it into the large padlock that secured a thick chain around the gate. All the while his gun was trained on her.

With shaking fingers, she did as he asked and after pushing the gate open, they climbed back into the car.

Wang didn't bother getting her to close the gate behind them and Sally-Ann worried that he didn't intend to be there very long. *Would he take her inside and shoot her, leaving her for dead with nobody the wiser?* The thought was terrifying and one look at his closed expression and the coldness in his eyes and she could very much believe him capable of doing just that.

"Why are you doing this?" she asked quietly. She wanted to know why her life was about to be cut short so tragically. In the back of her mind she thought that if she could get him talking, distract him from his purpose, he might think twice about killing her or perhaps an escape route would present itself. She didn't know which, but anything was worth a shot.

"Your father broke the rules by having more than one child and is also a traitor to his country. He paid officials to look the other way when you were born, but that doesn't make it right. For sixteen long years I have been searching for him. Finally, the end is near."

The cold certainty in his words filled her heart with fear, but she needed to keep him talking.

"You talk in riddles. My father is no traitor. You've mistaken him for someone else."

Wang looked at her with eyes so dark and emotionless, she shivered. "I don't make mistakes and neither does the Chinese government. Yu Zhang was wanted by the police for selling state secrets. He confessed to the authorities. He was to be executed three days after his confession, but he escaped." Wang spat out the words and his lip curled in disgust.

"The stupid guards released him so that he could say good-bye to his family. One of the guards had been a client of his in the past. He believed your father's fork-tongued promises that he'd return before the sun rose. Surprise, surprise… He never showed."

She brought the car to a halt outside the warehouse. Apart from a rusted car body and a few large drums, there were no other signs the place was inhabited.

"What is this place?" she asked in an effort to keep him talking.

"It belongs to a freight company."

"How are they connected to you?"

"I needed somewhere to contemplate and plan the job I'd been sent here to do. I sourced a few places and this one suited my purposes best. I managed to talk my way in one day and stole the key. Then I made a copy and returned the original before anyone noticed it was missing. I set up in an unused corner of the warehouse, behind a pile of junk. Nobody even knows that I'm here and of course, I'm careful to only come by when the place is empty. That's the good thing about freight," he smirked. "They always run on a schedule. It's not difficult to know when the place will be unoccupied."

"How did you know my family came to Australia? We could have gone anywhere."

"My superiors tracked your father and his family to Sydney. I arrived with a government envoy a few days later under the pretext of a state visit. By then, you'd disappeared. We knew your father was most likely living in the city, but we didn't know for sure. Still, it was a gamble I was willing to take. I've spent the past sixteen years combing the streets, searching databases, accessing all manner of official records in the hope that I'd stumble across one of you."

She stared at him in sudden comprehension. "That's why you became a police officer, isn't it? So you could access government files."

He didn't bother to deny it. "Very clever of you, ChangChang. That's exactly why I murdered the real Detective Hung Wang and assumed his identity. It eventually led me straight to your family."

Sally-Ann gasped. "Do you mean to say you killed someone in order to pose as a police officer?"

Wang chuckled. "That's exactly what I'm saying. And just so you know, it wasn't the first time I'd killed."

She stared at him and tried to hold the encroaching terror at bay. The longer she kept him talking, the better. "So you're employed by the Chinese government. Why were *you* the one sent to find us?"

This time, he smiled, but it was a bitter kind of smile that showed no mirth. "My cousin was the head of the Chinese People's Armed Police Force. He was responsible for arresting your father. Though he wasn't on duty the night your father was released, my cousin was held responsible. He disappeared not long after your father. There were no guesses where my cousin went. The Chinese government doesn't like to be bested. Someone had to pay."

Once again, Sally-Ann gasped in shock. "You mean, they killed him?"

"Yes. And then they came for me. My cousin's shame became my shame; I was the one held responsible for your father's disappearance. I was a bright young officer employed in the People's Liberation Army. I was among an elite band of men and part of the largest military force in the world."

Wang's smile was soft and sentimental. She could only guess he was caught up in memories of his glory days. She looked around her, seeking possible escape routes, but nothing materialized. And then her captor shook his head as if to clear it of his reminiscences and his expression hardened once again.

"I was also a member of the original team of interrogators that tortured your father. You can't imagine how gratifying it was to watch his pain and anguish."

She stared at him in horror and tried to think through a cloud of confusion. "I don't understand. Why did you hate my father?"

He chuckled and it was far from a pleasant sound. "A long time ago, your father represented my ex-wife in a rather nasty divorce. He poured all his energy and significant professional skills toward convincing the court to give custody of my son to my ex. He succeeded but I finally got my revenge. My cousin knew how much I hated Yu Zhang. When your father was arrested for treason, my cousin contacted me. He was sure I'd jump at the chance to be part of the interrogation team. Naturally, I accepted his offer."

Wang smiled a satisfied smile. Sally-Ann shook her head in horror at the thought of what her father had endured at the hands of this man.

"Then, to my great disappointment my cousin and his officers managed to let your father escape and the commander-in-chief came to me with this mission of atonement. He told me it had come directly from the president. He had every confidence in my ability to find your father and bring him back to face justice. Failure wasn't an option."

Wang paused and his eyes took on a distant look, like he was once again beset with memories. After a moment, he continued, his voice low and determined. "It's taken me sixteen years, but I will return triumphant to my home country. I will erase the dark cloud of shame that has haunted my family ever since your father escaped—and this time, everyone will know my name for the right reasons."

Sally-Ann shook her head in disbelief. Everything her father had warned them about had been true. He'd been adamant the Chinese authorities wouldn't forgive and forget and he was right. If only she'd listened harder, believed in what he'd said. If only she hadn't said anything to James...

No, this wasn't James' fault. Besides, she'd only told him to help her father out of a fix. It wasn't right that her well-meaning actions had resulted in *this* and that even now, her parents might be on their way to join her. What had Wang said in his second letter? Would it be enough for them to set aside their inherent distrust of the police and seek help from someone who could make a difference? *Would they turn to James?* She wanted to hope they would, but knowing how they felt about law enforcement didn't fill her with much confidence.

The thought sent an icicle of fear trickling through her veins. It pooled in a thick lump in her belly. Perhaps her parents were even now waiting somewhere nearby for Wang? He'd mentioned something to that effect when he'd first captured her.

And what about her sister? Sweet, darling Aimee, at a complete disadvantage in her wheelchair. Had she also been targeted? Was she also close by, awaiting her fate? All of a sudden, she needed to find out.

"Where are the other members of my family? My sister, my mom and dad?"

Wang turned to her and chuckled and the evil sound of it sent icy shards of terror straight through her heart. "All in good time, Ms Zhang. Now, enough of this chatter. It's time to get on with the real reason you're here. Get out and just remember, I have this gun trained a few inches from your spine and let me assure you, I'm an excellent shot."

James checked the GPS and made sure he was taking the fastest possible route to the address Chao had given him in Mascot. He murmured desperate prayers heavenward that he'd get there in time and that Sally-Ann would be okay.

He hadn't been lying when he'd told her father he loved her. It had happened so quickly and without him even being aware of it, but it was true. He couldn't imagine being with anyone else. He wanted to wake up beside her every morning and he wanted hers to be the last face he saw at night. It was over the top sappy, but it was the way she made him feel. Now that he'd found her, the thought of losing her filled him with cold, hard dread.

With lights and siren blazing, he swerved into the next lane and then the next, zig-zagging back and forth in an effort to move forward in the congested traffic. He cursed aloud at the cars piled up in front of him and once again, prayed that he wouldn't be too late.

The moment he had gotten the address details from Chao, he'd bolted from the station in a panic, racing to his squad car. He hadn't even paused to let his boss know what was going on, or to organize backup. Somewhere enroute, he had put in a call to the station and done both. After explaining what had happened, including Wang's treachery, his boss assured him that he'd have all hands on deck. James could only hope the police arrived in time.

He glanced again at his GPS and noticed he was only a couple of blocks away from his destination. Switching off the lights and siren, he slowed the vehicle and though he itched to floor the accelerator, from that point on stealth would be his friend. No doubt Wang was on the lookout for Sally-Ann's parents. He'd directed the elderly couple there, after all. It wouldn't do for the rogue detective to spot James instead. Chao had confided in him his fears that Wang was one of the original officers who'd interrogated and tortured him in China. Wang's second letter hinted as much. The thought made James' blood run cold. *Who knew what the maniac might do if he thought he was surrounded by heavily armed police?* Being spotted too early was the last thing James needed.

With that thought uppermost in his mind, he pulled over and killed the engine. For the rest of the way, he'd go on foot. He picked up his service revolver from the passenger seat, climbed out of the car and made sure the safety was still on before slipping the gun into the holster on the belt around his waist. With a quick glance up and down the street, he jogged the rest of the way until he arrived at the address he'd been given.

He was in an industrial area not far from the airport. The corrugated aluminum-and-steel warehouse looked much like all the other warehouses that lined the street. He knew from other investigations that most of the businesses in the area contracted out services and supplies to the airlines, such as catering, moving freight or providing private cleaning services.

The gate to the compound area around the building was open and an unfamiliar navy-blue BMW was parked outside the main door of the building. James couldn't be sure, but from this distance, the vehicle appeared empty. He wished he had his squad car nearby so he could run the plates through the system, but for now he had to work on the assumption that the vehicle belonged to Wang—and given the doorman's description of the man she'd left with, James believed there was a good chance Wang and Sally-Ann were somewhere inside.

The thought sent a surge of adrenaline rushing through him. The rush was laced heavily with dread. As soon as Wang caught sight of him, he'd know the game was up. There was no telling what he'd do under such circumstances. All James could do was be more than careful...and hope...

He felt terribly exposed as he strode quickly through the open gate, then jogged the rest of the way to the door. The front yard was a vast open space. If Wang was on the lookout and spied him, he'd be dead in the water. With his ears tuned to the slightest sound, he made a run for it and arrived at the warehouse out of breath.

Plastering himself against the side of the building, he noticed the door was ajar. He waited a moment until his heart rate had slowed and he'd gotten his fear back under control. Slipping off the leather tab on his holster, he eased out his gun, flicked off the safety and crept through the doorway.

He blinked hard to adjust his eyes to the sudden dimness. Almost immediately, he heard voices. He recognized Wang's. He strained to hear better and then heard Sally-Ann. Her voice was still strong, but there was no doubt she sounded scared. His heart went out to her and he sent a silent prayer heavenward that all would end well.

Please, God. Please take care of her...

He snuck behind a pallet of boxes, his boots barely making a sound on the concrete floor. The building had that musty, closed-up smell that came when a place was shut for long periods of time and there wasn't enough air flow. Dust rose from beneath his boots and tickled his nose. He clenched his fists and breathed hard against a sudden urge to sneeze. All the time, he crept closer to the voices.

And then he stepped around a corner and ran straight into a solid crate. His knee took the brunt of the impact and he couldn't suppress a groan. Pain radiated from his knee up his thigh and it was all he could do not to collapse on the floor. Through sheer strength of will, he forced himself forward. Then he put weight on his injured leg and a howl of pain tore from his mouth. He stumbled and fell hard onto the concrete. Tears of pain burned behind his eyes.

The voices fell silent and he was left to wonder how long it would be before Wang found him. With gritted teeth, James worked his gun hand free and held his weapon out in front of him. Chances were, he'd only get one shot. He'd best pray it was a good one...

CHAPTER 22

Sally-Ann froze when a sound snagged her attention. Wang had forced her into the bowels of the warehouse. He'd taken her to his office, the place he'd told her he went to when he needed to clear his mind and focus on nothing but the search for Lu Zhang and his fugitive family. He'd frequented it often over the years.

The hideout was some kind of tiny storeroom. When Wang had flicked on an overhead light, she'd gasped in horror at the pictures that were plastered across every wall. Photos of her father taken many years ago. Pictures of her and Aimee when they were little girls. Photos of her mother going about her daily business, both in Beijing and more recently, in Australia. There was even a photo of her and James outside her building. She wondered how long she'd been under surveillance.

The sound came again, and this one was more guttural, like the howl of an injured animal. Wang heard it, too. A smile of anticipation curled up his lips and the look in his eyes turned feral.

"Ah, it sounds as though your father has finally made it to our meeting place. It appears he cares for you as much as I thought he did. I do hope he followed my instructions and brought your mother with him. What kind of reunion would it be without the lovely Fen—or should I say, Lihua? She was as much to blame as he was. She was his secretary, you know. She answered the phones and made the appointments and worked hard to keep up the cover that your father was running a legitimate business. Ha! I can't believe they thought they could get away with it! Lucky for me, they won't get away with it for much longer."

His cackle of glee was pure evil and Sally-Ann stared at him in horror as realization dawned. He'd used her to lure her parents into a trap from which there'd be no return. Likely they were there on the pretext that he'd let her go if they gave themselves up. His next words confirmed it.

"Everything is falling into place. I have you and very soon, I'll have your parents, too. My little note, alerting them to the fact that your life was in danger, did the trick. I didn't think they'd risk losing you forever." He laughed again. "It's really quite touching. And after taking care of the three of you, I still have poor little Aimee to look forward to."

Sally-Ann's fear morphed into terror. It was one thing to threaten to harm her and her parents. The three of them had some chance of defending themselves, even though she was yet to work out how to put that into practice. Yet her sister had no one and nothing. It wasn't fair.

A huge surge of anger flooded through her and with it, a supernatural strength. She took advantage of Wang's lapse in concentration and lashed out at his hand that held the gun. The contact she made with his forearm was jarring. He yelped in pain, but the gun remained firmly in his hand. Realizing she'd failed and with nothing to lose, she spun on her heel and ran.

Ducking and weaving through the dimness of the warehouse, she stumbled along in her high heels between the towering shelves, now empty of freight. The sound of a shot ricocheting off something beside her head made her scream. She ducked lower and frantically tore off her sandals, ripping a fingernail in the process. The pain barely registered as, once again, she took off at a run.

"Sally-Ann!"

Her name was said so low and urgent, she nearly missed it. If she hadn't been so close, she probably would have. She peered into the darkness and saw the figure of a man sprawled on the ground. He lifted his head and she skidded to a stop.

"James? Oh, God! What happened? Are you hurt?" She whispered the questions frantically, bending down on one knee to see him better.

"I'm fine," he replied.

He sounded anything but.

"Then what are you doing on the ground?"

He tried to move and grimaced. "I ran into

something and busted my knee. I can't walk."

Panic nearly overwhelmed her. "Oh! My God!" she whispered frantically. "We need to get out of here! It's Wang! He's got a gun! He says he's going to kill my entire family!"

"Yes, your dad called me. He told me about the second note. It had been slipped under his door. By then, I'd worked out that Wang was in the employ of the Chinese government. I believe he was deployed here as a spy."

"He said he was sent here to find my father and bring him back to China to face justice."

James nodded grimly. "Just like your father told you they would."

A sound, not far away from them, drew their attention. They fell silent and stared at one another. Sally-Ann tried desperately to come up with a plan. With James incapacitated, it was almost impossible to get him out of there. He was far too heavy for her to lift, or even partially carry. She let out a tiny sound of distress and jammed her fist against her mouth in an effort to force it back in. James reached out for her in the darkness and pulled her close against him.

She breathed in the warm male scent of him and immediately felt safer. The irony of the situation wasn't lost on her. They were being hunted by a madman with a gun who was determined to kill them.

"You can't hide from me forever, ChangChang," Wang crooned from somewhere in the dark. "Sooner or later, I will find you and then I will shoot you dead. It's taken me sixteen long years to find your family, but I never, ever gave up. And now I have you in my sights."

The sound of his triumphant cackle of glee sent shivers down her spine. She crouched low, frozen in place, as he continued.

"Victory is but a moment away, my little ChangChang. I will return to my homeland a hero, to claim my rightful place. My cousin's reputation as a great soldier will be restored, his memory glorified. There will be rejoicing in my family and in the land. I will settle for nothing less."

James stared at her in confusion. "What the hell is he talking about?"

"I'll tell you later," she whispered.

"He sounds unhinged."

"*Shh.*" Sally-Ann frowned at him in the darkness. She'd heard a noise and it wasn't very far away.

James must have heard it, too. He stilled and then, with a finger pressed to his lips, he eased his arm from around her and slowly pushed himself into a sitting position. A gleam of light appeared in the distance, in front of them. It bounced off the barrel of James' gun. Sally-Ann swallowed a gasp and then realized the distant light was coming closer and she was suddenly grateful that James was armed.

"Lie still and keep your head down," he whispered in her ear.

Her stomach did a somersault and then clenched in fear. Her pulse took off full speed and it felt like her heart would thump clear out of her chest, but clamping her lips together to contain her panic, she did as he directed.

"Ah, my little ChangChang. There you are," Wang sang.

With her head buried against James' chest, she couldn't see her tormentor, but his voice sounded closer with every step he took. Her terror increased.

She knew the exact moment Wang realized it was James on the ground and not just her or her parents. He gasped in surprise and then started to chuckle.

"Well, well, well. What do we have here?"

"Stop where you are, Wang, or whoever you are and put your hands where I can see them," James demanded. "The warehouse is surrounded. There are snipers watching your every step. One false move and you'll be history."

James sounded so sure of himself, she almost collapsed against him in relief. If what he said was true, it was only a matter of time before the police stormed the building and rescued them. She tightened her hold and kept her head down and prepared herself for whatever was to come. She didn't have long to wait.

Wang laughed. Loud and long. She couldn't see him, but she could almost imagine him throwing his head back and succumbing fully to his mirth. James tensed beside her. His muscles clenched beneath her hands. He reminded her of a tiger waiting for the right moment to unleash his power and tear his tormentor to shreds.

The laughter came to a sudden halt and when Wang spoke there was no mirth in his tone.

"How *dare* you threaten me? *Me!* One of the brightest soldiers in the People's Liberation Army.

You're not fit to wipe the dirt off my boots, Shepherd. All these months I've been forced to treat you as an equal. *Ha! An equal! You could never hope to gain such lofty heights."

He moved closer and Sally-Ann's fear increased. *Where were those snipers and their rifles? How long were they going to wait?* Wang had a gun and had made it clear he intended to use it. They needed to act before it was too late.

"I must admit, I'm surprised you managed to work it all out," Wang continued in a conversational tone. "I thought I'd done a pretty good job of being Hung Wang and throwing you off my scent. I worked by your side for months and you never once suspected. All the hours I spent on the computer and you never once asked me why. You were lazy, Detective Shepherd," Wang jeered, "and now it's going to cost your life."

Sally-Ann heard the sound of a gun being cocked. In horror, she lifted her head. There was no way she could sit by and let him shoot James in cold blood. Not without doing something about it. She sat up and stared down the barrel of Wang's gun. He was a handful of feet away, grinning like a madman. Frozen with fear, her heart simply stopped.

"Ah, brave little ChangChang. I love that about you," Wang tittered. "I was so glad that you and your family were cleared of the Hanley murder. It would have made my job so much harder if I'd had to arrange for your demise in jail. I'm lucky that while my esteemed partner might be lazy, he managed to find the real killer. That made it so much easier for me to carry out my orders to eliminate you and your family."

Wang raised the gun until it was pointed right at her head. Unable to help herself, she whimpered in fear. *This was it.* He was going to pull the trigger. Her life had come to an end. She cried out in distress. She and James had only just found each other and now it would all be over...

A loud report sounded in her ears at the same time James shouted and pushed her back down. Pain seared through her shoulder, pain like she'd never known. She screamed, but her distress was drowned out by the sound of more gunfire. The gun in James' hand flashed fire.

Another shout and her heart stopped again and then she saw Wang fall. He landed hard on the concrete floor and she collapsed against James in relief.

It was over.

Wang was dead, and if not dead, severely incapacitated. He'd be arrested, charged and hopefully convicted. The nightmare was over. Her family would be safe.

James leaned over her, his face filled with concern. "Sweetheart, are you all right?"

She gave him a shaky smile. "I-I'm fine. How are you?"

"All good. Wang's shot went wide. I was a bit luckier. I hit him squarely in the chest."

"I'm glad. He sounded like he meant business, now and earlier."

"I'm just glad it's over. He's not going to hurt anyone again."

Sally-Ann glanced at the lifeless body on the floor. "Is he...dead?"

"Yes."

She shuddered as the reality of the past few moments set in. Sweat popped out on her forehead, despite the cool, dank air. She thought she made a sound of distress, but couldn't be sure. James' face hovered over her, at once blurry, then clear, then blurry again.

"Sally-Ann! Sally-Ann! Talk to me! Honey, please look at me! Are you okay?"

The worry in his eyes was disconcerting, but she was beyond caring. She closed her eyes on a heavy sigh and everything faded to black...

EPILOGUE

Sally-Ann had to sneeze. Her chest was tight and her nose tickled. Her eyes watered with the effort to hold it back. She gasped once, twice, a third time before the sneeze exploded from her nose. And then pain blasted through her shoulder and she cried out in agony.

"Hey, sweetheart. Take it easy. The pain meds are still kicking in."

She opened her eyes and stared up at James who sat in a chair beside the bed. He looked down at her with tenderness in his eyes.

"W-what happened?"

"You're in hospital. Your shoulder was grazed by one of Wang's bullets. I can't believe I didn't realize it at the time. The surgeon's been by and he's pleased with how things went. There should be no lasting complications."

She frowned up at him in confusion. "Surgeon?"

"Yes. They thought it best to take you to the OR to make sure there was no internal damage. You've been given the all clear. Once the stitches are removed, you'll be as good as new, thank God."

His eyes darkened with emotion and his voice went rough. "For an instant, back in the warehouse, I thought I was going to lose you. In the dark, I had no idea you'd been shot. And then your eyes rolled back and you fainted. I thought you'd died."

He offered her a lopsided smile and reached for her hand, giving it a squeeze. "You wouldn't believe how crazed I was trying to find a pulse. I nearly collapsed with relief when I found one."

His gaze became more intense and she couldn't look away. "I don't know what I'd do without you, Sal. We've known each other for such a short time, but it doesn't seem to matter. We're connected in a way I never dreamed I'd find with anyone and I think you feel the same way. We met in unusual circumstances but I hope that won't matter to you. It doesn't matter one little bit to me." He paused and for the first time, looked uncertain. "What do you think?"

She stared at him in wonder, hardly daring to believe what he was saying. "You mean, you want a relationship with me? Something more than a casual fling?"

He leaned over and cupped her cheek in his hand. His voice was husky with emotion. "You could never be just a casual fling. I didn't plan it, but it's like I told your father... I've fallen in love with you, Sally-Ann."

Joy filled her heart and her lips stretched wide. "Oh, James! I don't know what to say!"

"Say you feel the same way!" He laughed.

Her smile widened and tears burned in her eyes. "Oh, I do! I can't believe it! I can't believe we've found each other when it was the last thing I expected. I love you, too."

He leaned in toward her and pressed a soft kiss on her lips. Forgetting about her injury, she reached up to hug him. They cried out together.

"I'm sorry, I didn't realize I squeezed you so hard," she said.

"You didn't. It's my leg. I fractured the fibula just below the kneecap while I was in the warehouse, when I collided with something solid in the dark. It's the reason why I couldn't stand. Fortunately, the news about my injury is just as positive as yours. They've put on a plaster and given me some crutches. The doctor's confident I'll regain full use of my leg within six weeks."

She shook her head in disbelief, but was relieved the news was good. "Wow, we're a sorry pair, aren't we?"

"At least we're still alive. Wang wasn't so fortunate. Do you know he assumed someone else's identity? All these years, he only pretended to be a detective."

She nodded somberly. "Yes. He told me he'd murdered a detective and stolen his identity. He even lived in the man's apartment, wore his clothes, used his phone. He needed to be employed as a police officer so that he could have access to government records otherwise unavailable to him. I guess it worked. If he hadn't been a detective, he wouldn't have found my family." She paused in thought. "I feel so sad for the man he murdered."

"We're opening up an investigation. I only hope we find the poor man's remains."

"Do you know Wang was also part of the interrogation team that tortured my father in China?"

Surprise filled James' face. "No. That's awful! I can't believe he told you that!"

"Gloated, more like it," she said dryly. "Apparently my father represented Wang's ex-wife in a divorce and custody proceeding. It got ugly. Dad won custody for his client. Wang was furious."

She went on to tell James about Wang's cousin and how he'd allowed Wang to torture her father. James shook his head in disbelief.

"I can't believe I worked with the man for so long and didn't have a clue."

"I guess we only see what we think is there," she said quietly. "You're not the only one who was fooled."

A knock on the door was followed by a young woman coming shyly into the room. James turned toward the door and smiled.

"Hi, Lizzie. I see you got over your dislike of hospitals enough to pop in for a visit. Is Dad with you?"

"No, Anita dropped me off."

James nodded. "I'm glad to hear you're getting along better."

The young woman pulled a face, but didn't argue. She looked toward Sally-Ann and James stepped forward and made the introductions.

"Sally-Ann, I'd like you to meet my kid sister. Lizzie, this is Sally-Ann."

Sally-Ann smiled at her. Even without the introduction, she would have guessed the woman was related to James. She had the same dark hair and deep green eyes and her mannerisms were also quite similar. It was a little weird to see the man she loved replicated in a feminine form. Still, the smile the girl shared with her was pleasant enough. She'd never had a younger sister and she looked forward to spending time with Lizzie and getting to know her better. She was sure they'd become friends.

All of a sudden, she yawned and then blushed with embarrassment. She was dismayed at how worn out she felt. She studied James. He didn't look a whole lot better...and he was wearing *pajamas.*

"Oh, James! I just realized you're a patient here, too! What are you doing here with me? You need to rest!"

He merely chuckled at her concern. "I'm fine. I might have to take the weight off this leg shortly, but I wanted to see you. I bribed the nurse with a box of chocolates to let me come up here."

He winked at her and gave her a smile so sexy, warmth spread from her chest to her toes. She wanted so much to kiss him and hold him and never let him go... But that would have to wait until both of them were a little further along their road to recovery, when it didn't hurt so much to hug him tight. She prayed that time would come soon...

Note To Readers

I do hope you have enjoyed reading James and Sally-Ann's story. If you've enjoyed this book, please feel free to leave a review for At the Hand of Her Father at Goodreads and your favorite digital retailer. Every review is very much appreciated.

Receive a free book when you sign up for my newsletter if you would like to receive news on upcoming stories, release dates, book launches and other snippets. I love to receive feedback from my readers. Please feel free to contact me at chris@christaylorauthor.com.au

Lies and Deception is the next book in The Sydney Legal Series.

Here's a sneak peek:

Monica Radford wants a baby. At thirty-two, though not exactly ancient, she longs for a child before it's too late. The only problem is, she doesn't have a partner and has no intention of signing up for one. In her usual no-nonsense style, she decides to go out and find the perfect baby daddy.

Colby Shearer has a successful, demanding career as a lawyer and crown prosecutor. By chance, he meets Monica at his younger sister's wedding on the exotic island of Vanuatu. Immediately drawn to her stunning beauty, they engage in a torrid fling. But then the holiday is over and they return to their separate lives. While Colby is keen to remain in contact, Monica blows him off. He's confused and upset, but there is nothing he can do about it.

Monica returns to her previous life, thrilled in the knowledge that she's pregnant. Determined to keep it a secret from Colby, she's shocked and horrified when she runs into him outside the court room. Relieved that she's only two months along and not showing, she then discovers he's prosecuting her brother for murder and will be in their lives for weeks to come.

What will happen when he discovers her treachery? Will he demand to be part of her baby's life? To exert his rights as a father? It's her worst nightmare come true and the thought makes her sick – almost as sick as the realization her brother might be a murderer....

CHAPTER 1

Colby Shearer picked up his scotch glass and drew it to his lips. Ice clinked as he took a sip, relishing the slow warm burn as the whisky glided down his throat. He settled against the steel and rattan bar stool and surveyed the wedding guests who filled the pool area. Most of them were well into their cups. The wedding had ended hours earlier. The bride, his little sister, had danced what could be loosely described as the bridal waltz with her new husband on a small wooden platform set up in front of the house band who had been playing soft, slow love songs most of the evening.

It had been a nice ceremony as far as weddings went. In the past, Colby hadn't bothered to take much notice of all the details, but this was Katie's special day and he knew firsthand how much time and effort and organization had gone into the event, right down to the candles and frangipani decorations that graced the white linen-clad tables.

So what was he doing sitting all alone at the bar, feeling introspective and morose and downing his third scotch? He should be out on the dance floor—what there was of it—kicking up his heels with one of the bridesmaids. The three girls had been friends with his sister since kindergarten. He knew them almost as well as he knew Katie. And therein lay the problem. All three of them were smart, funny and attractive, but he looked upon them as he did his sister. The thought of getting romantic with one of them just seemed plain wrong. It was too bad. At thirty-three, he was feeling the need to settle down. He guessed it had something to do with the fact he was at a wedding. They seemed to highlight the fact he was still single and all those gooey words of love and the look of adoration on the happy couple's faces made him yearn to have that for himself.

What would it feel like to be so in love with someone that you couldn't imagine wanting to spend a second of time apart? On days like this, he wished he knew.

"Colby! What are you doing over here all by yourself?"

He turned slightly on his stool and offered his mother a lopsided grin. "Feeling sorry for myself?"

She *tut tutted* and pulled up the stool beside him. "What are you talking about? Surely you're not unhappy about Katie and Jason? I've never met a couple more in love."

"Of course not," he hurried to assure her. "I think they're great together."

She tilted her head and looked at him. "Then what?"

Colby sighed and emptied the contents of his glass. The bartender materialized and asked if he wanted another. He shrugged. *Why not?*

"Would you like a drink, Mom?"

"No, I'm fine, thanks. I've already had too much champagne." She smiled and he smiled back at her. His mother had never been a drinker.

The bartender collected his empty glass and set a fresh drink in front of him. Colby handed over a few bills and murmured his thanks. The bartender moved away.

"Talk to me, Colby," she said softly. "Tell me what's wrong. It's your sister's wedding. You should be celebrating, not sitting here looking all forlorn."

He lifted his glass and sipped at his drink. "I am celebrating, Mom."

She shook her head and rolled her eyes. He grinned. She held his gaze, her dark brown eyes that were the exact same shade as his remained serious. He looked down at his drink and cleared his throat.

"I'm happy for Katie and Jason. I really am. It's just the whole wedding thing. Sometimes it gets me down."

"How come?"

"I'm thirty-three, Mom. I'm not exactly young. I want to get married, have a family. What if I never meet the right girl?"

"Colby Albert Shearer! Stop talking such nonsense! You're sweet and kind and sinfully good-looking. You have a great job, a nice apartment.

What are you talking about! Any girl would fall over herself in order to call you hers."

"Thanks for the pep talk, Mom, but it's not necessary. My self-esteem's still intact. I'm not feeling unloved, just... I want to *be* loved. I want to know what it's like to be so totally in love that there will never be anyone else. Like Katie and Jason. I want to have a girl look at me the same way Katie looks at Jason and I want to feel the same way."

He stopped, a little embarrassed by his revelations. He'd had way too much to drink. He ought to stop talking right now, kiss his mother goodnight and retire to his room before he said anything more. Intent on putting that thought into action, he set his glass down on the bar and pushed back on his stool. His mother's hand on his arm stilled him.

"I understand, Colby, truly I do. But you don't need to worry. You're going to make someone a fine husband and father one day. I know it."

He grimaced. "You have to say that. You're my mom."

She looked affronted. "Of course I'm not just saying that because I'm your mom! Yes, I might be a little bit biased in your favor, but let me assure you, there are plenty of female guests who've been watching you all night. Any one of them would welcome an invitation to dance."

She looked toward a table where a group of Katie's work colleagues were gathered. At least three of them were young, attractive females who appeared to be unattached. Colby thought about what his mother had said and wondered if he should try a little harder to socialize with them. As if reading his thought, his mother patted his arm.

"See? All you have to do is go over there and speak with them. Don't you remember the way I met your father? If he hadn't found the courage to come over and ask me to dance at my cousin's twenty-first birthday, we'd have never gotten together! Imagine that!"

She laughed and Colby gave her a reluctant grin. He'd heard the story of how his parents had met many times over. He had to admit. It was a nice story.

"Okay, Mom! You win! I'll make an effort to speak to at least one of them. There. Are you happy?"

She leaned over and pecked Colby on the cheek. "That's my boy! Now, head over there to that table. I'm sure you won't be disappointed. I'll look forward to meeting her!"

She gave him a cheeky grin and he shook his head and smiled. "Mom, you're incorrigible."

"Have a good night, Colby," she replied unrepentantly. She turned away and disappeared into the crowd.

Colby finished his drink and then stood and left the bar. The tableful of girls beckoned him and he found himself making his way toward them through the crowd of wedding guests. He took a step forward just as a woman pushed back her chair and stood. The chair came into contact with his hip and he stumbled, along with the blonde who wobbled precariously on outrageously tall high heels.

"Oh! Oh! Oh!" she squealed in alarm.

Colby reached out to steady her. Her arms were slim and tanned and toned in her sleeveless black dress. Her skin was warm beneath his hands. She turned and looked at him and his breath caught in his throat.

"I-I'm sorry. Are you all right?" he stammered and silently cursed the blush that crept up his neck and spread across his cheeks.

The woman laughed, her blue eyes twinkling with good humor. "Of course. I'm fine. And please, *I'm* the one who should be apologizing. I should have looked before I pushed back my chair."

Colby smiled down at her and tried to steady his heart beat. Her golden hair was swept upwards in a sophisticated style. Gold hoop earrings matched a necklace that hung around her neck. Her lips were perfect and round and shimmered with glossy pink lipstick. When she smiled, he caught a glimpse of even white teeth. His gaze drifted lower, across the firm tanned skin of her exposed neck and lower still, to the impressive bust line that strained against the bodice of her dress.

His body hardened in response. He couldn't remember ever seeing a more beautiful woman. He wondered if her outer beauty matched the beauty in her heart. All of a sudden, he wanted to find out.

Releasing her arms, he stepped back and offered her a bow. It was embarrassing and corny and no doubt he looked ridiculous, but for some reason, it felt right.

"Colby Shearer, at your service, ma'am. And you are?"

"Monica Radford," she replied and graciously shook his proffered hand.

Her skin was soft against his. Her nails were long and well-manicured, gleaming with polish that matched the color of her lips. She smiled and his heart skipped another beat. "It's nice to meet you, Monica Radford. Are you a friend of the bride or the groom?"

"The groom. Jason and I work together. I'm his PA."

Colby nodded. "That's why we've never met before. I'm pretty confident I know all of Katie's friends. At least, the ones she invited here."

Monica looked around her. "It's a beautiful place. I've never been to Fiji. I can understand why people have their weddings in places like this. The island is absolutely amazing. I've never seen water so clear. It's just like the photos in all those glossy tourist brochures, isn't it?"

Colby grinned, delighted at her enthusiasm and lack of artifice. And then she blushed and he was absolutely certain he was in love.

"I-I'm sorry," she stammered, averting her gaze. "I sound like a wide-eyed school girl. You must think me terribly unsophisticated."

He shook his head. "To the contrary. I find you refreshingly honest." His gaze roved over her from head to toe. He took his time, liking everything he saw. "And very, *very* sophisticated."

Her blush deepened and he was even more intrigued. She looked like a million dollars and yet she blushed like a young woman who felt awkward and uncertain in her skin. A rush of curiosity went through him. Who was this woman who worked with his new brother-in-law? He very much wanted to find out.

"Would you like to dance?" he asked.

Her eyes widened in surprise, but to his relief, she nodded. "Yes. That would be lovely."

"Great."

Moving the offending chair back beneath the table, he took her hand and led her to the makeshift dance floor. The tiny square of faux wooden flooring was already occupied by two other couples. Colby moved them into the only space available and took her in his arms.

She danced well.

The thought was only one of about a million others that flooded through his mind. She was almost as tall as he was and fit snugly beneath his chin. His hand rested on the small of her back, pulling her close but not too close. He didn't want to scare her off. The band was playing a slow love song and it was just as well. Anything faster and his scotch-soaked brain might not have been able to keep up.

He closed his eyes and enjoyed the feel of the beautiful woman in his arms. The music flowed over them. A gentle breeze lifted his hair and brought with it the tang of salt and the sweet scent of frangipani. The pleasant smells mingled with the perfume that wafted toward him every now and then.

"So, are you a friend of the bride or the groom?" she asked.

He opened his eyes and blinked her back into focus. "The bride is my sister."

"Oh." She smiled in reply. "I didn't notice you on the main table."

"Well, there wasn't really a main table. My parents are divorced and both of them remarried years ago. Mom and Dad are civil toward one another, but apparently there haven't been enough years yet for them to share a table at their daughter's wedding. Katie and Jason and their attendants sat at one table and Mom and Dad each hosted a table of their own. I sat over there, with my brother, Eamon and a group of our friends."

She looked in the direction he pointed and nodded. "I heard you laughing through the speeches. You sounded like you were having fun. Are you and your brother married?"

"Nope. Katie's the youngest and the first one down the aisle. Go figure."

She looked up at him from beneath impossibly long lashes. "Where do you fit in?"

"I'm the oldest. Eamon is three years younger. Katie's another four years younger than that."

"Ouch." She laughed. "I bet you've been getting sidelong looks from the elderly relatives all evening. They'll be wondering what's going on with you and when it will be your turn."

Colby grinned. "Oh, yes, don't worry, Eamon and I have already had an earful from old Aunty Mavis and I was bailed up by Aunty Nellie for more than an hour while she quizzed me about why I wasn't married. It almost made me wish I'd brought along a pretend fiancé, maybe even a couple of kids. At least I would have warded off the well-intentioned but nevertheless irritating lectures from my relatives about being left on the shelf."

She laughed again and the musical sound of it sent ripples of desire shivering along his veins.

"Do you *want* to get married?" she asked lightly.

He stared down at her and all of a sudden, people, the music, the whole damn island disappeared. It was just the two of them: him and Monica.

"Of course I do," he answered softly. "But I was old enough when my parents' marriage fell apart to realize it isn't something I want to rush into. I don't intend to become another statistic, like them. I want to make sure that the woman I choose is prepared to be in it for the long haul. She'll be my partner for life."

"What about kids?" she asked and her voice was a little breathless.

"Kids are great. I love kids. Two, three, four. As many as she wants."

The woman gazed at him, her eyes a deep cobalt. A soft, sexy smile played around her lips. "You sound like every woman's dream man. Are you *sure* you're still single?"

Monica stared at the man whose hand was still pressed firmly against the small of her back and wondered if he would answer. She'd posed the question teasingly, but waited on tenterhooks for his reply. From their earlier conversation, she guessed that he was probably single, but she didn't know for sure and one thing was certain: She needed to be sure.

After all, she might be desperate for a baby and to find the man who could make that dream come true, but she drew the line at married men or men involved in serious relationships. She hoped Colby Shearer was neither.

He'd attracted her from the moment she'd set eyes on him and that initial attraction hadn't waned while they'd been dancing. He was tall and dark and handsome—very dark and handsome. His hair was midnight black and his eyes were a shade of brown that could only be described as dark chocolate. He was smart and pleasant and polite and it was obvious he was part of a caring family.

His parents might be divorced, but they'd both seen fit to attend the wedding and support their only daughter, albeit from separate tables. She'd seen the identical expressions of love and pride on their faces as they'd walked Katie down the aisle and the way she'd talked and laughed as she danced with her father. Divorce or not, this was a family who were close and who cared about each other and that was an important attribute in the father of her unborn child, although not essential. It wasn't like the father of her baby would ever be part of the baby's life—or even know about it, for that matter.

His arm tightened around her and he pulled her

up close until her breasts were crushed against his chest. He bent his head and his lips grazed the soft skin of her ear.

"Let me assure you, I am *very* much single."

His voice was a low and husky drawl that sent heat flooding to her core. His hand moved from the small of her back to her ass and curved around her cheek. He pressed her forward and her belly brushed against the unmistakable feel of his erection.

She swallowed a gasp of excitement and desire rushed through her veins. Her nipples tightened from the delicious friction caused by his tuxedo jacket. She ought to be shocked at his forwardness, at the unspoken invitation in his eyes. But the truth was, he was the epitome of what she'd been searching for and she couldn't believe her dreams of having a baby had just taken a huge leap forward.

"I'm glad to hear it," she replied. Her voice was soft and breathy, foreign to her ears. Her pulse beat a fast tempo in the side of her neck. He spun her around and then dipped her low and she gasped in surprise and clung to him. His strong arms held her easily and then he drew her back up.

She draped her arms around his neck and laughed at the sheer fun of it. If she were ever looking for a husband, Colby Shearer would be at the top of the list. Too bad she wasn't in the market for a life partner. No, a baby was all she needed. And he was the best baby daddy she'd found.

Chapter 2

Colby slid his keycard into the hotel room door slot and listened for the beep. Turning the handle, he pushed the door open with his shoulder, all the time maintaining contact with Monica. His arm was around her shoulder and hers was around his waist. They'd shared their first kiss in the elevator.

He couldn't believe he'd asked her up to his room. They'd met barely twenty minutes earlier. But there was something about her that he couldn't resist—or rather, many somethings. There were the long tanned legs that went up to her armpits, the cloud of golden blond hair. The wide blue eyes, the perfect lips. The bountiful breasts he longed to touch that almost spilled out of her dress.

He was rock hard and aching. He burned with need and anticipation. When she'd agreed to his suggestion she might like to join him upstairs, he'd almost thrown back his head and roared with excitement. The scotch had left him feeling warm and fuzzy, but he had no fear it would impede his performance. He prided himself on his skills in the bedroom. He couldn't wait to taste, to lick, to touch.

The door closed behind them and she came into his arms like she'd been born there. He cupped her ass in his hands and pressed her close. She draped her arms around his neck. His head came down and her lips parted in silent invitation. She tasted as good as she looked.

He groaned as the kiss deepened. Tongues ventured out and tangled in wild need. Releasing her, he reached behind her and fumbled with the knot of fabric that was tied around her neck. At last, he got it free and the front of her dress fell forward. The golden glow from the lamp he'd left on beside the nightstand illuminated her skin. She wore a strapless lacy black bra. He glimpsed part of one pink nipple.

Without conscious thought, his hands went out and he cupped her luscious breasts and squeezed. They filled his hands to overflowing. His cock strained against his pants.

"You're so beautiful," he breathed, his voice husky with need. She merely stood in silence and let him look his fill.

Unable to help himself, he pushed her dress down further and was pleased when she stepped away and shimmied out of it altogether. The black lace bra was matched with equally sexy panties. Within moments, she stood naked except for her underwear.

Another rush of desire surged through him and

he shucked off his jacket and loosened his bow tie. He fumbled with the tiny buttons on his pleated shirt and cursed when they resisted his efforts. Finally, he got them free and tugged off his shirt and sent it the same way as his tie and jacket. Undoing the button at the top of his pants, he slid down the zipper, stepped out of the pants and kicked them away. At last, he was also naked, but for his silk Homer Simpson boxers.

Her eyes widened in surprise at the sight of them. Her lips curved upwards in delight. "Homer Simpson? Really?"

"Hey! What's wrong with Homer Simpson?"

She laughed. "There's nothing wrong with Homer Simpson. I'm one of his biggest fans."

"Then we have more in common than we realized," he replied and then drew her hard against him.

Once again, their lips met and opened in a rush of need. His hands stroked her back, her hips, the sweet curve of her ass. His cock throbbed almost painfully, but he wanted her to set the pace. Thankfully, she appeared to be every bit as eager as he was and when she pulled away and took his hand and led him to the bed, he almost sighed in relief.

They sank together on the soft mattress and immediately resumed their kiss. She tasted of wine and chocolate. He smiled inwardly. She must indulged in his sister's wedding cake. Katie had turned her nose up at the traditional fruit and marzipan concoction and had insisted on a chocolate mud cake with lashings of chocolate icing. He could taste remnants of it on Monica's lips. She tasted delicious.

Finding the clasp of her bra, he released the hooks and tugged gently at the fabric. He sighed as her breasts sprang free. They were even larger than he imagined. He buried his face between their softness and couldn't hold back a groan. There were some men who were intimidated by large breasts. He sure as hell wasn't one of them.

He kneaded them, squeezed them, flicked his tongue across her nipples. He licked them, sucked them, loved them. He couldn't get enough.

"*Mm*, that feels good," she murmured and he thought he might explode.

He moved lower and kissed his way down her sternum, paused at her belly button and then buried his face between her legs. Breathing in her unique scent, he pressed his hand against her mound. Not satisfied with feeling her through the black lace, her tugged at her panties. She lifted her hips to assist him and he slid the underwear over her hips. She kicked it off and he returned to his position between her legs. As much as he wanted to linger, this was going to be quick.

He licked her soft folds up and down and tasted her musky need. Dipping his tongue inside her, he relished the sound of her excitement. Her breathing had quickened, her hands had tightened into fists. Her eyes were closed and her head moved slowly from side to side.

"Please, Colby. I need you."

And he needed her.

With his cock painfully erect, he came up on his

knees. Her legs fell open, encouraging his approach. And then he thought about protection.

"Shit," he muttered.

In the dimness, he saw her frown. "What is it?"

"I don't have a condom."

She struggled to a sitting position and smiled. "Then I guess it's lucky I do."

With that, she swung her legs over the bed and hunted for her abandoned purse. He'd noticed it draped over her shoulder earlier. A moment later, he heard the crackling sound of plastic and then her hands were on his cock. She sheathed him quickly and then paused a moment to cup his balls.

He shuddered at the feel of her soft hands on his heated flesh and gently pushed her hands away. Anymore of that and he'd disgrace himself and that was one thing he had no intention of doing this night. For whatever reason, this angel had stumbled in his path. Who knew if she was looking for forever? He intended to spend with her whatever time she was prepared to give him. He hoped like hell she was staying on the island for a few more days...

Pushing her gently backwards, he positioned himself between her legs. His cock probed her entrance and with a single thrust of his hips, he pushed all the way inside. She was warm and moist and wonderful. She felt like heaven on earth. A mere hour ago, they were strangers. Now he couldn't ever imagine her not in his life.

He stroked in and out and held onto his control, despite the urgings of his body. And then her legs tightened around his hips. Her arms clung to his shoulders. She groaned in ecstasy and called his name and he was lost. Together, they reached for the stars.

It didn't last anywhere near as long as he wanted it to, but it was magical just the same. She cried out her release moments before he found his and together, they crashed back to earth.

———

Monica slowed her breathing and did her best to get her heartbeat back under control. When she'd set out on her plan to find a baby father, she had no idea it would feel so good. She didn't even know the man who now lay curled up against her side and yet, it felt like she'd known him forever. Once again, she felt a stab of regret that her future didn't include a husband.

No, there wasn't any room for a husband in her neat and ordered life. She liked the independence that came from being single, having no one to answer to, no one to pretend to care. She knew all about divorced parents and hers had been a hell of a lot nastier than the situation Colby had described.

No, she didn't need a husband, and her unborn child didn't need a dad. After all, *she'd* grown up without one. The last time she'd seen her father, she was three. And she'd grown up okay, hadn't she?

She'd graduated from college with Honors and had secured a good job that she enjoyed. She owned a condo in a nice suburb and was financially secure enough that she could give a child all that it might need. And the bottom line was, she was thirty-two. Her biological clock was clanging. Time was running out. There was no way she wanted to risk losing her ability to be a mother. It was the most important thing she could do.

Thirty-two wasn't ancient, but it wasn't young, either. Health risks to both mother and baby increased exponentially when one skipped over the other side of thirty-six and that was a mere four years away. Besides, she didn't want to be an old mom. As much as she loved her own mother, she could still remember how embarrassed she was whenever her mom visited at her school. Audrey Radford was a beautiful woman with a cloud of beautiful hair, but she'd gone gray very early and Monica had wanted to run and hide rather than admit to her young friends that the woman with the gray hair was her mother.

It was immature and silly, but that's the way she'd felt and she didn't want her child embarrassed, either by a mom who was older than most of the mothers of the kids who shared the classroom. It was the reason she didn't feel the slightest amount of guilt when she'd pricked holes in her box of condoms, including the one she'd used on the man who now snored gently beside her, sated and oblivious…

Lies and Deception will be released on 29 October, 2017 and is available for pre-order from your favorite digital retailer.

About the Author

Chris Taylor grew up on a farm in north-west New South Wales, Australia. She always had a thirst for stories and recalls writing her first book at the ripe old age of eight. Always a lover of romance and happily-ever-afters, a career in criminal law sparked her interest in intrigue and suspense. For Chris to be able to combine romance with suspense in her books is a dream come true.

Chris is married to Linden and is the mother of five children. If not behind her computer, you can find her doing the school run, taxiing children to swimming lessons, football, ballet and cricket. In her spare time, Chris loves to read her favorite authors who include Richard North Patterson, Sandra Brown, Kathleen E Woodiwiss and Jude Devereaux.

You can find out more about Chris and sign up for her newsletter at her website:

http://www.christaylorauthor.com.au

9 781925 119503